I0778390

THE LIGHT OF OTHER DAYS

The Accidental Time Travel Agency

The Light
of
Other Days

DEBORAH CARROLL

Danbury House
Franklin, Tennessee

For Ann Brown

"There is nothing I would not do for those who
are really my friends."

~Jane Austen

PROLOGUE

Then up she rose, and forth she goes, all in that fatal hour,
And bodily was borne away, and never was seen more.
~Traditional, "Sir James the Rose"

"David's bones!" Raven swore as he studied this latest rift in the Timeline. The rift was fresh enough—maybe two hours old, and someone had obviously come through it. That in itself was not particularly irksome, or even all that unusual, but they had come from his least favorite of all centuries, the twenty-first.

Not only that, but on this side of the rift, the year was 1813. It was the worst of all possible time combinations, it was. How many daft people had he dealt with who wanted to stay in the Regency Era for a while, like it was some kind of vacation destination? The men, thinking they could "just watch" Napoleonic War battles as if they were action flicks, were annoying enough, but it was the women, dreaming of finding real-life Regency romance, who really got him moithered. They'd seen Colin Firth in a wet shirt on the telly, then they wanted to lark about in the nineteenth century, on the hunt for Mr. Darcy.

Worst of all, whoever had entered through this rift was nowhere to be seen. *Bobol bach*, good grief! Why couldn't this have been an easy one? Grab the body— dead or alive, shove it back through, mend the rift— done and done. Not counting the paperwork, of course, of which there was plenty. He was supposed to go on holiday this weekend. To have a scarper now was the end of enough!

He could just do the repair and be done with it, vow or no vow. He deserved that blasted holiday on the blasted beach in Ramsgate, didn't he?

No, blast it, he couldn't take the risk. Chances the traveler had survived were too good; he had to find them and shove them back through to their own time. One of the Accidental Time Travel Agency's mottoes, "A Shove in Time Saves Nine," was running through his mind like the refrain of a catchy song. Not that Raven gave a fig for the agency's stupid mottoes; it had a hundred of them. The truth was, it was more than his job, and maybe even his life, was worth to leave the shoving bit undone. It was a good job, too, with full government benefits— much better than working the coal mines back in Wales, it was. No black lung at the end of it, either.

Raven sighed, scrubbing the top of his head with one grubby hand until his hair stood up in black spikes. This rift was at the intersection of several roads, one of which went through a tiny village. Good. He could wait things out there, if need be.

He flipped back his government-issued black cloak, shifted the tool bag on his back, and knelt on one knee in the road. He scanned the area within the circle of light cast by his hooded lantern. Yes, there was a depression in the vegetation at the roadside, where the body must have lain. He stood again and moved his lantern slowly over the carriage wheel tracks, hoofprints, and footprints in the muddy road, then brought the lantern in close to study the hoofprints: one set of impressions got deeper after a certain point, as if the horse had taken on additional weight. Bingo.

The prints led Raven down the lane opposite the one-street village, heading west. They ended at a stone bridge and picked back up again on the other side of the river, finally leading to a set of grand pier gates— locked, of course. "David's bones!" he swore again, lifting his lantern high in the mad hope that he could see anything beyond the gates in the nearly moonless night. Bah, nothing. With gates like those, it was clearly some toff's estate, though— it shouldn't be hard to find out whose.

Raven could do no more at the moment, and the time traveler wasn't going anywhere for at least a day or two. He headed back towards the tiny village to look for a pub.

CHAPTER 1

My Mary's asleep by thy murmuring stream,
Flow gently, sweet Afton, disturb not her dream.
~ Robert Burns, "Afton Water"

Janie Jones returned to consciousness and immediately wished she hadn't. Pain was everywhere. Was someone kicking her in the head? She couldn't move her arms; they felt like they were strapped down. She couldn't open her eyes. Were they taped shut? Oh, God! Was she being worked over by thugs? Why? She was just a musician! What had she done to them? And why did it smell like lavender? Nothing made any sense.

Janie finally got her eyes to open. What came into focus was an intensely blue pair of eyes, only a couple of inches away from her own. Janie screamed. So did her supposed assailant, a pale little ginger-haired girl who couldn't have been more than twelve.

"Miss Sackree! She's awake!" the girl shrieked, bolting upright and dropping an armful of bedding on Janie's stomach. The girl rushed out of the room, leaving the door open.

Okay, so that little kid had obviously not beaten her up. Why was she in so much pain, then? Was she in a hospital? It sure didn't look like one. There was a yellow canopy above the bed— nothing like the frilly pink one she'd had when she was a kid, more like something you'd see in a museum. It was silk, maybe, and covered in embroidery. The bed was something George Washington could have slept in, with massive mahogany posts at the corners. It was also the lumpiest, most uncomfortable bed imaginable.

Janie's arms were pinioned by a thick sheet that was tucked in too tightly. The room was stiflingly hot. She tried to squirm her way out of her linen cocoon, but she was too weak. She shut her eyes to keep the room from spinning.

She opened them again at the sound of someone closing the door. A matronly, aproned woman strode over to the bed. "Well, Miss. It's high time you woke up. We were all starting to wonder if you ever would." She spoke with a British accent. "You've caused ever so much trouble around here," she said, but her smile belied the cross-sounding words. She laid cool fingers gently against Janie's forehead for a moment. "I am Sackree, the children's nurse. Here, you need to drink some of this, love." She held something resembling a little teapot up to Janie's lips.

Janie *was* terribly thirsty, so she drank what was in it— a warm, chicken-y broth with a bitter aftertaste. "Where am I?"

"You're at Godmersham Park, Miss."

It sounded vaguely familiar. "Is that near Nashville?"

"It's near Canterbury, Miss. In Kent."

She was in England! Goodness, how had she forgotten that? She had just started classes at Newcastle University. Wait—what day was it? "How long have I been asleep?"

"You've been here nigh on two days."

Two days!

Sackree gathered up the blankets the young girl had dropped on the bed and left the room before Janie could gather the wits to ask her any more questions. Janie's skin prickled; it was super weird how both the girl and the nurse looked like they were dressed to film an episode of *Downton Abbey* or something, in their starched aprons and mob caps. Had she gotten sick while touring some living history museum, like Williamsburg? Why wasn't she in a hospital? She couldn't remember anything. Pain throbbed in her temples, the room spun around, and everything went dark again.

When Janie awoke, it was no longer daylight. A light, whuffling snore emanated from someone nearby, and a soft light danced on the wick of a very old-fashioned lamp on the nightstand. Jeesh, was that an actual oil lamp? Who even used those anymore? Oh, yeah; she was in some kind of living history museum. The snore came from the nurse, Sackree, who was sitting in a chair near the fireplace, opposite the bed. There was a fire glowing in the fireplace now. Janie was glad of it, for she was chilly now, though she had been so hot before.

Someone had also added a woolen blanket and plumped up the lavender-scented feather pillows behind her, making it easier for her to see her surroundings. Her head still hurt, but Janie let her eyes travel around the room. Either this was a very old building, or it was made to look old. It was a really beautiful room. There was ornate white trim where the walls met the ceiling and above the fireplace. The walls were painted a pale yellow. At the two windows, brighter yellow silk draperies that matched the ones on the four-poster bed cascaded to the floor. Wow, there were some seriously expensive-looking antiques, too. Against one wall stood a marble-topped mahogany washstand which held a large chinoiserie bowl and matching pitcher. Like everything else in the room, they seemed to be in perfect condition, in spite of their age. Against the other wall was a neoclassical-style dressing table. The mirror above it had an ornately carved and gilded antique frame, but the glass itself had to be new; there was no damage to the silvering. On either side of the dressing table were two gorgeous little English landscapes in oil, also in gilded frames.

Her mom would have loved this place! She had been a history professor who loved old things that she said "told a story." Janie had often gone to antique fairs with her when she was a little girl. Her earliest memory was of being pushed around in a stroller and gradually being crowded in by her mom's purchases. They couldn't afford furniture like the stuff in here, but her mom had liked finding small, beautiful things that were priced low enough for her; she wasn't the haggling type. "Score!" Mom used to say whenever she found a treasure.

Tears prickled behind Janie's eyes. Sure, she missed her mom, but she had been gone a long time, seven years now; it wasn't just that. Where was her dad? At twenty-two, Janie was used to being on her own, but her father had never failed to be there for her when she was really sick or needed any kind of help. Could he be on his way?

When she was a little girl, her father used to sit on the side of her bed and pray with her each night. "God, are you still there?" Janie whispered. She pulled the blankets up close under her chin and drifted off to sleep again.

Janie awoke the next morning in far less pain, but in dire need of the bathroom. The nurse was gone; only a set of knitting needles and what looked like a sock occupied her chair. Janie managed to get shakily to her feet, noticing for the first time that she was wearing a long, white linen nightgown. She didn't own a nightgown; usually she slept in oversized t-shirts. She tried not to think about a stranger having apparently undressed her, even if she was a nurse.

Janie walked across the room to the rather narrow door next to the washstand, her bare feet cold on the wood floor. She unhooked the latch that held it closed. No, it wasn't a bathroom at all, just a sort of cupboard with three shelves, two of which were bare. The third shelf had something small wrapped in tissue on it. The bathroom must be in the hall. Ugh! She went back across the room to the door. She saw there was a keyhole in the shiny brass plate below the knob and felt a second of panic, but the door wasn't locked, and it swung open very quietly for such an old door.

Janie peered out into a wide corridor lined with doors, all of them closed. There didn't seem to be a sign on any of them. How was she supposed to tell which one was the bathroom? Her rising panic was quelled by the sight of someone leaving one of the rooms: it was the ginger-haired girl she had seen in her room earlier. "Excuse me," Janie called out to her. "Can you tell me where the bathroom is?

"Och, Miss! You startled me! I didn't expect you to be up and about." It sounded more like "aboot" the way she said it.

Probably Scottish, then, not English. "I need to use the

bathroom," Janie said, a bit more quietly this time. She felt strangely apologetic. Was it the unaccustomed grandness of this place making her feel so shy? She shook off her embarrassment.

The girl looked confused for a moment, then gave a quick half-curtsey and said, "I'll tell Miss Sackree you want a bath right away, Miss." She whisked down the hall and around the corner before Janie could explain.

Shoot! She should have said, "W.C." That was what the English called bathrooms; probably the Scots did, too. Janie hoped Sackree would come soon. Not only was her bladder on the point of bursting, but she was feeling rather dizzy again.

Thank goodness, it was only a moment before Sackree came bustling down the corridor, a look of alarm on her face. "Why, Miss! You oughtn't be out of bed yet, I'm sure!" She herded Janie back into the bedroom.

"Sorry, but I need the W.C."

Apparently that wasn't right, either; Sackree looked just as confused as the girl had.

Good grief! Shouldn't it be obvious? She apparently hadn't peed for days. "The Loo!" Janie said, her voice rising into a squeak.

Whether it was the terminology, the tone, or the desperation that was surely evident on Janie's face, comprehension finally dawned in Sackree's. "Why, there's a chamber pot right here, Miss." She whooshed past Janie, opened a door in the front of the elegant little bedside table, and produced a lidded porcelain pot with two handles and a delicate floral design all around it. She handed it to Janie.

Was she serious? Even Williamsburg had toilets! The chamber pot looked suspiciously like the antique "soup tureen" in their china cabinet back home, used on special occasions. The implications were too hideous to contemplate.

"Elspeth will be back in a trice to take care of it. If you need anything else, one of us will help you." She hurried out of the room, closing the door behind her.

How long was a "trice"? And how exactly did you pee into this thing?

Very carefully, with your borrowed nightgown hiked up over one shoulder.

She slid the pot back into the cabinet. Completely exhausted, Janie fell more than climbed back into the bed. Lumps notwithstanding, it felt wonderful. Just then, there was a little scratching sound at the door, and the girl, who Janie now knew was Elspeth, came in. "Miss Sackree says to tell you the doctor will be in to see you later today, Miss."

"Thanks. Hey, my name's Janie, by the way."

"Aye, Miss," Elspeth answered with a quick bob. She opened the cabinet, got the chamber pot, and went back out again, just as if she carried other people's pee around every day.

Mr. Scudamore, the doctor, couldn't have been a day over thirty, but something about him made him seem much older. Maybe it was his formal manner, or maybe it was his habit of clearing his throat as if he were about to make an important pronouncement. Instead of a lab coat, he wore a green jacket, a green and gold striped waistcoat, and knee breeches.

He reached for Janie's wrist and took her pulse with two fingers. She pulled the covers up to her chin with her other hand. She had only ever had female doctors before. She needn't have worried, though, because he made no move to check anything else. Maybe he wasn't even a doctor, just a historical reenactor.

"Are you really a doctor? Where's your stethoscope?"

He ignored the questions. "Your color is better, and your pulse is much stronger. Very good."

"Wait, 'better'? Did you see me before?"

"Certainly. I examined you two days ago. The application of leeches to the cranium seems to have been quite efficacious."

"*What?* You stuck *leeches* to my head? Are you *kidding* me?"

He looked serious enough as he peered at Janie through his small, wire-rimmed spectacles. "How have you been feeling?"

"Like I've been run over by a truck. Actually, not so much anymore. I feel a whole lot better than I did at first. But about the leeches—"

"Incoherent, I see." He cleared his throat. "Hmmph. It's not unusual to have a certain amount of—" He waved his hands around his head— "confusion, after a cranial injury. Do you remember your name?"

"Sure, it's Janie."

"Full name, please."

"Jane Austen Jones."

He raised his eyebrows. "Related to the family, are you then?"

"No, not as far as I know. I've never been here before. I don't know how I even got here."

"Hmmph. I was recently privileged to attend a lecture on cranial traumas by the renowned surgeon, John Abernethy, in London. Confusion and memory loss may be caused by concussion to the brain. Miss Jones, will you please relate to me all that you can recall about what happened to you?"

"I don't remember anything. I think maybe I was driving to a gig. Maybe I got in an accident." It was her best guess, anyway. Trying to remember made her head hurt.

His eyebrows shot up again. "Driving a gig, were you? Not the vehicle for a young lady, in my opinion. Overturns much too easily if the driver hasn't enough experience with the ribbons. At any rate, it's my understanding that no one found a carriage. More likely your horse threw you, and it ran away. A servant found you, alone and unconscious, on one of the roads leading to this estate."

No, that wasn't what had happened. Her horse would never have run off and left her. Jack wouldn't have thrown her in the first place. Janie had had him since he was a yearling, and she was a little girl. Anyway, Jack wasn't here in England; Janie's little sister was taking care of him, back home in Tennessee. Tears came to her eyes, but she blinked them away.

Mr. Scudamore's rather abrupt manner softened. "Miss Jones, it's important that you not try to force yourself to remember; that will only bring on headaches and possibly cause further damage. Your memory should return naturally, after you've had enough rest. If not, I will apply leeches again."

"Um, I don't—"

"I'll ask a servant to bring you some gruel. Food and rest are what you need right now. Then some fresh air. But be sure not to overexert yourself; resume your normal activities gradually. Aside from driving gigs, of course."

"When can I go home— back to school, I mean?"

"Hmmph. You shouldn't travel any distance for a few days, perhaps a week. I'm sure the master of the house will extend his hospitality as long as need be; Edward Knight is a good man."

"The semester just started, and I'm missing classes. Can you write a note for me?"

Mr. Scudamore smiled indulgently but did not answer.

He bowed. "Your servant, Miss Jones," he said, and then he left.

So formal! If he was an actor, he did a good job of staying in character.

Sackree must have been waiting for permission to bring in food. She arrived only minutes later, bearing a silver tray. Janie thanked her and pushed herself up into a sitting position. She was suddenly very hungry. The tray contained a bowl of watery oatmeal, two thin slices of buttered toast, a cup of tea, and a newspaper. Only old people read newspapers, she thought. Everything was on your phone, anyway. Oh, shoot! She hadn't asked anyone about her phone! She needed to call her dad; he obviously didn't even know about her accident yet, or he would be here already. Or if he couldn't get a flight, he would've at least called. Wow, her brain really was messed up! Why hadn't she called him right when she woke up? Sackree had already left the room, but she would ask her about it as soon as she came back.

Janie admired the china pattern as she picked up the delicate pink teacup, another lovely antique. She only ate a little of the runny oatmeal, which was salted. She usually had hers with lots of sugar. The toast was delicious, though, made from thin slices of homemade bread. Out of curiosity, she opened up the newspaper, *The Kentish Gazette*. Wow, the print was so tiny! Was this from today? She hardly knew what day it was anymore. She peered at the minuscule date: 27 September, 1813.

The china teacup slipped from Janie's fingers, rolled off of the bed, and shattered on the floor, as she fainted dead away.

CHAPTER 2

He has set her upon his steed and roundly rode away,
And ne'er loot her look back again the live-long summer's day.
~Traditional, "Bonnie Barbara Livingston"

As he rubbed down and fed the pair of bays that pulled the Knight family's barouche, Duncan MacKinnon found himself wondering what the master would make of the lady who had turned up at Godmersham Park three days earlier. Duncan had heard from the house servants that she had finally regained consciousness, and the doctor had come to check on her a second time. He was relieved, for he had been the one who first discovered her, half covered by the furze that grew along the roadside. His first horrific thought had been that he was looking at a dead body, but upon dismounting from his horse, kneeling in the mud, and checking for a pulse, he discovered that she still lived.

The poor lass had been wearing nothing but a sleeveless sort of green shift in the damp chill. She didn't even have shoes or stockings on her feet. Her long, chestnut hair was unbound, and some of it lay in waves across her face. Duncan tried to brush it gently back from her bloodied brow with his fingers, grimacing when he saw it was stuck to the wound in her forehead. At least the gash wasn't deep and probably didn't need stitching. Still, he needed to get her to the great house right away, where they could take care of her and send for a doctor. It would be easier to take her to one of the houses right there in the village, but something he couldn't define made him want her to be much closer to home.

He gathered the lady up in his arms, but in order to mount his horse without dropping her, he needed to free up at least one of his arms. "My apologies," he said, grimacing again, as he slung the lady over his shoulder like a sack of oats. He was fully aware of the indelicacy of the situation—what if she woke up while being handled in such a fashion? But she did not awaken, and Duncan stepped up into the stirrup, landing rather more heavily than usual into the saddle. His horse protested with a snort. "Extra oats for this, Bruce me lad," Duncan promised.

It was odd how protective Duncan still felt towards the lass, although she had no connection to him. Several times he had found himself stopping by the servants' door of the great house for news of her. He couldn't help wondering who she was and where she had come from. How had she come to be there, clad in so little, injured and alone?

The silky garment she wore spoke of wealth and luxury. He blushed as he remembered her bare shoulders. The lady's jewels testified that she hadn't been the victim of a footpad or a highwayman; those were emeralds and diamonds of the first water. He thought wryly that the Duncan of ten years ago would have slipped the necklace into his pocket before bringing her to the house, but he wasn't that person anymore.

The lass was indeed a mystery. He wondered what color her eyes were. Och, he needed to get back to work.

After he finished with the horses and put the tack away, Duncan left the tack room and headed towards the great house.

Fanny's Diary- 28 Sep. 1813

Lizzy, Marianne, Sayce, and I got home from Goodnestone last night. We had fine weather for the fair, and I bought four yards of lace, some ribbon, and pink and green Persian, for I couldn't decide which color I liked better. I fell ill on Saturday evening and had to miss church on

Sunday, but I was better yesterday, and coming home has cured me altogether. I am happy to report that the fresh paint smell has left the house at last.

However, none of that is the exciting news. It is this: we have a mysterious houseguest!! Three days ago, a young woman who is entirely unknown to us was found on our property, in such a state that no one could say if she would live or die! I hardly slept a wink last night for wondering about her! I finally got a look at her this morning before breakfast, although she wasn't awake yet. Sackree has put one of my nightgowns on her, so I guess we are of a size. She looks to be about my age, as well. She has a plaster on her forehead, no doubt covering some ghastly wound. How my heart goes out to her! I wonder what happened to her. She is very pretty, with abundant, reddish brown hair and a heart-shaped face. I would even call her beautiful, if not for the ~~hideous~~ unfortunate freckles across her nose. Perhaps she doesn't know about using strawberry water for the complexion. I must loan her some of mine.

Aunt Jane says that Papa was rather vexed about our houseguest at first. He said, "Why do I always have something unpleasant to deal with when I arrive home?" Of course, dearest Papa still did the right thing, as always. He sent right away for Mr. Scudamore to come and attend to her and said she could stay with us until she is fully recovered. How enjoyable it will be to have someone my age staying with us!

Sackree says the lady did finally wake up but couldn't

stay awake. She must really be quite ill. I tried to get more information from the chambermaid, but the dull girl couldn't even tell me what color eyes the lady has! How can anyone be so unobservant, so utterly lacking in imagination? My guess is her eyes are grey, like Guinevere's.

I did get something interesting out of Elspeth, though. She said the lady had been wearing a satin gown and jewels when she was found, so she must be a person of some consequence. Aside from her name, Miss Jones, which I had to winkle out of the doctor, I still know almost nothing about her!

I have the front parlor (I think I shall call it the Rose Room, now that it is pink) all to myself this afternoon. The younger ones are back to their lessons with Miss Clewes. Papa and the older boys are out hunting, and John is in the nursery. Aunt Jane is in the library, as usual. In short, all is quiet. I should have written all of my letters by now, but I have only managed one. I could hardly keep my mind on the page; my thoughts were too busy wondering about Miss Jones and, I must confess, playing matchmaker for Papa. He certainly won't do it for himself. I used to think he was so romantic in his devotion to my late mama. Now I think he's not so much romantic as content, happy to keep things as they are forever. I've done my best to be the lady of Godmersham Park for five years now. As dearly as I love this house and all ten of my younger brothers and sisters, I want to marry, to have children and a home of my own. Dare I hope that the lady upstairs has been sent here by Providence?

"There, she's coming 'round!" Janie heard someone say.

"Sackree, help me sit her up and get her some water. Miss Jones, are you alright?" asked a pale, brown-haired young woman Janie hadn't seen before. She was dressed like a character from a Jane Austen novel, minus the bonnet, in a long, high-waisted pastel blue dress with puffed sleeves. A furrow of concern showed between her slender brows.

"I can sit myself up," Janie said, but her voice sounded shaky to her own ears. She pushed herself up as the young woman fluffed the pillows behind her.

"Here you are, dearie." Sackree handed Janie a glass of water. Janie took it with both hands, which were shaking as badly as her voice.

"I will stay with her," the young woman said. "You go get Mr. Scudamore, Sackree. I think he is still playing billiards with Papa."

"No! No more leeches!" Janie yelled. Oops, that came out a bit loud. Both of the other women were frozen like frightened rabbits. "I mean, no, thanks. I'm fine, really I am. I don't need the doctor." Janie certainly didn't plan on losing any more blood, anyway. No wonder she kept fainting! Her head was itchy, too. Gross.

Sackree unfroze first, nodding her head vigorously and setting the lace of her cap to fluttering. "That's right. I always say those leeches do nary a bit of good. Not like a nice, hot, mashed onion poultice."

Not having any opinions on poultices, Janie looked at the young woman, who was still wide-eyed. "I don't think we've met, but there's a lot I can't remember, so maybe we have. My name's Janie Jones. I really like your dress. You look like Elizabeth Bennet."

The young woman's hazel eyes opened even wider, and she broke into a smile. "So you've read *Pride and Prejudice*! That bodes well for our friendship, Miss Jones." The ringlets that framed her face bounced as she made a quick curtsey. "My name is Fanny Knight, and I'm so pleased to make your acquaintance at last." She blushed. "That is, I'm happy to see you're awake, and I hope you're feeling better."

Fanny Knight– Janie was sure she had heard that name before, but she was also sure that she didn't recognize the young lady. That was weird.

"You're welcome to stay in our home until you're fully recovered," Miss Knight said with a smile.

"This is your house, then, as well as a museum? Thanks so much for letting me stay here. I hope I haven't put you out of your bed."

Miss Knight laughed brightly. "Indeed not, Miss Jones!

I assure you, we have guest rooms aplenty here. It's no trouble. But we should let you rest now. Is there anything else we might do for your comfort before we go?"

"I don't think so. Wait— yes, there is! What a mess my brain is in— my phone! Do y'all have it? I need to call my father. I don't think he knows where I am. I usually call him every few days, so he may be worried about me."

Miss Knight and Sackree exchanged a look, eyebrows raised.

"Actually, I may need to borrow a phone. I bet mine has lost its charge."

"It sounds to me like you need to rest, love," Sackree said. "I will get you pen, ink, and paper, and you may write to your father whenever you feel up to it. We'll see that it is delivered." Miss Knight nodded her agreement and slipped quietly out of the room.

Why would she want to write a letter? "No, that's okay. I'm looking for my— oh, I forgot! Y'all call them mobiles, don't you? Did someone find my mobile?"

"I'm sorry, Miss," Sackree said. "I don't know as I've ever heard of mope isles, but you had nothing with you but the clothes on your back when you were found, except for that fancy necklace. I sent them out for cleaning—the clothes, that is. Miss Knight will loan you some of her gowns. And I put your necklace safely away in that corner cupboard, so don't you worry. You should get some rest now, Miss. I'll just clean this up and be out of your way." Sackree stooped to pick what looked like broken pieces of pink china up off of the floor. She wrapped them up in a newspaper and carried them out with her.

She hadn't heard of mobiles? That was carrying the reenactment thing a bit far, wasn't it? Maybe their employer didn't allow them to make any modern references. Still, it was very unsettling to hear she had nothing with her when they found her. So was seeing the newspaper in Sackree's hands; something about it was prickling Janie's memory in a disquieting way. Why that should be, she couldn't say, since she rarely ever saw newspapers, other than the ones the antique dealers wrapped delicate things in after you purchased them. A memory flashed through her mind, as bright and clear as a scene from a favorite DVD, of her mother unwrapping something she had found for Janie on one of her antiquing trips. It was a sweet little bone china horse, dapple gray, just like her beloved Jack. "He looked like he wanted to come home and live with you," Mom had said with a grin.

But that wasn't the memory that was playing hide-and-seek with Janie now. It was ironic that she could recall something that had happened a decade ago as if it were yesterday, yet not be able to remember things that had happened yesterday, or even today— ironic, and really, really frustrating. Janie had the strangest urge to call Sackree back, to ask if she could take a look at that newspaper she was throwing out, but she didn't.

CHAPTER 3

____

Oft, in the stilly night, ere slumber's chain has bound me,
Fond memory brings the light of other days around me.
~Thomas Moore. "Oft, in the Stilly Night"

Janie followed the doctor's advice insofar as she stayed in bed the next day, but she ignored it in spending that day forcing herself to remember everything she could. Anyway, the so-called doctor used *leeches*, for goodness' sake! Did she really need to listen to him?

Some things came back to her fairly easily: she had just started graduate school at Newcastle University, where she had a scholarship to study the traditional folk music of the British Isles. Her new flatmate, Anne, was from Yorkshire. Anne played the cello and was studying classical composition. She and Janie had been texting one another even before Janie got to England, and they were already becoming friends.

It took much more effort to recall why she was in Kent, so far away from the university. Something was telling her it was because of a music gig, but why would she have a performance right at the beginning of classes, in a place where she only knew one person? She poked and prodded her mind over and over again, but all she got was a massive headache.

Janie was relieved when the nurse came in with some soup and tea on a tray. She sat up and Sackree put the tray in her lap.

"Thank you." Janie said. "Do you have some Tylenol, or whatever y'all call it— Paracetamol? Something for a headache?"

"The doctor said you would have the headache. That tea has willow bark and chamomile in it, Miss."

"Okay. I guess I'll try that first, then."

"Elspeth will come in later for your tray," Sackree said, and she left the room.

The soup was a thin but savory beef broth. The tea wasn't exactly nasty, but it had a woody, medicinal flavor, and it made Janie's mouth feel a little numb. When she was finished, she slid the tray onto the bedside table and closed her eyes.

Janie woke from her nap feeling much more like herself. Maybe it was that stuff in the tea, or maybe it was her subconscious working overtime in her sleep, but her memory was returning at last. She had been right— she *was* here in Kent because of a gig.

The violinist in Anne's string quartet had broken her arm, and Janie had taken her place at an afternoon wedding in Chilham, on the grounds of Chilham Castle.

Against the backdrop of the manor house's Tudor architecture, the terraced gardens, designed by the famous Capability Brown, were stunning, even in autumn. The sky was full of dark, tumultuous-looking clouds that brightened the colors in the flower-filled urns and highlighted the happiness and hopefulness of the occasion by juxtaposition. The rain did them the honor of waiting until the ceremony was over before coming down in cold, fat drops.

Janie had to drive back to school afterwards because she was the only one without a reservation to stay at the castle. Even the violinist with the broken arm, who, like Anne, was a close friend of the bride, was staying there overnight. Every bed was taken. Since Janie didn't know anyone there but Anne, she really didn't mind leaving early, although she imagined the castle's guest rooms— probably more luxurious than anything she'd ever stayed in— with a pang.

The other details of the evening came flooding back, filling the gaps in her memory. Janie had been tired after the reception, and rather than do the whole five-hour-plus drive that night, she had called the inn in Chilham. It was booked solid, so she was going to have to drive to nearby Canterbury.

She remembered getting into the blue Mini Cooper and feeling the usual sensation that the driver's seat was on the wrong side. She remembered she was wearing the green satin evening gown she wore whenever she did weddings, instead of her usual black; she felt damp and chilly and wished she had worn a jacket. She remembered slipping off her new shoes, which had rubbed blisters on her heels. She remembered throwing her wet umbrella onto the back seat, then reaching over to snug her violin case carefully into the space under the passenger seat, where it fit exactly. She remembered the feeling of the little brass chain sliding over her wrist as she let her black beaded evening purse fall into the passenger seat. She remembered starting the car, turning on the windshield wipers, and driving through the castle gates and into the parking lot, where she stopped to set the GPS on her phone. She remembered leaving Chilham and getting onto the A2 at the roundabout, then realizing she was heading away from Canterbury a few minutes later when she heard the GPS reroute. She remembered peering through the darkness and the rain, looking for a good place to turn around.

Try as she might, beyond that, she remembered nothing at all.

Where was her violin now? It was her most precious possession, handed down to her by her mother's father when Janie was just a little girl because he knew how much she loved its music. It had belonged to his father, and to his father's father before him. Seven year old Janie, unaware that her grandfather was nearing his end, had known only joy at the gift. Wearing her favorite blue sundress and pink cowgirl boots, with her long hair in braids and a huge smile on her freckled face, Janie had hugged that battered old fiddle tightly to her chest. She had never let it go, not even years later, when she could have bought a much nicer looking instrument. Some people might not understand, but Grandpa Jim's fiddle had her family's music in it—years and years of music and love. Why would she want anything else?

Janie heard the scratching noise at the door which always announced the entry of the little chambermaid.

"Hello, Miss! It sure is good to see you sitting up, and not dead or anything," Elspeth said as she entered with her arms full of clothing.

Janie laughed. Elspeth gave her a puzzled look, then she

began laying some of the garments across the end of the bed. There were two long, white dresses, as well as a pink one and a blue one. "Miss Knight said to bring you these gowns to choose from. If you feel well enough, you're to come downstairs and meet the master this evening. Can I help with your hair, Miss? I want to be a lady's maid, like Miss Sayce. She doesn't mind; she has enough to do taking care of Miss Knight and her aunt. Please, Miss?"

Janie started to protest, but she couldn't resist the chance to dress up in a beautiful gown like the one Miss Knight was wearing. Why not play along with the whole living history game? She had always wondered what it would be like to live in the past. Besides, hadn't Sackree said Janie's clothes were at the cleaner's? It would be fun, even though she would probably look ridiculous, unlike Miss Knight, who looked completely natural wearing this sort of thing. "Sure, why not? Which dress do you think I should wear?"

The maid was all seriousness. "The pink one, Miss. Most assuredly. It will bring out the color in your cheeks, Miss."

Janie smiled at Elspeth's manner; the girl had gone from twelve to twenty, all at once. "Pink it is, then. Is it possible for me to have a bath first?"

"Aye, Miss. I'll just get the tub set up for you." The maid scurried out and returned a few minutes later, carrying a large copper tub like a turtle shell on her back. Janie helped her set it down on the floor. "I'll be right back with the water, Miss," Elspeth said.

Janie had not realized how much trouble she would be putting the poor girl through, but there was no backing out now. Besides, Janie was in no fit state to be meeting anyone. She was sure she looked terrible and smelled even worse.

The maid made three trips with two buckets of hot water, Janie's feelings of guilt increasing with each one. "Okay, that's enough. Thank you, Elspeth."

"Are you sure, Miss? Miss Knight usually has eight."

"Yes, it's plenty."

"I'll come back in a little while to help you get dressed then, Miss," Elspeth said brightly, setting a bar of soap, a sea sponge, and a towel next to the tub.

Janie wanted to say she could manage by herself, but the girl seemed so excited about playing lady's maid. "Okay, thanks."

As it turned out, Janie was more than glad she had help. Not only would she never have figured out how to fasten the dress, which closed at the back with a mysterious combination of drawstrings and straight pins, she wouldn't even have known how to put on the underclothes. It turned out that the corset, which Elspeth called "stays," wasn't worn next to the skin at all, but on top of a shift, a kind of underdress made of linen. It was a surprisingly comfortable outfit. Why did those actresses in historical movies always complain about not being able to breathe? The dress fit her perfectly. Janie loved the lace details around the neckline and the cuffs, and the narrow satin sash around the high waistline.

After Elspeth helped her into a pair of silk stockings that were secured with ribbon garters just above her knees, Janie slipped on a pair of Miss Knight's white leather flats. They were a tiny bit snug on her, but the leather was very soft. She hoped they wouldn't stretch out too much for their owner's feet.

"Now sit down at the dressing table, if you please, Miss. I watch Miss Sayce do this all the time."

Janie sat, and Elspeth reached for a comb. She parted Janie's hair deftly down the middle and started combing it out.

"I predict a great future for you as a lady's maid, Elspeth," Janie said.

The girl giggled. "Och, don't speak too soon, Miss. I haven't finished doing your hair yet."

"I'm not sure I should be letting you. What if you burn a chunk of it off with the curling iron like Jo did in *Little Women?*

Elspeth looked shocked. "I would never, Miss! I'm ever so careful!" The strokes of the comb through Janie's hair became noticeably gentler. "Of course that lad Joe didn't know what he was doing; it's a lass's job! Anyway, your hair curls naturally. I just have to pin it up and put in some wee pearl combs. I'll be done in a trice, Miss."

There was that "trice" again. The girl was quick,

though. When Janie saw herself in the mirror, she was surprised at how good she looked. Elspeth had pinned her hair in such a way that some curls covered the gash in her forehead, and she had left some tendrils of hair loose at her temples. The rest of Janie's hair was swept up on top of her head in a style that reminded her of the ancient Greeks. She looked very nice indeed, even without her usual mascara and lip gloss.

"Och, I almost forgot, Miss." The maid poured something from a glass bottle onto a piece of cloth, which she wiped all over Janie's face. It smelled like strawberries.

It was a good thing that Miss Knight had stopped by Janie's room to show her the way to the parlor; the house was even bigger and grander than she had supposed, and more than one room looked like a parlor. As they came down the staircase, Janie gasped. The central hall was enormous; her whole house would practically fit into it! It would have been perfectly at home in a palace, with its stone floors inset with squares of black marble. The upper walls and ceiling were decorated with elaborate white trim, and each doorway was topped with a marble lintel and flanked by Corinthian columns. The tremendous fireplace had a marble overmantle carved with a classical frieze. A crystal chandelier above their heads held dozens of candles. Janie hoped she would have a chance to see it when they were all lit.

They went through one of the grand doorways into and through another room before entering the parlor, where a handsome, dark-haired gentleman who looked to be in his forties was sitting on an antique empire couch upholstered in gold velvet. His elbow rested casually on one of its rolled arms. Like Miss Knight, he did not look at all like an actor wearing a costume. He belonged in his surroundings. In Hessian boots, buff breeches, embroidered waistcoat, impeccably tailored green coat, and starched cravat, he looked for all the world like Mr. Darcy waiting to receive guests at Pemberley. He stood when they entered the room, as did the black and white spaniel that had been sleeping on his boot. Four young men, similarly attired, jumped quickly to their feet from their seats at a card table on the far side of the room.

Miss Knight said, "Miss Jones, may I present to your acquaintance my father, Mr. Edward Knight, and four of my brothers: Mr. Edward Knight, Mr. George Knight, Mr. Henry Knight, and Mr. William Knight." Mr. Knight and his good-looking sons each made an elegant bow. Fanny's oldest brother was particularly cute. He looked like a younger version of his father, with thick, wavy brown hair. The spaniel waved its flag-like tail and trotted over to Janie. She bent down to stroke its silky ears. "And that is Flossy," Fanny said.

"I'm pleased to meet y'all," Janie said, still trying to place the name Edward Knight. She was sure she had never seen him before. Maybe he was reenacting the part of someone from history. That made sense.

Mr. Knight said, "I trust you are feeling better," Miss Jones."

Oops! She probably should have curtsied before this. She attempted a curtsy now. It wasn't as smooth as their bows, but not too shabby. The dress probably helped. "I am feeling better, thanks. And thanks so much for your hospitality. Everyone's been so kind."

Mr. Knight invited her to sit on the couch, and she and Miss Knight sat down. He moved to a rosewood chair opposite them, and his sons resumed their seats at the card table. Miss Knight took some needlework out of a compartment in the sewing table next to the sofa and began stitching on it.

Janie smiled politely at Mr. Knight, trying not to be distracted by the number of beautiful antique pieces in the room. She should have expected it, considering the gorgeous things that had been relegated to the guest room where she was staying. Those were the cast-offs, she supposed; the real treasures were in here. She had seen less perfect Meissen figurines in a museum than the ones over on that mantelpiece.

Wow, the window still had its original wavy glass, too! Not a single pane appeared to have been replaced. It framed a view of gardens, an extensive lawn, and a wooded hill that must all be stunning in full daylight. Near the window stood a beautifully carved harp; she wondered if anyone played it, or if it was just for decoration.

"... have an American staying with us," Mr. Knight was saying.

Shoot! She had obviously missed something. Janie turned her attention to Mr. Knight.

"Tell me a little bit about your family, Miss Jones," he said.

"Well, we live near Nashville, in Tennessee. My father is the pastor of a church. My mother died six years ago. I have two sisters and a brother; I'm the oldest."

"I'm sorry about your mother. That is something you and my daughter have in common."

"Oh. I'm sorry for your loss, too." She looked at Miss Knight, then back at her father.

"Thank you. What was your mother's family name?" he asked.

"McIntyre. It's Scots-Irish."

"Hmm. Is your father a gentleman?"

Janie squirmed under the pointed gaze that slid down Mr. Knight's long, aristocratic nose. What a weird question! "If you mean does he give up his seat for old ladies and things like that, then yes. But he's also—" She searched for a word— honorable? That sounded so archaic. "He has integrity. He's the best man I know."

"High praise indeed. More to the point, does your father own land there in America?"

Another weird question. "Yes, sir."

"How much land?"

"Well, our house in Tennessee is on five acres. We also have a horse farm in Kentucky that was my grandfather's. It's on 2,500 acres. We raise American Saddlebreds."

"So he is a gentleman, then."

"*That's* what makes him a gentleman? Not that he's honorable?" There, she'd said it, and she was glad of it. "That's ridiculous!" Janie was pretty sure she heard a little gasp from Miss Knight.

"You give your opinion very decidedly for so young a person," Mr. Knight said.

"I suppose I do, Mr. Knight." Janie grinned. "Or should I say, Lady Catherine?" Yeah, that was definitely a gasp from Fanny, and one of her brothers snorted.

Edward Knight burst out laughing. "Touché! You know *Pride and Prejudice*, I see. You will do very well. I am happy for you to stay here with us for as long as you like, Miss Jones. My daughter and my sister shall enjoy your company. I daresay, we all shall."

Miss Knight sagged with relief beside her. "Shall I ring for tea?"

CHAPTER 4

Go daughter of Megan to castles of splendour;
Each eye that beholds thee thy presence shall bless.
~Traditional, "Daughter of Megan"

Fanny's Diary- 29 Sep. 1813

My matchmaking scheme proceeds apace! I admit that introductions this evening made a poor beginning, but then our guest made Papa laugh so heartily that I was quite taken with her, and I think Papa was, too. Sadly, Miss Jones declined my invitation to have dinner with the family, in favor of a tray in her room. I'm afraid Papa wore her out with all of his questions. Miss Jones asked me, does he "grill" everybody that way, or was it just her? (Her expressions are so amusing!) I had to admit I'd never seen him do so before, but we don't usually have complete strangers staying in our house. I want so much to introduce her to Aunt Jane, who dearly loves to laugh, but she's been sequestering herself in the library since our arrival. We sometimes tease Aunt Jane that she prefers the company of her characters to her family's! Still, she must come out for meals, and we must content ourselves with seeing her then.

I asked Miss Jones to meet me in the breakfast room this morning. Afterwards, we plan to go for a drive, if the weather is fine. I lent her my bonnet with the cherries on it, as well as my green spencer, since she has none with her. She was very disappointed that her own clothes were not ready, though she said she was enjoying "playing dress-up."

But I've gotten ahead of myself. Before we decided to take a drive, Miss Jones actually asked me if I knew where Chilham Castle was! I answered how could I not, when it is a mere two miles away, and the Wildmans such friends of the family? Her astonishment and happiness at this news were so extreme that I feared she might faint again! I pulled out my vinaigrette just in case, but she regained her composure. I told her our estate is far prettier, whatever she may have been told, but she still insisted we drive there at once. Of course, I said we couldn't, as it would be the height of rudeness at that hour, so near to dinnertime. Whether Miss Jones' odd ways are due to her cracked head, or simply because she is American, I find them to be exceedingly diverting!

P.S. Her eyes are not grey, as I supposed, but green.

Janie was already awake and in danger of dislocating both of her shoulders while trying to fasten her dress when Elspeth came in the next morning. "Och, nae, Miss! That's not the way!" the maid said, after opening the draperies.

"Well, you'll have to help me, then. It looks like I absolutely can't manage without a lady's maid."

Elspeth grinned and fastened her up. "Will you be wanting a breakfast tray now, Miss?"

"No, I'm actually going downstairs for breakfast this morning, so you may need to draw me a map to the breakfast room. Miss Knight and I are driving to Chilham Castle today. It's the last place I remember being before waking up here."

"Oh! Then you need someone to do your hair, too." Elspeth's grin widened, and she fairly bounced in anticipation. "The breakfast room is simple, Miss. Take the door on the left after you come down into the great hall, and you'll be in the dining room. Go through the door on your left, turn left again, then you'll see the door to the breakfast room on your right."

"Yikes! I definitely need a map. And you don't need to do my hair. It'll be covered up, since I'll be wearing that bonnet over there as part of my costume. I can just twist my hair up and be done with it."

"Och, nae, Miss! That will never do! What if you meet the love of your life today, and you with your hair all twisted up? What then?" The girl looked genuinely pained at the thought. She was actually wringing her hands.

Janie laughed. "In that case, I guess you'd better do it. I wouldn't want to ruin my date with destiny. I'm all yours." She sat down at the dressing table.

"Aye, Miss," Elspeth sighed happily, and she got to work.

"The carriage should be ready for us by the time we finish eating," Miss Knight said when Janie finally found the breakfast room. They would be going in an actual carriage instead of a car? Cool! They sure did go all the way around here.

Janie looked around the room, which was light and airy, with lovely chintz curtains on its windows. Imagine having a room just for breakfast! Along one wall, a sideboard held an urn filled with a huge arrangement of fresh flowers. On the wall opposite was a matching sideboard, bearing dishes and a variety of breakfast choices, including toast, muffins, fruit, sliced ham, and a pound cake.

Following Miss Knight's example, Janie chose a muffin. A pretty, blonde-haired maid wearing a bored expression stood mutely next to the wall, perhaps waiting to clear things away afterwards. "Hi," Janie said.

Had the maid rolled her eyes? Maybe she imagined it.

"Would you like tea, coffee, or chocolate, Miss Jones?" Miss Knight asked.

"Yum! Chocolate, please." Miss Knight poured her some steaming chocolate from a tall, blue and white pot into one of a set of four matching cups. The cup was taller and narrower than a teacup and was made of china almost as thin as an eggshell. It made Janie feel clumsy to pick it up by its tiny handle and carry it over to the table, which had already been set with four places.

"Is anyone else joining us?"Janie asked.

"One never knows; breakfast is a casual affair around here. My father and my Aunt Jane often take theirs later, after Papa has met with his steward and such. The older boys are doubtless out with the beaters on a shoot already. One can never expect to see them until evening. My youngest brothers and sisters take their breakfast in the nursery. You should be able to meet them later today."

"On a shoot?"

"They are always shooting something. Pheasant, partridge..." She waved her hand dismissively. "They are mad for any kind of sport and fancy themselves 'top o' the trees Corinthians.'"

Janie nodded, although she had no idea what Miss Knight meant, and she took a sip of the chocolate. It was positively divine— much thicker and richer than any she'd had before. She closed her eyes and savored another taste. "This is amazing hot chocolate! I could drink this stuff every day!"

Miss Knight's eyes opened wide. "Do you not have chocolate in America?"

Janie laughed. "It's not as tragic as all that! We've got chocolate; it's just nothing like this."

"Oh, I see. Are you still set on viewing Chilham Castle? Of course, it's too early to pay a morning call, but if you like, we can call on the Wildmans this afternoon. I should do so anyway, now that we've returned. Fortunately, there is a good prospect of the castle from the town square. After you've seen it, I can show you around our estate; we have some beautiful walks. If you are up to it, of course. I don't want to tire you."

"That sounds really nice, actually."

As they ate, Miss Knight was skimming a newspaper that lay on the table. Once again, something stirred in Janie's memory. She glanced over at the front page. The date was 30 September, 1813. 1813! The memory of another headline hit Janie like an unexpected wave at the beach, but she quickly regained her footing. Of course, the museum must have an antique press that printed these! They probably even copied actual historical headlines. For a second there, she'd had the crazy thought that she had traveled through time! Janie laughed aloud at herself.

"I daresay you think me the most dreadful bluestocking, Miss Jones, but I assure you, I only read the news to keep up with the battles. When one has relatives in the Royal Navy, it is only natural to take an interest. Have no fear, I don't intend to gain enough knowledge to be indelicate."

Janie said, "No, of course not," but she wasn't about to confess what she had really been laughing about.

What Janie noticed first was not the lovely carriage, which looked to be freshly painted in green with gold trim, but the magnificent pair of bays that was harnessed to it. They both had white blazes on their noses and were groomed so immaculately that they shone in the sun. Janie reached up and stroked the nose of the horse nearest to her. "Hello, there! Aren't you beautiful? I wish I had brought you some sugar lumps from breakfast. Maybe I can just run back and— Oh, sorry."

The man Janie had almost plowed into smiled at her as if he was glad to see her, his eyes wide with what looked like recognition. Maybe he thought she was someone else. Janie felt her face flush with warmth. She would definitely remember if she had ever met this guy before; he was gorgeous. He removed his hat and bowed to her. Like everyone else at the museum, he looked like he belonged in the 1800's. He wore a long, caped coat of dark green wool. His dark, curly hair was cut in a typical Regency style, short with longer layers on top and sideburns coming down almost to his well defined jawline. He opened the carriage door and held his hand out to her. "Let me help ye, Miss." He spoke with a Scottish accent.

"Um, thank you," Janie said. She placed her hand in his. He helped her step up into the carriage, but he didn't close the door right away. Her hand lingered in his for a moment, and Janie found herself looking into his warm, brown eyes.

"Your goon, miss."

"My goon?" Oh, her gown— its long skirt was hanging outside of the door, so he couldn't close it. Good grief, what an idiot she was! She pulled the hem of her dress up out of the way, and he shut the door.

Janie loved the sound of the gravel crunching under the carriage wheels as they pulled away from the house— it was like something from a Jane Austen movie. She leaned forward to look out of the window. "Oh, wow!" she exclaimed. A herd of fallow deer was grazing out in the meadow in front of the house! She turned to look through the back window at the Palladian mansion as they drove away from it. Godmersham Park, with its bricks glowing a fiery orange-red in the soft morning light, looked even more impressive from a distance, when she could see it presiding over the surrounding landscape. The gravel drive turned into a dirt road. On her side of the carriage, there were farms and sheep meadows. Miss Knight's side was more wooded. They must be avoiding the main roads to keep the horses away from cars; she hadn't seen a single car.

They passed a young man driving an ox cart in the opposite direction. He obviously also worked at the living history museum.

"We are on the Pilgrim's Road now," Fanny said. "It goes all the way from London to Canterbury."

That explained it. This lane probably hadn't changed since Chaucer's day. Janie was surprised it hadn't ever been turned into a highway. Then again, the Brits were good at preserving their history. "How far are we from the castle?"

"Not far; we are only about ten minutes away now."

Soon, they were on a cobblestone street lined with charming old buildings. Janie adored English villages like this that were virtually unchanged from the past. She hadn't seen this part of the village before, on the way to the wedding. There were probably a lot of things she missed when driving, though; she was always concerned with keeping to the left side, but not too far left, on the narrow roads. How long would it take her to feel completely comfortable with driving in England? Making turns on roundabouts was the hardest part. Maybe she would be used to it by the end of the semester.

It really felt like time travel to be riding in a carriage through a village like this, though!

"Here we are," Miss Knight said, as the carriage pulled to a stop in front of the White Horse Inn. She and Anne had stopped here for a delicious lunch the other day. It was at one corner of the big parking lot, which Anne called a "car park," in the center of the village. The gorgeous carriage driver opened Miss Knight's door and helped her step down, then he came over to Janie's side and did the same for her.

Janie glanced around the parking lot. This was definitely the same pub, and there was St. Mary's church with its clock tower, and the Medieval buildings around the lot looked pretty much the same as they had a few days ago, except there was no scaffolding on any of them. Had they finished the renovation work already? Something felt very different. Wait, what had happened to the wine shop with the peacock sign? Her eyes traveled around once more, and her disorientation was complete: she was standing in a cobblestone village square, not a paved lot full of cars. In fact, there were no cars to be seen anywhere. Sudden dizziness caused her to stumble, and someone's arm— the carriage driver's— steadied her.

A man wearing Regency clothing rode by on a horse. He tipped his hat, saying, "Good day, Miss Knight," as he passed them.

Miss Knight called after him, "Good day to you, Mr. Tylden," then she turned to Janie. "There's Chilham Castle," she said, pointing across the square. There, beyond a gate with only one gatehouse where there had definitely been two a few days ago, was the castle where Janie had played at the wedding.

Like everything else in the village, it was, but it wasn't. It was impossible, unless it really was 1813.

49

CHAPTER 5

Oh, I am like the turtle dove who flies from tree to tree;
As he waits for his own mate, so I will wait for thee.
-Traditional, "Turtle Dove"

Raven was not, generally speaking, a favorite of Dame Fortune. Not only did that blasted, tiny village have no pub, but he had to backtrack to the toff's gates and then walk three miles north from there to find this one. However, his rotten luck had finally turned— his quarry had actually come right to him! He'd seen the trio enter the tavern but thought nothing of it at first. The man and the woman were supporting another woman, who was near to swooning. They all sat down, and the man ordered an ale for the sick woman. Raven wasn't close enough to hear their conversation distinctly, but his ear caught one word: "Okay." It was a dead giveaway; the swooning lady was definitely the one he was looking for.

David's bones! If only he could get her away from that broad-shouldered fellow— there was no way he was going to take him on. Raven was no lightweight, but he was half that man's height and twice his age, he was. He had to settle for studying the girl's face. He now knew what she looked like, as well as where she was staying. He would have to be patient.

On the drive back to Godmersham Park, Janie was seeing everything with new eyes. This was probably not a back lane at all, just a regular road without the tarmac, signs, and cars. She was still a bit shaky, but it was as much with excitement as anything else. She was in the past! It was incredible, but so much made sense now— the house full of antiques that looked brand new, the leech doctor, everything! Of course, Janie wanted to go back to 2025, and she was a little worried about missing classes, but this was freaking amazing! How had it happened? Had she come in a time machine, like the Tardis in *Doctor Who*? Had she fallen into some kind of wormhole or time vortex? She would have to figure it out so that she could go back, but in the meantime, she wanted to experience everything!

Duncan couldn't help being concerned about Miss Jones. He felt her hand trembling in his when he handed her down from the carriage, and her eyes looked fever-bright. (Her eyes were extraordinary— they looked green at first, but up close, they were actually blue with tiny streaks of yellow right around the irises.) At the tavern, she had smiled and tried to reassure them that she was fine, or "oh-kay," as she put it, after drinking the ale, but she still seemed restless and unwell. She kept looking about, muttering odd things like, "That wasn't here before," and "Where are all of the books and the fairy lights? It must be true."

Books in a tavern? Duncan would have laughed aloud had she not been his superior, and had he not been so worried for her. And *fairy lights?* She had to be feverish. He was glad when Miss Knight insisted they return home.

He was spending entirely too much time worrying over the lass. Och, just because he had held her in his arms a few days ago, it didn't mean she was his responsibility now, did it? More importantly, he had no place worrying about a lady who was above his station, who didn't even know his name and probably didn't care to. He needed to remember that and get to work; the horses still needed to be rubbed down, walked, and groomed.

A woman Janie hadn't seen before was crossing the great hall as they entered the house.

"Aunt Jane!" Miss Knight exclaimed. "I thought we'd never see you! May I finally introduce our house guest? This is Miss Janie Jones. Miss Jones, this is my favorite aunt, Miss Jane Austen."

The Jane Austen? She couldn't be, could she? Oh, my gosh, yes, she could— it was 1813! Janie remembered to say, "I'm so pleased to meet you," but inside, she was doing cartwheels. This was insane! Jane Austen looked much prettier than her pictures. She was slender and a little taller than Janie, with glossy brown curls, hazel eyes, rounded cheeks, and a lovely smile. She had the same aquiline nose as Mr. Knight.

"I hope you are comfortable in the yellow room, Miss Jones. I'm usually in that one, but I shocked everyone by choosing another room that has recently been improved by the application of the most delightful wallpaper." Miss Austen said. "I was just about to take some tea. Why don't you both join me?"

"That's just the thing we need," Miss Knight said. "Miss Jones was feeling unwell when we got to town."

"I'm fine now," Janie insisted, "but I won't say no to a cup of tea."

They went into the breakfast room. Following Miss Knight's example, Janie took off her bonnet and gloves when she sat down. The pound cake from that morning was still sitting out on the sideboard, and next to it was a steaming pot of tea. Miss Austen poured a cup for each of them, and Miss Knight cut each of them a slice of cake.

"Mr. Knight is your brother, isn't he?" Janie asked Miss Austen, just to be sure.

"Yes, he is. I know the difference in our surnames is confusing. He was adopted by my father's second cousin, who had no children. I, for one, am very happy with the arrangement, since it means I get to come and visit this lovely place, use its extensive library, eat its excellent food, and drink its superior wine," she grinned.

No wonder the names Knight and Godmersham had seemed so familiar! She must have heard them in connection with her favorite author! Janie tamed the ridiculously big smile on her face so that Jane Austen wouldn't think she was a wacko.

"Why don't I see if the children can take a break from the schoolroom and join us?" Miss Knight asked.

"Yes, I'm quite certain they will prefer cake to doing sums," Miss Austen said with a chuckle.

After Miss Knight had hurried out of the room, Janie couldn't resist the chance to fangirl just a little bit. "Miss Austen, it really is an honor for me to meet you. *Pride and Prejudice* is one of my all-time favorite books."

It was as if a cloud had suddenly moved across the sun. The author's smile was gone. "How did you know that was my work? I published anonymously!"

Oops. Janie had totally forgotten that.

Miss Austen bit her lip and blushed. "Do forgive me, Miss Jones. My niece let something slip, didn't she? She's rather proud of me, you know. I'm actually surprised that you've read it. It has only just been published this year."

"I promise not to tell anyone."

"Think nothing of it, Miss Jones. Your admiration is very gratifying, I assure you. It's only that I value my privacy." She sighed, then her smile returned. "I shall have to become accustomed to the recognition, anyway. My brother Henry hasn't been able to help himself, either. I think he has told everyone of his acquaintance already."

Miss Knight returned with six kids in tow, stair-stepping from a girl who was maybe a year older than Elspeth down to a wide-eyed little boy of about five. "Miss Jones, allow me to introduce Miss Elizabeth, Miss Marianne, Master Charles, Miss Louisa, Miss Cassandra Jane, and Master Brook John Knight." The children curtseyed and bowed charmingly.

"What a lot of names! I am pleased to meet all of y'all."

"Who is Olive Yawl?" Brook John asked.

"I think she means you, John," Miss Austen said, patting his head. The little boy frowned. Before he could voice his objection to her answer, or possibly the pat on the head, Miss Austen asked, "Who wants cake?"

As the children clamored for cake, Miss Knight said, "I invited Miss Clewes and Sackree too, but they said they'd rather not spoil their lunch. I got the feeling they welcomed the break, though." She turned to Janie. "Miss Clewes is the girls' governess. You've already met Sackree, our nurse. You'll also hear her called Caky. She's been with us since I was a baby."

"A nuncheon of cake, on occasion, never hurt anyone," said Miss Austen, as she helped herself to a large slice.

Janie had to agree, but she felt sorry for the invisible servants, who would rather have a few minutes away from their charges than enjoy a treat. From all the novels she had read, she had the impression that to be a governess was a particularly dreadful and lonely fate. Socially, they were above the servants, but lower than the family, and they had to spend every waking moment with only the children for company. At least Miss Clewes would have a companion in Sackree until John was too old to need a nurse. What happened to servants once their charges outgrew them? She hoped Mr. Knight was the sort of employer who would make sure they were taken care of.

"Do you want to see my aviary, Miss Jones?" Miss Knight asked. "We can walk through the gardens afterwards, if you like."

"Sure! I've never known anyone before who had an aviary."

"I love birds; some of them I've had for years."

They donned their bonnets again and left the house by way of the back door. To the left of the portico was Miss

Knight's aviary, a charming structure topped by a cupola. It looked like a palace for birds.

As if she had heard Janie's thought, Miss Knight said, "When Papa ordered it, he told the man to design the house he would make for King George, if he were a bird. Papa is so good to me." She opened the latch on the door, which was tall enough for a person to enter. "You may come in, if you like. I don't recommend going in when wearing one's best bonnet, though."

"I hope you didn't loan me your best bonnet, but I won't risk it, anyway."

Miss Knight did go in, and a pair of turtle doves and several smaller birds flew down right away to perch on her shoulders and arms. "I usually have some seed to give them," she said. "They are going to be disappointed." They all seemed very tame; one little goldfinch allowed Miss Knight to stroke its tiny head.

Janie couldn't help thinking what a lot of work it must be for someone to clean up after all of these birds, and she was quite sure it wasn't Miss Knight herself. How many servants did they have in all at Godmersham Park? It was probably rude to ask, so she didn't.

Miss Knight closed the door to the aviary and latched it after she came back outside. "I was positively mad for animals when I was a girl. We also have a rabbit hutch. It's over there—" she pointed to a line of trees in the distance— "under the limes. My sisters keep rabbits there now. Of course, in the stables we have horses, and the children have a pony. Oh, and I hope you aren't afraid of big dogs; Papa has two huge mastiffs that help him keep poachers away. They look scary, but they will be quite sweet as long as they know you're with me; I've played with them since they were puppies. Papa also keeps a pack of deerhounds for hunting, but they aren't really pets. They're kenneled over on the other side of the river."

"I like dogs," Janie said. "And I am 'positively mad,' as you said, for horses, so I hope you'll show me the stables later, too."

Miss Knight agreed, then she showed Janie through the gardens, which were impressive. There was a kitchen garden with vegetables, herbs, and espaliered fruit trees, as well as a cutting garden filled with a variety of flowers, many of which were still blooming. Janie wasn't very expert at flower identification, but she recognized asters, black-eyed Susans and dahlias. The last were particularly beautiful.

Next they walked through a rose garden. Roses were Janie's favorites. Some of the bushes had finished blooming, but the varieties that remained smelled nothing short of heavenly. She bent down to each bush, breathing in their scent. Miss Knight was grinning at her.

"I don't know why, but roses don't smell this good where I come from," Janie explained. Miss Knight still looked amused.

"It's true, they don't! Your green is greener, too," Janie said, as they came into another garden with perfectly trimmed ornamental hedges. "This is so cool! I've always wanted to go through one of these."

Miss Knight giggled. "You have such funny expressions."

Okay, Janie really needed to try not to say things like "cool" while she was here. "This is a maze, right?"

"No, but it is laid out in a design that one can see from the upper stories of the house. The shrubberies would have to be much taller, up over our heads, for it to be a maze."

Bummer. "Oh, yeah, of course." As they walked down the path through the immaculately trimmed hedges, Janie mused again about how much work it must be to keep everything so nice; they must have at least one full-time gardener. Sure enough, it wasn't long before they came upon an older man pulling weeds in one of the beds. He stood up and took off his straw hat when he saw them. "Good day, Miss Knight. Good day, Miss."

"Hello, Thomas," Miss Knight answered. "The dahlias are still quite lovely, aren't they?"

He beamed. "Thank you, Miss," he said with a nod that was almost a bow.

Wait, why was this guy just plain Thomas? Everyone else was Mrs. This or Miss That, even Miss Knight's own younger siblings, at least when she was introducing them. Wait, Janie had forgotten the chambermaid, who was just Elspeth, too. And the nursemaid and the butler only used their last names! What on earth was the rule, then? Once again, it was probably rude to ask, but she would need to figure it all out if she was going to be in 1813 for a while.

Janie was a little out of breath. At her own request, they had walked up the slope of the hill behind the house and were resting on a bench under the portico of what looked like a Greek temple in miniature. Miss Knight called it a folly. According to her, follies were "all the rage." Janie had been silent most of the way up, thinking about the debt she owed to the Knights for taking her in, and wondering how she would ever repay it. The view from up here was stunning, and she wished she could just enjoy it, but once the thoughts had started intruding, she found she was helpless against them. What could she do? She had no money, though perhaps there was a way for her to make some. And she had nowhere else to go, so she hoped they would let her stay here until she found a way to get home.

They sat for a few minutes in silence, then Miss Knight asked, "Do you play any instruments, Miss Jones? I love music. I play the pianoforte. I began studying the harp when I was a girl, but the music master moved from Kent, and I became busy with other responsibilities. Perhaps I may learn it yet. "

"I can't play the harp, but I play the violin and the piano." Janie was about to mention her music studies at the university, then she thought better of it— women in this time couldn't attend a university. She was going to have to tread carefully not to reveal she was from the future, wasn't she? If she was lucky, everyone would attribute any slip-ups to her head injury, or to her oddness as an American. If she wasn't lucky, she could end up in a place like Bedlam. She shivered. Didn't people in this century actually pay money to see the poor souls in mental institutions, like they would animals in a zoo? Suddenly, everything felt less like adventure and more like danger.

"Are you unwell, Miss Jones?"

"I'm just tired." She really was, she realized. The adrenaline rush from discovering she had time traveled was long gone. "Would it be okay if we go back to the house? I think I should rest for a while."

"Of course. I forgot to show you the greenhouses, but we can walk through those some other time."

"Thanks."

As they started down the hill, Fanny continued, "We have some neighbors coming to dine with us tomorrow, and we might have some music afterwards. On second thought, perhaps we should play cards instead; then we would have more time to practice a duet for later. I'm sure we can find a violin for you to play. That would be fun!"

Janie smiled, both because she agreed that would be fun, and because she finally had an idea about how she could earn her keep in 1813.

CHAPTER 6

When all were at the table set, then not a bit
Could this lady eat;
When all made merry at the feast, this lady wished
She were at her rest.
~Traditional, "Gil Brenton"

Fanny's Diary- 31 Sep. 1813

I sent invitations on Tuesday to the Colemans and the Ingrams to come for dinner tonight. I've planned the meal with Cook: mock turtle soup, roasted partridge, filet of fish, ragout of asparagus, and whipt syllabub. Afterwards, Papa is for playing Whist, and I am for Lottery. I will have tables set up for both.

Poor Miss Jones has slept through both breakfast and lunch! I am afraid we did too much, too soon yesterday, and now I hope we shall not have to answer to Dr. Scudamore for it. I've been enjoying Miss Jones' company more and more, especially since I've hardly seen Aunt Jane, who is still totally preoccupied with her writing.

Sometimes she suddenly laughs and then rushes over to her writing box and scribbles like a madwoman. Aunt Jane usually shares the funny bits with all of us, but she has been very secretive indeed about this new novel, probably because Miss Jones is in our midst. Aunt Jane does not want it generally known that she is the authoress who penned *Sense and Sensibility* and *Pride and Prejudice*. We are all sworn to secrecy. All I know about her latest book is that the new heroine is to be named Emma. I think I can safely predict some very amusing passages in it, though.

I almost forgot! I am going to seat Miss Jones next to Papa at dinner tonight. Who knows what may develop?

Janie's first formal dinner at Godmersham Park was an unnerving experience. She was sure she wouldn't get anything right. Weren't there particular forks for certain things? She decided she would just watch which utensil the people around her were using before she picked hers up. Sitting next to Edward Knight was going to be awkward, too. On their way into the dining room, Miss Knight had whispered, "Ask Papa how the shooting went this morning. He loves shooting," with an arch look. Was she trying to set Janie up with her father?

Miss Knight's possible matchmaking plans aside, Janie was all too aware that she was entirely dependent upon

Mr. Knight's hospitality, under what she increasingly felt were false pretenses. She thought of the cheeky comments she had made to him when they first met, when she thought he was a twenty-first century person playing a role; they seemed so rude now. He had laughed, but still.

There were dishes of food all down the table, and a large, brownish, molded Jello-looking thing with bits of who-knows-what suspended in it, in pride of place at the very center of the table. It was strangely fascinating, and Janie had to force herself not to stare at it.

Four footmen, all in matching green and white livery, including matching white powdered wigs, lined the wall behind the table on one side. They came forward to pour the wine for the guests. The first course was soup. Janie asked the server pouring her wine what kind of soup it was.

"Mock turtle, Miss," he said.

What? Like that creature in *Alice in Wonderland?* But those weren't real. She thought of the illustration of the woeful Mock Turtle crying into its handkerchief. "Um, what's in it?" she asked.

"Veal, I believe, Miss."

"Oh, Okay. Thanks."

The soup tasted unusual, but not bad. The servers removed their bowls, and then the gentlemen served everyone from the various other dishes that were on the table. Mr. Knight offered Janie something from a tray of birds with the heads still on and feathers sticking out of their rumps. She shuddered. There was *no way.* "No, thank you," she said. She had been quite hungry when they finally sat down to dinner, since she hadn't eaten all day, but she wasn't starving enough for that.

She sipped her wine and decided she would surreptitiously watch how the others managed their birds, in case she ever had to eat one in a time of true desperation.

"Fish?" Mr. Knight asked.

"Sure. Thanks."

He served a fish filet onto her plate. Yikes! It still had its head on also. Janie casually moved the garnish with her fork so that it covered the fish's eyes. At least that way, it couldn't watch her eating it.

"Asparagus, Miss Jones?"

"Oh, yes, please!" No body parts involved, thank goodness.

The asparagus was covered in some kind of sauce. It tasted delicious. Janie relaxed and remembered she should be trying to make conversation. "Mr. Knight, how was this morning's shooting?"

"Very good indeed, Miss Jones. The partridge that you just declined was one result of our efforts."

Janie nearly choked on her asparagus. "I'm so sorry! I'm just not used to the kind of food you have here. In my time—I mean, in America, everything is so different." She wished she were back upstairs in her room, eating toast and porridge alone, until she realized Mr. Knight was grinning good-naturedly.

"I daresay it must be. What foods do you typically dine on, then?"

"Well, my very favorite food is pizza. I also like burgers and fries and stuff like that. I do try to be healthy occasionally, but I'm afraid I just love junk food too much." Ugh, what was wrong with her? None of that probably made a bit of sense to him. This was torture.

Mr. Knight looked puzzled, albeit in a polite sort of way. "I must say those are new to me. I suppose I should be quite at a loss to know what to eat myself, if I were in America," he said with a smile. "Most Americans are of English descent, are they not? Surely there are a great many things we have in common."

"Yeah, like our language."

"True, although your accent and expressions are *surprisingly* different."

A footman set a small bowl of water in front of her. Janie thanked him, though she didn't know what she was supposed to do with it. She looked around. Everyone was dipping their fingers into their bowls and wiping them on their napkins, so she did the same. The server removed her bowl and set a yummy-looking whipped dessert down in its place. "Mmm, that looks great! Thanks so much!"

"Apparently, your customs also differ from ours. Do people always thank the servants so profusely for every little thing in America, Miss Jones?"

"Of course people thank the— um, servants. Nice people do, anyway."

"It's not necessary here."

Was he offended? No, he was smiling, and there was a twinkle in his eye. He seemed to be the sort of person who might be joking half the time, but she couldn't be sure. Whew! This was exhausting. She just had to make it through dessert. She looked across the table, where lucky Fanny was having a much more fun conversation with her Aunt Jane. They were both giggling.

"I find cultural differences to be quite fascinating, Miss Jones; please forgive my curiosity," Mr. Knight said. "I confess that is one reason why I am happy to have you staying with us, though we have been at war with America these many months. It's not as if you could be a spy. If you were a man, I would be more wary, of course."

What? Oh my gosh, she had totally forgotten about the war of 1812! Janie bit back her words before saying that women could be spies, too. Once again, she was struck by how potentially dangerous her position really was.

"I was just reading this morning that a young pup from Kentucky has routed our British forces at Fort Stephenson. You have property in Kentucky, do you not? Are you acquainted with the Croghans?"

Janie shook her head. "No, sir." She didn't remember diddly-squat about the War of 1812. She should change the subject. "Do you think the fine weather will continue, Mr. Knight?"

They were in the drawing room at the front of the house. With its elaborate white moldings of acanthus leaves and scallop shells alternating with female masks, pale pink walls, and touches of gold everywhere, it had a more feminine look than parlor at the back. Even the furniture looked more delicate. Janie especially loved the beautiful secretary desk topped with lots of little compartments that stood in one corner. Miss Knight's, she supposed.

The ladies had already been there for an hour when the gentlemen, who had stayed in the dining room with their port wine, finally joined them for cards. Most of the ladies spent the time catching Miss Austen up on the local news, while Miss Knight explained the rules of Whist and Lottery to Janie. Whist sounded more complicated, while Lottery was based on luck rather than skill. Janie chose the latter. It involved placing bets using some cute little counters shaped like fish. Janie hadn't really played cards since she was a kid, but Miss Knight had never heard of Go Fish or Old Maid, much less Uno.

"What quaint names!" Miss Knight laughed when Janie told her those were the only games she knew. "I hope you know I mean no offense. It is just so diverting! Everything in your America is quite different, is it not?"

"You have no idea how different, Miss Knight."

"Please, call me Fanny, will you?"

"Sure! And you can call me Janie, Miss— um, Fanny."

"Now pick three cards from this parcel, without looking at them, and place them face down in the center, Janie," Fanny said, with a slight emphasis on her name that made Janie smile. It was nice to have at least one person calling her by her first name.

The Colemans, who had joined their game, were a lively couple, and Lottery turned out to be great fun. Fanny's brothers, who were at another Lottery table, got so boisterous that the Whist group twice asked them to quiet down. Whist was a much more serious game, apparently.

After Fanny won the game, the Colemans excused themselves to see what was happening over at the Whist table. Fanny scooped up all of the fish she had won.

Yikes! Why hadn't it occurred to Janie before that actual money might be at stake? "Do I owe you real money now?"

"Do you have any?" Fanny asked.

"Not a farthing."

"No, then," Fanny grinned. Eyebrow lifted, she asked, "So, did you ask Papa about today's shooting?"

"Yes, I did. Look, Fanny," Janie lowered her voice to a whisper. "I'm sure he's a great guy and everything, but he's old enough to be my father!" That should have been obvious, seeing how he was Fanny's father, but whatever.

"Why should that signify?" Fanny gave a nod and made a slight gesture with her fan to indicate the girl seated across from Mr. Knight at the other table. She whispered, "Miss Ingram– not Miss Eliza Ingram, the one in pink, but the one wearing that unbecoming shade of yellow— is our age too, and she has obviously set her cap at Papa." She nodded again. "Just look."

Janie glanced that way. The young lady in question either had something stuck in her eye, or she was batting her eyelashes mercilessly at their host. She was fluttering her hand of cards like a fan.

"To be honest, I can't imagine him choosing someone like her," Fanny whispered with a grin. "If he chooses anyone, that is. Papa hasn't yet shown any signs of wanting to remarry." Her expression turned wistful. "But how else am I ever to leave him and the children and have a home of my own?"

"I totally get it. I feel a lot of responsibility for my younger sisters and brother, too. I've been the only mother they've had for six years."

"Exactly," Fanny said. "Let us see if the Colemans want to play Whist now, so that you can learn it. My family often plays Whist in the evening, and I'd love for you to join us while you're here."

Janie would have responded, if not for the sudden appearance of a light in the large window opposite her.

A hooded man, whose scowling, black-bearded visage was eerily lit by a lantern, was clearly framed in one of the panes of glass. He was staring right at Janie. Miss Ingram obviously saw him too, for she stood up, screamed, and fainted dramatically. Seeing Mr. Knight rush immediately to the lady's assistance, Janie had the rather uncharitable thought that Miss Ingram was probably faking it.

Then all was in an uproar. Outside, dogs started baying deeply and loudly, and the face disappeared from view. A couple of gentlemen leaped from their seats and ran towards the window. Everyone else began talking excitedly, all at once. Fanny said something to her, but Janie couldn't make it out over the cacophony of sound.

Edward Knight took charge, ordering two footmen to help him check on the disturbance outside and calling on a maid to attend to Miss Ingram, who quickly recovered without need of assistance.

The other tables finished their games. There was still a nervous energy in the room, and the party broke up early. After Fanny and her father had seen all of the guests out, they came back into the room and Fanny sat down rather less delicately than usual. "Did they catch that man, Papa?" she asked.

"No, but the dogs ran him off. There's no need to worry,

dearest," he said, patting his daughter's shoulder. Then he turned to Janie. "Miss Jones, occasionally we have a problem with gypsies camping in our woods. This is the first time one has come up to the house, but as you can see, the dogs know what to do. Just as a precaution, though, I would ask you ladies not to walk the grounds alone. I will assign one of the servants to accompany you whenever you wish to go out."

Janie nodded along with Fanny. It was just prejudice that attributed evil motives to all gypsies— Romani people, rather. Still, a frisson of fear crawled like a spider up her spine when she recalled the look of pure malice on that face at the window.

CHAPTER 7

If any creature's face had ever worn a look of pure malice, Raven thought, it was that blasted, monstrous dog that had bitten him in the leg and then chased him up an ash tree in the woods last night. Generally, Raven liked dogs. He even had one himself— a little grey terrier he called Scrap, who sat companionably with him in front of the fire in the evenings and kept his place free of rats.

That demon of a leg-biting mastiff, though, had sat at the bottom of the tree for over an hour, champing its jaws, drooling, and staring up at him with eyes that Raven could have sworn were gleaming red in the moonlight. Finally, the dog had lifted its massive head, as if hearing some far off sound, and trotted away.

Now, sitting in the White Horse Inn with his throbbing calf bandaged in a strip of brandy-soaked linen, Raven took stock of his situation. This job should have been finished days ago. The girl needed to be returned to her time *now*; the Lotus Effect was more likely to take hold with every day that went by. She had almost certainly already entered the phase where fascination with this century overrode the desire to return to her own. He would have a devil of a time getting her cooperation once she lost the sense of her past's reality, and ten devils of a time once she forgot it altogether. He hated using physical force on a girl. He didn't happen to have a bottle of memory tonic on him, either. Even if he had, it would have to be administered by trickery. Not that Raven was all that troubled by lying; it was just such a bother.

What he needed was someone on the inside, someone who knew what went on in the toff's household. "Know anybody who works for the gent in yon big house?" he asked the pretty barmaid when she brought his breakfast to the table. Ah, fresh bread and a mug of ale. Things were looking up, they were.

"Chilham Castle, across the square?"

"No, the place a few miles south of here."

She nodded. "Godmersham Park, then. Sure, some folks around here work for Mr. Knight."

"Any of them in here now?"

She glanced around the room. "Well, not just now, but

my brother runs errands for them sometimes." She called loudly over her shoulder. "Johnny!"

A sturdy-looking fellow of eleven or twelve years galloped down the stairs. "Wot, Mary?"

"This— she looked Raven up and down. Her mouth quirked. "Gentleman— needs you. He has business with Mr. Knight."

Fair enough— Raven had caught a glimpse of himself in a looking glass earlier, and he knew that he looked the worse for wear after last night's ordeal. He fought the urge to smooth down the unruly hair and beard that framed his face like a shaggy, black lion's mane. *Twp* hair, he growled inwardly. He turned to Johnny and pulled a farthing from his pocket and set it on the table. "Sit down, boy. I have a job for you."

Janie's first thought upon waking was that she should remind Fanny about borrowing a violin; there had to be someone in the neighborhood who would pay her for lessons. Her second thought made her smile— Fanny had promised to take her riding! Fiddling and riding would put Janie back into familiar waters, which she needed if she was going to make it in 1813. Wait a minute— what was she even thinking? She needed to remember that making it in 1813 wasn't really her goal. She needed to know how she got here, so she could figure out how to get back to 2025! She would start her search today.

Elspeth scratched at the door and entered her room as if on cue, bearing a new outfit, complete with boots, hat, and riding crop. "Here's your riding habit, Miss," she said. "Miss Knight says you're to wear it so you can go riding with her after breakfast."

Fanny had not forgotten! Janie was surprised at how excited she felt. "Alright, Elspeth, do me up."

The outfit was different from the others Janie had borrowed. Instead of being all in one piece, it had a long, green skirt and a separate white top. Unlike a blouse, it was open at the sides. The skirt was held up with straps that were hidden by the jacket, which was also green. The hat resembled a man's top hat.

After she was all dressed, Janie said, "Thanks. I can take it from here."

Elspeth gave a little cry of dismay. "But your *hair*, Miss!"

"What, can't we just shove it up into this hat? I'm just going riding. If you could only see what I usually wear for that, you'd have a heart attack."

Elspeth held her ground. "Nae, Miss, we can not 'just shove' your hair. What if—"

"Oh yeah, I forgot. Today is the day I might meet the man of my dreams, and all that."

Elspeth sighed. "Aye, Miss. I'll have you done in a trice."

In her eagerness to go riding, Janie nearly tripped when the heel of one boot caught on the hem of her dress as she was going down the stairs to breakfast. She yelped and grabbed onto the bannister with both hands. Good grief! All she needed now was to take a tumble down this elegant staircase! The dress seemed longer than the others had been. She hiked the skirt up and held it, along with the riding crop, in her right hand, so she could still hold onto the bannister with her left.

"It has a train," Fanny called from the hall below. "There are ties on the side to hold it up when you aren't riding." She helped Janie tie the skirt up when she reached the bottom of the stairs.

"I don't get it. Why do I need a train when I'm riding?"

"To make sure your legs are covered when you are sitting side-saddle, silly."

Of course! Janie had forgotten ladies didn't ride astride in 1813. Her spirits fell into her boots. There had been a side-saddle club back home where the girls learned to ride that way, but Janie had never been interested in joining. It had seemed so snooty.

Once again, they had the breakfast room all to themselves, and the usual offerings were on the sideboard, except that there were scones and blackberry jam instead of muffins. Janie loved scones, but she was halfway through hers before she even realized how delicious it was, tainted as it was by her disappointment at not being able to ride. Not like a proper lady in 1813, anyway.

How hard could it be to learn, though? Riding was second nature to her. Maybe she could pick it right up. "Fanny, do you think you can teach me to ride side-saddle?"

"What are you talking about? I thought you said you've been riding since you were a little girl."

"I have, but not like that."

Fanny's eyes widened. "Surely you can not be saying you ride like a—" She whispered, "*man!*"

"Actually, um, yeah. That's how we usually ride in America, even ladies. We don't wear outfits like this, either. We wear— oh, never mind." That was a close one! God only knew what Fanny would think of her wearing pants.

Fanny was blushing. She took a deep breath and let it out again. "Well then, Duncan and I shall have to teach you. It would not do for you to ride— that other way. Papa would definitely not approve."

"Who is Duncan?" Another first-name basis person.

"Our stableboy. He is the one Papa has asked to stay with us today when we are outside, on account of that gypsy last night. This should work out quite well, actually. Duncan is a wonder with horses; I almost think he can speak their language. I can't think of anyone who could do a better job teaching you."

"Okay." As long as she was riding again. "Oh, I almost forgot— Did you find a violin?"

"Not yet, but Papa thinks he may be able to find one for you. There are generations of the Knight family's possessions stored in this house."

At Mr. Knight's request, one of the footmen was ready to accompany Janie and Fanny out to the stables.

"Joe, before we go, could you ask Cook for some bones for me to give to Castor and Pollux?" Fanny asked him. "I think they deserve a treat after chasing off that gypsy last night."

"Yes, Miss," Joe answered, and he went to the kitchen.

"We are going to stop by the kennel before we go riding," Fanny explained, "so you can meet the watchdogs."

Joe returned in a few minutes, holding two huge beef bones in his ungloved hands, and they all walked to the kennel, which was on the far side of the stable-yard.

"Here are Castor and Pollux. They're brothers," Fanny said.

The two brindle-colored mastiffs were the most enormous dogs Janie had ever seen in her life. They whined excitedly when they saw Fanny approaching.

"Let me and Miss Jones give them the bones," Fanny

said to the footman, taking off her gloves and holding them in the crook of her arm. Janie did the same. Joe handed each of them a bone. "You give yours to Castor, Janie," Fanny said. "He's the one with more black on him; Pollux is more brown." Fanny held her bone out to Pollux, who snatched it eagerly. "Good dog for chasing away the gypsy."

"Hi, there, Castor," Janie said, holding the bone out for him to take it. "Good boy." A six-inch rope of slobber hung from his mouth. Gross. He seemed sweet enough, though. He wagged his stumpy tail and took the bone from her hand with more gentleness than his brother had shown with Fanny.

The footman produced a handkerchief from his pocket, and they all wiped their hands on it before putting their gloves back on.

Duncan had groomed and saddled the mares for Miss Knight and Miss Jones, as well as his own horse, and he was waiting for them outside the stables. Instead of irritation at the interruption to his work, he felt anticipation. There were certainly worse ways to spend a morning than riding with two lovely young ladies. Miss Knight might be pampered and rich, but she was kind to animals, and that went a long way with Duncan. She was kind to the servants, too, albeit in that distant sort of way that people in her class tended to be. It was well known that she was charitable to the poor in the village, and she had a bright, sunny laugh that did one's heart good to hear.

It would be nice to see Miss Jones also, because— never mind, it was probably best not to let himself dwell on her. He had dwelled on her too much already.

Stable*boy*? This was definitely not a boy waiting for them, holding the reins of two mares— one grey, and one pied— in one hand, and those of a black Thoroughbred stallion in the other. It was the handsome coachman, only he wasn't wearing the long driving coat or the hat from the other day. He had on buff colored breeches, boots, and a white linen shirt with the sleeves rolled up. He looked even hotter than before; Michaelangelo himself could have sculpted those arms. And now he was probably going to see Janie fall sideways off a horse. Good grief! Hadn't she embarrassed herself enough in front of this man already?

Fanny waved at him and called out, "Duncan, guess what? We are going to teach Miss Jones to ride today!"

Duncan smiled. Janie did, too— it was hard not to smile at Fanny's exuberance, and Duncan had a really nice smile, with a dimple on one side.

Fanny had said "we," but Janie couldn't help noticing that Fanny's contribution to the lesson consisted of stepping up onto a mounting block and jumping onto the pied mare, saying, "See? That's all there is to it!" Fanny's long skirts made it impossible to see exactly how she was sitting in the saddle.

Luckily, Duncan did a much better job of explaining everything. He showed Janie what the stirrup and the two pommels were for, then how she should position herself in the saddle. "Your left leg should be in the stirrup, here, and your right one goes aroond that top pommel, and hangs doon." His voice was soft and low-pitched, his manner gentle and patient. Janie knew all of those things helped make him good with horses. Did the horses love the burr of his accent, too?

Duncan laced the fingers of both hands together to make a foothold for Janie to step into, and she jumped lightly up into the grey mare's saddle. So far, so good. She followed his instruction on where her legs should go and then shifted her skirts a bit so they looked like Fanny's. It felt so awkward to sit that way!

"Aye, just like that, Miss. That's grand." Duncan patted the mare's neck. "Nan here has a mild nature, so there's nae need to hang on tight wi' her, but ye can always clamp doon on those pommels if ye decide to take any fences," he grinned.

Janie laughed. "I definitely don't plan to jump any fences just yet, thank you!"

"Now that ye ha' the way of it, let's ride a bit. Use pressure from your leg on her left, or your wee crop on her right, to ask her to turn."

Everything felt weird, but it was good to be on horseback again. Janie patted Nan's neck. Now she just had to make sure she didn't fall off.

CHAPTER 8

The blood it flowed in torrents and never a blow was missed,
And they carried a bunch of thunderbolts well fashioned in
each fist.
~Traditional, "Heenan and Sayers"

Fanny gave Janie the grand tour of Godmersham, minus the woods, since her father had asked that they stay out of them until he could be sure that the gypsies had gone. She pointed out the best fishing spot on the Stour River, then they were off to see some "particularly fine" blackberry bushes nearby. Duncan kept his horse beside Janie's— the better to watch her fall off, she figured. Not that she really minded; his horse was a beautiful animal, at least sixteen hands high, shiny and black as jet, muscular, and spirited. He and Duncan made quite a pair.

"What's his name?" Janie pointed her crop at the Thoroughbred, who was obviously wishing he could have a go at something more than this slow walk.

"Bruce."

"As in Robert the–, I suppose? It suits him."

Duncan laughed. "Aye, could be. I didnae name him, though. He belongs to Mr. Knight. Bruce needs a lot o' exercise, so I ride him whenever Mr. Knight is busy. He's a grand horse."

"I'm pleased to meet you, Bruce."

"Och, ye met before this."

Janie stopped her horse. "What?"

Fanny kept on going down the path, but Duncan turned Bruce around and pulled him up beside Janie again. "Well done, Miss! You're a natural. I didnae even have to show ye how to use the reins."

"How could I have met Bruce before?"

"He, well, I—"

"You were the one who found me, weren't you?"

"Aye."

So Duncan had picked Janie up in his gorgeous arms and taken her to the house, with her looking like God-only-knows-what and not even conscious to enjoy the experience! Was there to be no end to her mortification?

Fanny came riding back. "There's no point. It seems the birds have gotten to the last of the blackberries."

They rode across a stone bridge over the river, then through Godmersham village, which had only one street.

It was not too small, however, to have both a school and an almshouse, whose residents Fanny said she and her Aunt Jane visited as often as she could. After they came back up the street, Fanny pointed out a hill to their right. "We have another temple folly up there, with a marvelous prospect of Godmersham Park. As you see, it's very wooded, so we won't be going up there today."

They rode back across the bridge and turned left on the lane to see the church. "We don't go this way on Sundays; we walk through the lime avenue."

Fanny's neck had to be getting sore from looking back at her every time she said something. Janie pulled her horse up next to Fanny's. She should have done so before, instead of letting herself get distracted by Duncan.

They rode past the vicarage. "Mr. Sherer is our vicar. You'll hear him preach tomorrow. I think you'll like him." Then they came to a large house that looked as old as the ones in Chilham. "This is Godmersham Priory. There used to be a convent here a long time ago," Fanny explained. "You remember the Colemans; they live here. We should probably call on Mrs. Coleman later this week."

Further down the lane was the Church of St. Lawrence the Martyr, where the Knights attended services. How old it must be, to look so old in 1813! "It must be ancient," Janie said.

"It is. Parts of it are Norman, and there may have been a

Saxon church here before that. It's even in the Domesday Book."

No way! She couldn't wait to see inside tomorrow.

They turned and headed back up the lane to the house in silence, listening to the birdsong and the rushing of the river. It was a beautiful autumn day, a perfect day, and Janie felt completely content, until she remembered that morning's resolution to find out how she ended up in 1813.

She pulled back on Nan's reins, so that she was riding beside Duncan again. "Um, I know this is a weird question, but I'm asking you because you're the one who found me after my accident. Did you happen to notice anything strange nearby at the time? Like maybe a big, blue— sort of um, box, taller than a person?"

To Duncan's credit, he did not laugh outright. He simply looked confused. Naturally. "A blue box? Nae, Miss."

Janie had the strangest sensation that she had left her body altogether and was hovering overhead, watching as she made an utter fool of herself, and helpless to stop it. "What about any kind of big— um, flying machine?"

"Nae." He wasn't laughing at her, but his eyes were twinkling like crazy.

Shoot. Janie took a deep breath. "A giant hole in the sky?"

"Nae, Miss Jones." Now he was grinning, showing that cute dimple. Maybe not out loud, but he was definitely laughing.

Raven had just missed them, but they had to come back to the stables sometime. Young Johnny had been a big help, winkling the ladies' plans for the day out of his little sweetheart, a chambermaid at the big house. More importantly, Johnny had informed him that the dogs were usually kept kenneled in the mornings. If Raven timed it right, he should be able to grab the girl on her way back to the house, while the groom was busy with the horses.

He decided to bide his time in the stablehand's quarters above the stables, which had a window with a view of the yard that would give him plenty of time to slip out when he saw them coming. He found nothing worth eating in the larder, but the bed was actually not too bad. There was a small bookshelf next to the bed. So the stableboy liked to read, did he? *The Holy Bible*, *The Compleat Horseman and Expert Farrier*, *The Breeding of Horses*, and *The Works of Robert Burns*. Bah, nothing worth reading, either. Robert Burns wasn't Raven's cup of tea, but he couldn't fault the fellow for his patriotism; one had to stand up for one's native poetry. Like all good Welshmen, Raven revered Taliesin as he ought, but if he were honest, there was only one Bard with a capital B for him. He pulled a small copy of Shakespeare's sonnets from his pocket, and he settled in to wait.

At least Janie hadn't fallen off her horse. Small comfort, considering Duncan thought she was loony now. As she and Fanny walked back across the stableyard, she was shocked to realize she was actually a little bit sore. Not that she would admit it to anyone. It had to be that weird position in the saddle. She was hungry, too; it must be lunchtime.

Suddenly, a man wearing a black cape stepped in front of Janie and grabbed her arm with a powerful grip. "You need to come with me. Now," he growled.

For a second, Janie was too shocked to do anything except try to pull her arm away. Then she recognized the man's face, surrounded by shaggy, black hair— it was the same one that had been peering at her so menacingly through the window last night! Janie tried beating at his head with her free hand. He yelped, but he didn't let go. She managed to grab a fistful of his spiky hair and yank some of it out. Franny was frozen beside her.

"Ow, stop it, you *twmffat*! Listen, you need to come with me. There's no time! It has to be now!" the man said, pulling Janie along with him.

Fanny's statue came to life with a little scream and broke into a ladylike run towards the house.

Janie yelled, "Help!" and Duncan appeared as suddenly

as an apparition. His face was a thundercloud. One hand clenched a currying brush, the other was fisted.

"Unhand her, villain!"

Unhand her, villain? Janie gave a snort of laughter, in spite of the fear that was still coursing through her like heavy volts of electricity.

The man let go of her arm, sputtering, "Wait a minute! You don't—"

Duncan's fist became a cannonball that caught the man in the jaw and spun him around into a stumbling run.

The caped man was shouting something as he ran into the woods: "Stay here, then, you..." Janie couldn't make out the rest; it sounded like some other language. She turned to Duncan, and then she was in his arms. She could feel his powerful heartbeat beneath her cheek, hear his ragged breath above her head.

"Miss Jones, I—"

What was she doing? Janie pulled away. "I'm so sorry, I just— um, thank you."

Someone called, "Miss Jones!" Mr. Knight was running towards them. "Are you harmed?"

Janie shook her head.

"Thank God! Here, take my arm."

Walking to the house with Mr. Knight, Janie looked back to see Duncan, who had already turned to walk back to the stables.

Fanny's Diary- 1 Oct. 1813

I have had a very shocking ordeal today!! Only think, my friend and I have actually been accosted by a gypsy!!!! It truly is like something out of one of Mrs. Radcliffe's novels!! (Papa doesn't know I read those. I am glad he has too much delicacy of mind to ever read someone else's diary.)

I declare, I am not over it yet, and I am sure Janie is not, for she was held in the monster's evil clutches while I went to find help! Papa has wisely suggested that she keep to her room for the remainder of today. I believe him to be quite solicitous for her welfare. Perhaps this frightful incident will be the thing that brings them together, for Papa must realize that she could have been lost to us forever.

Our stablehand bravely saved Janie from the hands of the gypsy, thwarting his nefarious plans. I must hear the whole story!!!

Janie was so shaken that she gladly took Mr. Knight's suggestion that she rest in her room. Everyone was being very kind; Fanny even brought her a piece of sponge cake layered with jam from Cook and a little bottle of something.

"It's another facial preparation."

Janie wondered what this one smelled like. She uncorked the bottle, and her eyes started stinging. "Thanks, Fanny." She was definitely sticking with the strawberry stuff.

"What happened after I ran for help? I want to hear every detail of the valiant rescue," Fanny said.

Janie told her everything, only leaving out the part where she ended up in Duncan's arms. Had Edward Knight seen it, though? He would certainly disapprove, and Janie was dependent on his goodwill.

Fanny seemed to think it was the most thrilling story she had ever heard. "I so admire a man who can take charge, do not you? Why, it's just like something from a novel, where the strong, romantic hero comes in and saves the day, is it not?"

Janie fell asleep soon after Fanny left and didn't wake until the next morning. She wondered if they would still be able to go riding after church. It looked like rain.

It was quite ordinary to use the chamber pot now, in spite of the difficulties she'd had at first, and normal to have a chambermaid come in and fill her bathtub and help her dress.

She was quiet while Elspeth did her hair. The truth was, Janie could no longer deny that 1813 was not only starting to feel more normal, it was starting to feel more *real*. It was not exactly that she had forgotten her former life, it had just taken on a dreamlike quality. Her life in the twenty-first century was something she still knew all about, but it was more like a story she had read somewhere, or something that had happened to someone else.

CHAPTER 9

He leapt on a horse and she on another,
And they rode on to the greenwood together.
~Traditional, "Lady Isobel and the Elf Knight"

When Janie entered the breakfast parlor, she was surprised to see Mr. Knight and his sons sitting at the table with Fanny. The men stood when she came in. "I do hope you had a restful night, Miss Jones, and that you've fully recovered from your ordeal," Mr. Knight said.

"Yes, thank you. I have." She walked over to the sideboard. Yum, more scones.

Mr. Knight continued, "I want to apologize again for what happened yesterday, Miss Jones. I never dreamed that such a thing could occur so close to the house, and in broad daylight. I blame myself. I should have arranged for someone to accompany you and Fanny back to the door after your ride."

"I'm perfectly fine, really I am. And it's not your fault."

He attempted a smile. "It is good of you to say so.

Sackree told me you wrote to your father earlier to let him know your whereabouts. Please reassure him in your next letter that you are in no danger. I will not allow anything like that to happen again. I assume he is visiting England as well?"

"Um, yes. He's in London," Janie lied, glad that Mr. Knight couldn't see her face as she got her scone from the sideboard. She hadn't actually written a letter. Today or tomorrow, she would write something to a bogus London address and leave off the return address so that it couldn't be sent back. Fanny sent out letters nearly every day; it would be easy to add one to her stack.

"I am going to organize a search of our woods for this afternoon, Miss Jones. Rest assured, the scoundrel will not escape justice when we find him. If you'll excuse me." He bowed and left, and everyone else sat down.

"Pater said that Duncan planted the brute a facer. 'Pon rep, I wish I had seen that!" George said, giving the air a punch.

Ned nodded. "Fellow's handy with his fives. Used to box in London, you know."

"Dordy and Ned, pray do not use boxing cant at the breakfast table," Fanny scolded. "Especially on a Sunday. You are putting our guest to the blush."

"Sorry, Fan. I beg your pardon, Miss Jones," George said with a blush of his own, either of contrition or embarrassment at his sister's using his baby nickname.

"Lud, Fan, no need to make a fellow feel like he's still

in leading strings," Ned said, but he apologized also. "Beg pardon, Miss Jones."

Janie's blush had nothing to do with the young men's slang. Had Duncan told his employer about punching her attacker, or had Mr. Knight seen it— and what happened afterwards— for himself?

After her brothers excused themselves, Fanny got up and went over to the table opposite the sideboard, on which rested a large, rectangular wooden box with a silver handle on the top. She picked up the box and returned to the breakfast table. "Janie, here is something that I think will lift your spirits. Papa had a servant search the house. Look at what he found!"

Was it a violin? Janie had never seen a violin case like this. It was made of polished rosewood inlaid with marquetry figures of musical instruments and scrolls of music. It looked like the Italian music boxes she sometimes saw at antique shops, only much larger. Ornate silver clasps on the side held the top closed.

"Open it," Fanny urged. Janie undid the clasps and opened the lid. Inside was a violin, nestled in a blue velvet insert. It was so beautiful! She lifted it out gently, turning it in her hands to admire the beautifully figured wood grain on the front and back. Then she peeked inside one of the f-holes to see if there was a maker's label. She gasped again when she read, "Joseph Guarnerius fecit Cremone, anno 1725 IHS." A Guarnerius del Gesù! Tears sprang to her eyes. She could have gone her whole life and never held a treasure like this in her hands, much less been allowed to play it!

"Papa says it's yours if you want it. None of us can play it."

"Oh, my gosh! No, I can't possibly accept it! It's worth mill— um, it's much, much too valuable! Y'all have to keep it. How about I teach someone in your family to play it? One of your little sisters, maybe. Promise me you'll never, ever get rid of this!"

Fanny looked crestfallen. "You'll at least borrow it while you're staying with us, won't you?"

"Of course I will!" Janie hugged Fanny. "Thanks so much! It's the most generous gift anyone has ever offered me!"

"And here are the new strings Papa got in Canterbury yesterday." Fanny opened one of the box's compartments to show her. "The only problem is the stick part." She pulled the bow from its niche in the lid of the box. It had lost most of its hair, but it was otherwise in perfect shape.

"That 'stick part' is called the bow."

Fanny giggled. "Oh, that's right. Anyway, Papa said to give it to Duncan today, and he will fix it."

"Really? I'm surprised your father's letting us out of his sight today."

"Only as long as we stay with a servant the whole time. Are you amenable to going riding after church?"

"Sure." Even though Janie seemed to embarrass herself every time she was near Duncan, she was most definitely amenable. Maybe she was a glutton for punishment.

As she stepped down the worn stone steps that led into the church and past the stone font, Janie had the impression that she was going still further back into time. The floor looked particularly old, with its uneven stones. The whitewashed walls were adorned with monuments and some framed Bible verses which looked hand-stitched. Each verse had a grotesque-looking face underneath it. How odd! Were they sort of like gargoyles?

Even the light slanting in through the Gothic windows seemed more ancient than ordinary light, but perhaps that was the effect of the overcast sky. Janie wondered if there had been stained glass in all of them before the Reformation. She followed the Knight entourage up the aisle to their raised family box, adorned with heraldic crests and more memorials. She held tightly to the handrail as she went up the five narrow steps and into the pew, where she sat between Fanny and Miss Austen. Janie looked through the box's arched window into the nave. The raised pulpit was directly opposite them. Behind it were oak boards on which were painted the Ten Commandments, the Lord's Prayer, and the Apostles' Creed. To her left, over the door through which they had entered, was a box running across the whole wall, supported by four columns. It had what looked like the royal coat of arms on it. "Who sits up there? The king?" she asked Fanny in a whisper, pointing.

"The musicians. That's the gallery." Fanny's facial expression added, *Of course.*

"My church looks very different from yours," Janie whispered back in self-defense.

Other villagers had entered the church after the Knights, and they were filling the box pews below on either side of the center aisle. She felt like a fraud. She should be sitting down there, too, not raised up like she was better than they were.

Finally she saw Elspeth, who was in the very back row. Janie gave her a tiny wave, and Elspeth grinned back. She looked very sweet in a blue dress and bonnet. Next to Elspeth sat Duncan, looking distinguished in a coat and cravat. A lady sitting on the other side of Duncan was leaning in to tell him something, touching his arm. Who was she? The lady turned her head again, and Janie saw the face beneath the bonnet. It was the Knights' pretty parlor maid. Janie felt a twinge of jealousy, then annoyance at herself. Why should she care if he had a girlfriend, anyway?

Janie stood up with everyone else to sing the opening

hymn. As she lifted her voice with the rest, she wondered how many people had sung this very psalm through the centuries under the ancient rafters of this beautiful church. A deep sense of history and of peace filled her soul.

It was turning out to be a dreich, dreary afternoon. The clouds that had gathered while they were in church were full of rain, but Duncan hoped it would hold off long enough for a short ride. Today he would make sure to stay behind the ladies. That way, he could see what was ahead of them and still be between them and danger should someone try to attack them from behind. He had changed his clothes and had the horses saddled and ready by the time Joe brought the ladies to the stables. He looked at Miss Jones, then quickly looked away again. He hadn't been able to stop thinking about how she had run into his arms yesterday.

"Duncan, Papa has a special commission for you. Can you fix this bow so that Miss Jones can use it?" Miss Knight handed it to him.

So Miss Jones played the fiddle, did she? It was an unusual instrument for a woman; most of them played the pianoforte or the harp. "Aye, I can fix it, but only with the help of Pretty Pie, since her tail's the right color. Do ye mind if I cut some hair frae her tail, Miss Knight?"

She looked doubtful. "Do you truly need to?"

"Aye, horse hair is what's used for fiddle bows."

Miss Jones said, "It won't take much at all, Fanny. I promise you won't even be able to tell it's missing."

"That's fine, then."

He glanced at Miss Jones again. "I should be able to get it done by Tuesday, if that suits ye, Miss. I ha' to wash and dress it before putting it in the bow."

Miss Jones nodded and smiled, and it was as if the sun had just come out.

Riding side saddle felt even more awkward than yesterday, just a different kind of awkward. Why, oh why, had she thrown herself at Duncan like that? Janie could hardly look him in the face. Not that she would even have the chance, since he was riding behind them today. She rode next to Fanny, only half listening to her talk about her father.

"...It's easy to see, is it not, why they chose Papa as their heir?"

"Um, sure." Was Duncan avoiding her? He definitely hadn't said much to her this morning, except, "Remember what you learned yesterday, Miss."

"...It has been difficult to become accustomed to a new last name, but that will happen again someday when I get married, will it not?"

"Um, yeah." Speaking of last names, why didn't Fanny use Duncan's last name? Janie thought ladies in 1813 couldn't call a guy by his first name unless they were engaged. Could they be secretly engaged, like Jane Fairfax and Frank Churchill in *Emma?*

"... and Papa's wonderful at managing estates, everyone says..."

No way. Janie would be able to tell if they were an item, wouldn't she? Besides, Fanny called him by his first name in front of everybody, even her father.

"... the only one of the Austens who got to do the Grand Tour. He spent over a year abroad. It makes such a difference, do you not agree?"

"Absolutely." What even was Duncan's last name?

"Was it not kind of Papa to say you could keep the violin? I think he must admire you."

That snatched Janie's attention. "I can't possibly keep it. He doesn't realize how valuable it is. And I think he is just kind to everyone."

"Well, that's true."

Duncan wished he could be riding further back, where

he couldn't overhear what the ladies were saying. Edward Knight must be courting Miss Jones, then; he had been a widower for a long time. Duncan sighed. Maybe it was time to think about moving on; he had never intended to spend his life working here, anyway. His sister did, though; she wanted nothing more in life than to be a lady's maid, right here at Godmersham, if possible. And Duncan was sure she would be a lady's maid— to the new Mrs. Edward Knight. It would be hard to leave Elspeth, but she knew he had always hoped to raise horses someday, and she wanted him to be happy.

He was relieved when the rain started and put an end to the conversation. They would have to turn around and go back home. The rain was coming down in sheets, having skipped over its usual preamble of drops.

Miss Knight squealed, but Miss Jones laughed. She laughed all the way back to the stable, turning her face up into the rain. By the time Duncan had helped the ladies down from their horses, they were all laughing.

Duncan only had one towel, but he had several wool blankets, and he handed one to each of the ladies. Should he have taken them to his quarters instead, where he could light a fire? Nae, it was too cramped in there, and there was only the one chair. At least in here, there were plenty of hay bales to sit on. Should he invite them to sit?

Thankfully, the ladies sat themselves down, so he didn't have to fash himself over the protocol. He began unsaddling the horses and laying their tack out to dry in the straw. Och, he was glad to have something with which to occupy himself.

"Look how hard it's coming down! This is what we call a 'gullywasher' where I come from," Miss Jones said, pulling her blanket more closely around herself.

"Here, we just call it typical weather," said Miss Knight. "The funny thing is, it could clear up in the blink of an eye."

Miss Jones looked lovely even when she was drookit, soaking wet. Her hat was hanging by its ribbons and her hair had started to come undone. She took her hat off, along with her hairpins, then started combing her hair out with her fingers and drying it with the edge of the blanket.

The memory of finding Miss Jones flashed through Duncan's mind—how he had brushed the hair away from her face with his fingers, how he had thought her the bonniest lass he'd ever set eyes on, and how he had carried her to the door of Edward Knight.

He turned his attention back to rubbing his horse down with handfuls of dry straw.

"We can help, can't we, Fanny?" Miss Jones was already grabbing straw and rubbing her grey mare with it. Miss Knight rolled her eyes, but she nodded and followed suit.

Duncan explained, "After that, ye will need to—"

"Put a thatch— a layer of hay— on her back, and then a blanket on top," Miss Jones finished.

Duncan felt like a brick had just hit him in the stomach. He thought Miss Jones had never ridden a horse until yesterday. How did she know something like that, then? He suddenly recalled how she had known exactly how to use the reins yesterday. She had played him for a fool.

He had always abhorred deceit, but this was somehow worse. Duncan knew he should let it go; he was just a servant. She was a lady, so she could treat him any way she liked. But he was sick with humiliation, disappointment, and anger; they were venomous things that he wanted to spit back out— at her, but mostly at himself, for being a fool. "Miss Jones, ye already kent how to ride a horse. Were ye having a joke at the stableboy's expense?" He knew he should stop, but he couldn't. "Does it amuse ye to pretend to need help frae those who are so far beneath ye?"

Miss Jones' face was now white, and Miss Knight's, red.

It looked to Janie like Duncan's jaw was chiseled flint, and sparks of anger were in his eyes. She had to tell him; it was far better to be thought indelicate than to be thought cruel. Janie looked at Fanny, who nodded her understanding.

Janie looked down at the straw clutched in her hands, rather than face those blazing eyes. "You're right; I wasn't honest with you. I already knew how to ride. I've been riding horses since I was four; I just didn't know how to ride side-saddle. Where I come from, women can ride astride a horse like men do, but here, you think it's not proper, so I needed someone to teach me. Believe me, I wasn't trying to humiliate you. I'm so sorry I lied, but I didn't know what else to do."

Janie risked a look at Duncan. All of the hardness had gone from his face; instead, he seemed now to be blushing. With embarrassment at being in the presence of such a floozy, probably.

When Duncan finally spoke, there was no anger left in his voice. "Now 'tis I who maun apologize, Miss Jones. I understand why ye didnae say aught before." He was quiet again for a moment. "I maligned ye. I condemned ye in my heart before hearing your side. Please forgive me."

Gracious, was that a tear shining in his eye? Janie was relieved that he no longer thought she was the kind of person who enjoyed humiliating others, but had he encountered people who were? "Of course I forgive you, Mr.— um, what's your last name?"

"MacKinnon."

"Mr. MacKinnon."

The rain had lightened considerably. Janie could hear the horses stamping, blowing, and chewing hay in the uncomfortable silence which followed.

The barn cat ran into the stable, shooting past them in a blur of wet, white fur, and the missing chunk of her memory struck Janie like a meteor.

CHAPTER 10

Her eye sae mildly beaming, her look sae frank and free,
In waking or in dreaming, is evermore with me.
~Traditional, "Ho Ro, My Nut Brown Maiden"

The white cat had come out of nowhere. Janie turned the steering wheel hard to the right to avoid hitting it, and her little car spun around on the wet tarmac with the lightness of a child's toy before running off the road and crashing into a signpost. Her forehead cracked the windshield before the force of the delayed and decidedly unhelpful airbag slammed her back into the seat.

Janie was shaken, but other than the painful injury to her forehead, she seemed to be okay— something of a miracle, considering she'd forgotten to buckle her seatbelt. After a quick prayer of thanks, she said another that she had only hit a sign, and not the historic-looking red brick building at the corner of the crossroad, nor an oncoming car in the right-hand lane. What she never could have imagined was what happened next— the crack spreading rapidly all over the windshield's surface like the roads on a map before exploding outward, and the airbag bursting like an overfilled balloon. Nor could she have imagined what she saw—the slit forming in the air in front of her like a rip in a plastic bag, pulling the rain into itself. Nor could she have imagined what she heard— a hollow sound like the hum of traffic driving through a tunnel, getting louder and louder. Least of all could she have imagined what she felt— as if a huge, invisible vacuum hose was stuck to her sternum, sucking her whole body in with a slow, excruciating force.

Janie's heart was beating fast, and the blood was drumming in her ears. Both Duncan and Fanny were looking strangely at her, as if they could hear the drumming, too, but of course they couldn't. "Janie, are you unwell?" Fanny asked.

Ugh! What *was* that? Janie pushed away whatever the pungent-smelling thing that Fanny was waving under her nose was. "I'm okay. I just remembered— um, something about my accident that I'd forgotten because of my head injury, and it kind of took me by surprise, that's all. It's fine. I'm fine."

Fanny put an arm around her. "Duncan, will you escort us back to the house?"

"Aye, Miss," he said, and they all set out across the stableyard together.

Janie and Fanny stood shivering in the hall in their wet riding clothes. Fanny said, "Let's meet in the dining room after we have both changed into dry gowns."

When Janie came back downstairs, what Fanny called a "cold collation" of sliced ham, chicken, and salad was spread down the center of the dining table. "Good! There's some soup to take the chill out of our bones, too," Fanny said as they sat down. Johncock lifted the the lid from the tureen and ladled some soup into their bowls.

Mmm. Forget the cold collation; soup was exactly what Janie wanted just then. It was potato and onion: thick, creamy, and most importantly, hot. "Where is everybody else?" she asked, before eating a spoonful of soup. It felt a little strange to be at such a large table by themselves.

"Papa and some of the men are searching the woods, remember? My brothers are helping. They will eat something later."

"What about your Aunt Jane?"

"She ate with Miss Clewes and the children. They love it when she visits. She is such fun! When I was a girl, she was always the one who would invent games for us to play. Sometimes, she and Aunt Cassandra even helped us put on theatricals in the evenings for our parents and neighbors. Not that they'd be doing anything like that on a Sunday, of course. Today she might be taking the children to visit old Mrs. Inman and bring her some fruit. Mrs. Inman is a widow, and she's blind now. Aunt Jane always visits her whenever she's here."

Janie smiled. Miss Austen's concern for women in need was just as evident in real life as in her novels. But theatricals? Obviously, Miss Austen didn't share the views of Mr. Bertram in *Mansfield Park*.

Janie and her brother and sisters had made up plays for the grown-ups, too. They had done *The Wizard of Oz* in their backyard with sheets hung between two trees for stage curtains, hadn't they? She tried to shake the disquieting feeling that it was someone else's memory, but she couldn't. Maybe it had never really happened at all.

It was still raining on Monday. Janie and Fanny had both slept late in the morning's darkness, but it didn't matter, since breakfast wasn't served until 10:00, anyway. The house was very quiet as they watched the rain run in rivulets down the wavy glass in the breakfast parlor. There was probably no way they would be riding today, but this hot chocolate was definitely the next best thing.

"Johncock said that Mr. Plumptre, my— a family friend,

has come to visit my brothers, and they have taken him shooting— in this weather! I hope they don't take a chill."

"They certainly couldn't be getting any wetter than we did yesterday, and we're fine."

"That's true. Oh! I almost forgot— we have several guests coming to dinner this evening, and I want to have some dancing. Since you play the pianoforte, would you help with the music?

"Of course! It would make me really happy to be able to contribute something. I owe y'all so much."

"Thank you! If you'll excuse me, I need to speak with Cook about the preparations for dinner."

"And I think I'd like to spend some time in your library."

A library was the perfect place to spend a wet day. Janie was stunned at how massive and beautiful it was. Rather than the dark, paneled walls she had expected to see, these were painted an airy Wedgwood blue which perfectly complemented the room's white trim and elaborate plasterwork. Marble busts placed around the room reinforced the impression that Janie was standing in a great box made of jasperware, in one of the classical patterns her mom had loved so much. The bright jewel tones of the leather-bound volumes in the floor-to-ceiling bookcases on each wall offered a beautiful contrast to their setting. There were so many books! There had to be over a thousand. It hardly seemed possible that a private home could contain such a library as this; it looked like it belonged in a university or some public institution.

Janie breathed in deeply, savoring the scent of the room. Mmm. It had a glorious smell, redolent of leather and paper, both old and new.

The cushioned sofas and tables and chairs that were arranged around the room gave a cozy feeling to a space which otherwise might have seemed too grand to be truly comfortable. Adding to the room's comfort were two stone fireplaces. It was a reader's dream, a sanctuary of quiet in which to escape. Janie sighed audibly.

"Wonderful, isn't it?" Jane Austen's voice startled her out of her reverie.

"It's amazing!" Janie agreed. It was hardly surprising that she hadn't noticed Miss Austen at first, since she was nearly hidden by the high-backed leather chair in which she sat in a back corner, near one of the fireplaces. "I hardly know how to choose from such a huge number of books!"

"If you haven't read it yet, may I suggest one of my favorites? Samuel Richardson's *Sir Charles Grandison*. My brother recently acquired a copy. Unless you disapprove of novels, that is." The last statement had a note of challenge in it, as if Miss Austen would be sizing Janie up based on her response.

"Are you kidding? I love novels! I think non-fiction

books are too much like textbooks; I can only handle so much at a time. But I can lose myself in a good story for hours and hours."

Miss Austen looked pleased. "Then do allow me to introduce you to *Sir Charles*." She went over to one of the shelves and selected a book that was beautifully bound in soft, burgundy Morocco leather, with gilded lettering on the spine. She handed it to Janie. "Here. I would love to know what you think of it."

Here she was, taking book recommendations from Jane Austen! Janie quickly tamed her ridiculous grin into something a bit more sedate. "Thanks. I'm sure I'll enjoy it."

"Shall I order us some tea?"

"Yes, that sounds great!" Janie settled into one of the other chairs near the fire, and Miss Austen left the room for a moment before returning to her own chair and book.

Soon the butler arrived with a tea tray, which he left on a nearby table.

"Thank you, Johncock," Miss Austen said.

So Jane Austen apparently thanked servants sometimes. How was Janie supposed to figure out the rules?

Johncock made a quick bow and went out again. Miss Austen poured the tea for them both and handed one of the cups to Janie.

"Thanks a lot. Now this is my idea of the perfect way to spend any afternoon, not just a rainy one."

"A comfortable coze in a well-appointed library? Indeed!"

They both smiled, sipped some tea, and opened their books.

An hour passed in companionable silence. Janie got up to stretch her legs and walk around the room. She gave a spin to the large globe held by a brass stand near one of the tall windows, then began looking over the book titles to see if any were familiar to her.

"Do you also enjoy poetry, Miss Jones?"

"I do, actually."

"I'm a great admirer of William Cowper's verse. Are you perhaps familiar with it?"

"'God moves in a mysterious way His wonders to perform,' right?"

"You do know him!"

"Well, no, not really. Only the poems that were made into hymns, like 'There is a Fountain.' I play the piano for services at my father's church, so I know a lot of hymns."

"Edward has two volumes of Cowper here, if you'd like to see them. This truly is the most marvelous library, is it not?" Miss Austen sighed. "Sometimes I scarcely leave it all day."

"I totally get that. I could hang out here forever."

Miss Austen laughed, then blushed. "Forgive me! I confess, sometimes I am at a loss to understand your American expressions."

"Sorry. How about—" Janie did her best British accent, which wasn't very good— "I am entirely in sympathy with you, Miss Austen. I would gladly spend endless hours among these splendid tomes"? She laughed at her attempt.

"Ah, yes. So much better!" Miss Austen said, joining in her laughter. She shut the book she had been reading with a *shwoop*. "I am curious. What is your opinion of the novel thus far?"

"To be honest, it's a little hard to get into, with everything being written as letters between the characters, but I'm getting used to it."

"I know the style has fallen out of fashion of late, but I think it has much to recommend it. I have sometimes enjoyed the challenge of writing stories that way, myself."

"That's right! *Lady Susan* is all in letters, isn't—" Janie stopped herself, but it was too late.

Jane Austen had gone completely white; whether from shock, fear, or anger, Janie couldn't tell.

"What manner of trickery is this, Miss Jones? How do you know these things about me?" Her voice was trembling, and it was edged in anger. "Do not tell me Fanny also told you about *Lady Susan*. She has never read it."

No, no, no, no, no! Janie put her face down into her hands. The weight of all the lies was pressing down like a goad on her shoulders, but how could she tell Miss Austen the truth? *I know all about you because you've been dead for two centuries?* Janie resisted the sudden urge to laugh. It was all so impossible.

"Miss Jones?"

"I'm really, really sorry. I didn't want to be deceitful, but I didn't think you'd believe the truth, and I was afraid. I still am."

"What is the truth, then?"

Janie felt something give way inside of her. "I know this stuff because I have traveled back through time. My time is more than 200 years after yours. I am from America, though. That much is true. I was staying in England when I um, came here." What a relief it was to finally tell someone!

"What exactly are you saying? You have come here from— the future? How is that possible?"

"I was— um, *pulled* into your time from mine, after my car— sort of like a really fast carriage— crashed into a post. I honestly don't understand how or why it happened."

"Why do you know about my manuscript?

"Because you're one of the most famous authors ever. You wrote— will write— six amazing novels. People all over the world know about you! In the future, I mean. Your books have been made into plays, movies— musicals, even! There are Jane Austen Societies. That's how my parents met, actually—"

Miss Austen's face was getting redder and redder. Her hands were gripping the arms of her chair, and she was making little rocking movements. Oh, no, Janie thought. Could she be having a stroke? "Are you okay? I'm sorry to be blowing your mind with all of this at once."

"What six novels?" She sounded as agitated as she looked.

Janie counted them off on her fingers. "There's *Sense and Sensibility* and *Pride and Prejudice*, of course, but also *Emma*, *Mansfield Park*, *Northanger Abbey*, and *Persuasion*. Not counting your unfinished novels and juvenilia."

"Juvenilia?" Now there was a note of hysteria in her voice. "You can't mean—"

"Yeah, the things you wrote when you were a kid. The *History of England* that your sister Cassandra illustrated, and all of that stuff. I'm sorry; I know you must be gobsmacked. It's a lot to take in."

Miss Austen stood up shakily and went to the door, holding onto its frame for support. Without turning her head, she said, "I must ask you to please excuse me, Miss Jones. I have the most dreadful headache. I must go and lie down."

Remorse and dread were like chunks of stone in the pit of Janie's stomach. What if she had just killed Jane Austen?

CHAPTER 11

Step we gaily, on we go, heel for heel and toe for toe,
Arm in arm and row on row, all for the sake o' Maire.
~Traditional, "Maire's Wedding"

Miss Austen had sent word to her brother that she was unwell and would keep to her room that evening. Janie felt guiltier than ever, especially when Fanny mentioned that the doctor had been called in to administer leeches for her aunt's migraine. "Poor Aunt Jane!" Fanny said.

"Yeah, leeches are totally disgusting!" Janie shuddered.

"No, silly! I meant that she has to miss the dancing this evening. She dearly loves to dance."

Fanny had gone a bit overboard with the dinner menu. The sheer quantity of food was unlike anything Janie had ever experienced, even at Thanksgiving, which was really saying something. Her family's Thanksgivings were epic, with every church member who didn't have a family to go home to, and often total strangers, too, being welcomed at the Jones' overflowing table. As on the previous night, many of the dishes were things Janie had never seen, much less eaten, before.

There were quite a few guests joining them for dinner, most of whom she had just met. Janie noticed that the order in which she and Fanny entered the dining room, as well as where they sat, changed each time guests were dining with them. Fanny's understanding of Janie's status was way off base— If only Fanny could see her family's little single-bathroom house and her tiny, shared flat at school!

Tonight, Janie sat between Fanny and a young man about their age named James Wildman, who lived at Chilham Castle. He was very interested in the fact that Janie lived in America, and he asked her a lot of questions. It was hard to answer them in a way that was appropriate for 1813. What were their primary crops? Darned if she knew— corn? Wait, she was forgetting that there would have still been slaves working in cotton, tobacco, and sugar cane fields in 1813. Janie mentioned those crops, too. "Of course, I'm absolutely against slavery, in case you were wondering."

"My family has slaves who work our plantations in Jamaica. Excuse me, Miss Jones." He pointedly turned to talk to the lady on his right.

What the heck? Did Fanny know about this? Janie

turned her attention to the food. Her strategy tonight was simple: accept the things that looked appealing (like that watercress salad), and pass on the ones that looked scary (like that roasted rabbit with the head still attached, ears and all!) She would also try not to ask questions about everything. She could only say, "Everything is different in America" so many times without raising eyebrows and suspicions. Luckily, everything she chose turned out to be delicious, except for the raw oysters. She had always wondered about those, and now she knew: they were as gross as they looked.

This time, Janie remembered not to keep thanking the servants, although it felt totally wrong.

After dinner, Mr. Knight invited his guests to move into the library. The footmen had removed some of the furniture and moved the rest against the walls, creating space for dancing. With the addition of Fanny's pianoforte, it made a wonderful ballroom. Janie sighed; it was just like the Disney movie where the Beast dances in the library with Belle. She couldn't resist doing a little twirl on her way into the room. The silk of her borrowed dress *swooshed* delightfully.

As lovely as everything was, though, she was no longer that disappointed to be missing out on the dancing. How on earth was anyone supposed to dance after eating so much? She went over to the pianoforte and sat down. Fanny had already set the sheet music up for her, in the correct order for each dance.

Janie knew she probably wouldn't recognize any of the songs, but this first one didn't look at all difficult. She silently thanked old Mrs. Beecher, who had made her learn to read music all those years ago. It seemed so stupid at the time because she could already play by ear, but she'd had many occasions to be glad of the skill since then.

Okay, Fanny and her father were now standing opposite one other at one end of the room, and the other couples were forming lines after them. It was time to start playing. The first few songs had a rather slow tempo, which made perfect sense after that big dinner. Then there were some faster-paced reels whose steps resembled square dancing. She would really have enjoyed playing some of these tunes on her fiddle; it was too bad she didn't have it here, or at least the bow for the borrowed Guarnerius. Would she even ever play Grandpa Jim's fiddle again? A wave of sorrow threatened, and she renewed her focus on the music in front of her.

After a few dances, Fanny came over and sat next to Janie at the piano with a sigh. "I am rather too warm now."

She pulled off her gloves and the fan that was dangling from her wrist by a cord, fanned herself for a moment, then flicked her fan shut and set it on top of the piano. "You've done wonderfully, Janie. I knew you would."

Fanny's fingers took over playing the notes at the lower end of the keyboard. "Here is a game that Aunt Jane used to play with me. You turn and face the other way so you can see the room, and I will play the music and guess what all the people who are here are doing at this moment. For instance, the woman in the violet gown is Mrs. Smythe. She is a widow, and her sons are friends of my brothers. Right now, she's probably waiting for my father to ask her to dance," she said with a smile, "but of course, he's too busy talking to one of the men about today's shoot. Am I right?"

Janie looked around the room. Some couples had resumed dancing, but most of them were still taking a break. Sure enough, there was Mrs. Smythe, standing at Mr. Knight's elbow. She seemed to be hanging on his every word. He, however, looked to be completely engrossed in a very animated conversation with another gentleman. "You got it exactly right!" Janie laughed.

"Now for my brothers. Ned and George are probably just talking to their friends, but I can safely say that Henry and Will are misbehaving."

"Right again! One of them seems to be trying to dunk the other's head into the punch bowl."

"I despair of them!" Fanny said in mock horror, then she

grinned. Her ability to talk so effortlessly while playing the piano would have been impressive in itself, but she further amazed Janie by describing the behaviors of the rest of the guests with such accuracy that they were soon both in stitches.

"One more," Fanny said. "I have saved the best for last: Mr. John Plumptre. He is the only one of the young men who is sitting down with the old ones. He looks miserable because he doesn't approve of dancing."

Yep, there he was, sitting in a lineup of gossiping matrons and elderly men, on the far side of the room. He had a handsome enough face, but also a receding hairline, unfortunate in one so young. His large, brown eyes looked earnestly but unsmilingly at the dancers. "He doesn't seem exactly *miserable*, just serious," Janie said. "I'm not sure I can give you full credit for that one."

"Oh. I'm glad, then. He's very amiable, actually." Fanny then proceeded to describe what she called Mr. Plumptre's "prospects"—which estates and how much money he stood to inherit— with a relish that sounded rather mercenary to Janie. Were those the things that made him so "amiable"?

Now that Janie could really see the dancing, she thought it looked like a lot of fun. Everyone obviously knew the steps to all of the dances already. Maybe she could ask Fanny to teach her some of them. She found herself wondering what it would be like to dance with Duncan MacKinnon. That bubble of a dream floated for only a moment before it burst. Of course, Janie would be stepping all over his feet. How was it that her fingers could move so nimbly over the fingerboard of a violin or the keys of a piano, while her feet were so clumsy? No amount of instruction from graceful Fanny could change that.

When Fanny came to the end of the song, she said, "Now it's time for a break. Come with me, Janie. I want to introduce you to someone."

Fanny scooped her arm through Janie's and led her over to where Mr. Plumptre was sitting. He jumped up at their approach. "Miss Knight! I have just heard news of the most troubling nature— that you have had a disturbance here at Godmersham Park involving a dangerous ruffian. You mustn't worry. That is, uh, you may depend on me for— for—"

Fanny and Janie waited.

"Protection," he finished lamely, as if he even doubted it himself. After this declaration, he made an awkward little bow.

"Thank you, Mr. Plumptre. That is very good of you." Fanny said. She was blushing.

"Please allow me to get you some punch, Miss Knight." Mr. Plumptre rushed away before Fanny even had the chance to introduce Janie to him.

What? Fanny was into this mousy guy, when her stablehand was a real-life Adonis? What about her "strong, romantic hero" comment earlier? Janie steered Fanny out of earshot of Gossip Row. "*He's* the one you like? That guy?"

Fanny nodded, suddenly demure. "We don't have an *understanding* or anything, but everyone expects it. He comes from a very good family." As if it were an afterthought, she added, "And I believe he cares for me."

"I bet you have plenty of options, though, right? Other admirers?"

"Well, there are a few beaux around here. Of course, I'm not saying I wouldn't consider an earl or a viscount if one happened to come along!" Fanny grinned.

Janie couldn't help herself. She had to know. "What about Duncan? He's really nice." She hoped she sounded more nonchalant than she felt.

Fanny's eyebrows shot up. "The *stablehand?*"

"Sure. Isn't he more your type?"

Fanny's laughter was like a sudden shower of sparkles. "Oh, Janie! You are too diverting! A servant!" She turned away then, for her gallant mouse was returning, holding a glass of punch before him like a chalice.

Was her new friend kind of a snob? Janie shrugged off

the disappointment; it was just her own modern, American way of looking at things. Besides, Fanny had also been very kind to her, even if it sometimes manifested itself in odd ways, like facial preparations.

At least Janie knew now that Duncan was fair game as far as the girlfriend code— probably the same in any century— went; Fanny was definitely *not* into him.

Not that it made any difference, Janie reminded herself. Duncan MacKinnon was still off limits. It was impossible, no matter how she felt. She was trying to figure out how to return to her own time, wasn't she?

CHAPTER 12

As I gaed in yon greenwood-side, I heard a fair maid singing. Her voice was sweet; she sang sae complete, that all the woods were ringing.
~Traditional, "The Duke of Athole's Nurse"

Elspeth had waited a little later than usual to come help her in the morning, but she needn't have. Unlike the rest of the household, Janie hadn't been dancing all evening. Elspeth opened the draperies to reveal a beautiful, sunny morning.

"Good morning, Miss. My brother says to tell you your fiddle bow is ready. He hopes he can hear you play, too, he says."

"Duncan MacKinnon is your brother?" How had she not heard that until now?

"Aye, Miss. I'm Elspeth MacKinnon."

"I never would have guessed. You look nothing alike." Wow, not even a little bit! Elspeth's accent was nowhere near as strong as his, either.

"Och, I know. He adopted me, Miss. Which gown would you like to wear today? The blue one, or the white one? The blue brings out your eyes, Miss. I think you should bring out your eyes."

Speaking of eyes, was it her imagination, or was there a twinkle in Elspeth's this morning? "The blue one then, by all means." What had Elspeth heard? "Has your brother mentioned that he has been taking me and Miss Knight riding, or— anything?"

"Oh, aye, Miss. I know all about it." Elspeth said nothing more on the topic, merely chatting about how muddy it still was outside while she helped Janie dress and did her hair. But she had a very knowing look.

"Elspeth, do you happen to know if Miss Austen is okay this morning? Feeling better, I mean?"

"Aye, Miss. She is *oh kay*," Elspeth giggled. "Miss Sayce says Miss Jane Austen is much improved this morning."

Janie made sure to bring the precious violin down to breakfast. She still couldn't believe she was going to play a Guarnerius! She laid the case down with care on one of the cushioned chairs before going over to the table.

Mr. Knight stood until Janie had seated herself. "I am looking forward to hearing you play, Miss Jones."

"Oh, yes, Janie! We should all do something for

everyone tomorrow night, while my brothers are still home! They must leave for Michaelmas term on Saturday. Miss Clewes and I have been working on some pieces with my sisters on the pianoforte; they can play, too."

"Splendid! Reserve a place for me in the front row, my dear," Mr. Knight said.

Fanny turned to her father. "Papa, may I go speak to Mrs. Kennett about those new table linens, while Janie gets the violin bow from Duncan? I'll come straight back to the stables afterwards, I promise."

Mr. Knight looked hesitant. "It's fairly wooded there. I think I should walk with you to the wash house. It's true that we didn't find any gypsies, and he is likely far, far away by now, but humor me, my dear."

Raven was a bit too far away for his liking. Luckily for him, though, young Johnny was a greedy little chap who would sell his own soul— or his friend's soul, at least, for a shilling, and he would keep his mouth shut about it for another.

After the "gypsy attack," as the villagers were calling it, Raven had to decide whether to shave his beard off and expose the damage that *cnaf's* fist had done to his face, or not. He decided the change to his appearance was worth it. He cut his hair— with regret, since he realized too late it was a blasted lot harder to do than it looked, and now he looked like a total *twmffat*, he did. David's bones, he couldn't bear to look in the mirror! He had also bought an ill-fitting jacket with more than one moth-hole off of the village rag and bone man.

The gypsy was no more.

Duncan held the bow out to Janie. It looked like such a delicate thing in his hands.

"It's wonderful! Thanks so much! I promise to pay you after I get my first paying student." Rehairing a bow usually cost about a hundred dollars. What was that in 1813?

"I cannae take your money."

"Please! It doesn't feel right. Not that I have any money to give you yet."

"Pay me with some tunes, then."

Janie laughed. "Now, that I can do! I wish I could pay for everything that way." She sat down on a hay bale, and Duncan sat down on another, a few feet away. She wondered if anyone would think they should have a chaperone. She was alone with a man in 1813! Scandalous.

"Och, I forgot." Duncan stood back up and reached into the pocket in his waistcoat. "I got some o' this frae my friend Charlie. He plays frae the village dances." He pulled out a little ceramic rosin holder and handed it to her.

"Oh, thank you! I do need that." Lord, it was a good thing he had no idea what his accent did to her. Janie heard the name Charlie nearly every day of her life, since it was her brother's, but the way Duncan said it, "Chairlee," with a burr on the r, turned her to butter. Okay, time to focus on the fiddle.

She took off her gloves and tightened and rosined the bow, then fine-tuned the fiddle. She played a few quick scales to warm up. Oh, my gosh! The tone was so beautiful! Better than beautiful! "You might even know some of these," she said. She played a set of reels, and after that, a jig.

Duncan was tapping his feet. He looked like he wanted to dance, and Janie didn't blame him. She could never resist tapping her feet herself, but she left the actual dancing to others, after a certain mortifying experience at the homeschool cotillion in junior high. Wow, it was so good to be playing again! And this violin was positively glorious!

"How is it that ye ken all of these Scottish tunes, Miss Jones?" Duncan asked when the jig was over.

"That music is in my DNA. My mother's family, the McIntyres, came from Scotland originally, and I've always loved traditional music. My grandfather played the fiddle."

"Och, I can ha' nought tae do wi' ye any mair, lassie! We MacKinnons ha' a blood feud wi' the McIntyre clan!"

"What? No, really? Our clans are feuding?" Wait, was he thickening his accent on purpose? "You're joking, aren't you?"

Duncan nodded, laughing. Janie grabbed a handful of hay and threw it at him, then another. He laughed harder. She was laughing too.

"Truce!" Duncan said, brushing the hay out of his hair with both hands. "What did ye mean, your dee and ae?

"Oh, sorry. You would probably say something is 'in your blood.' That's what it means."

"Och, aye. The same way working wi' horses is in my blood, then; my father and his father worked wi' horses. Will ye play one more tune? Then I maun get back to work."

"Sure. What's your favorite song?"

"I dinnae ha' a favorite. Play yours, instead."

"Okay, my favorite, then." She put her fiddle back to her shoulder. "Do you know the one called 'Afton Water'?"

"Aye. 'Tis in a book I ha' next to my— um, 'Tis in my book o' Robert Burns' poems."

"I thought you might know it. Anyway, it was my parents' song first, before it was mine. They heard it at a concert when they were—" She almost said dating, but he would have no idea what that was— "courting, then they danced to it at their wedding. My mother's name was Mary, like the girl in the song, though she went by Molly. After I was born, it was a lullaby she sang to me. Later on, when I formed a trad band– that's a band that plays traditional music, it was the first song I knew I wanted us to play." As a cringey teenager listening to her parents' old Nickel Creek CD, Janie had imagined what it would be like to have someone love her the way the guy in the song loved his Mary. Of course, she wasn't about to tell Duncan that, and not just because he wouldn't know what a CD was.

Duncan had never heard the song done to this tune before. It was a sweet melody, and she played it so tenderly that he thought his heart would break with the beauty of it. After she had played through the melody, she brought the violin down to rest lightly on her knee.

Then she started singing, and she took his breath away.

After she finished singing the last verse, Janie swallowed hard. Her heart was pounding as she positioned the violin again, then played the melody one last time to end the song. She had sung that song in front of a crowd of people so many times before, but it had felt very different to sing it for Duncan alone. It was as if she had let him look into the deepest part of her soul. What would he do with what he saw there?

The last, pure note on the Guarnerius lingered in the air. It was a moment before Duncan spoke.

"That was the bonniest thing I've ever heard in a' my life," he said in that low, soft voice of his. His dark eyes looked almost black.

Fanny stuck her head in the door. "Janie, are you ready? "Let's go practice our music."

Practice was apparently something Fanny didn't devote a great deal of time to. They had only played through their duet twice when Fanny closed the lid over the pianoforte's keys with a dramatic flourish and said, "I think that's enough, Janie. It is far too lovely a day to be spent indoors! I want to take you shopping. Too bad we haven't time enough to go all the way to Canterbury. Chilham only has a couple of shops, but it is better than nothing. I will order the carriage to be ready for us after lunch."

Judging from the window display, this shop was fancier than the last one, and they had spent half an hour there, as tiny as it was. Fanny could shop with the best of them. She had commented on nearly every item in the store before settling on her purchases. The footman, Joe, had carried her parcels back to the carriage.

"This one's even better. You'll see," Fanny said.

"Do you mind if I stay here this time? I'd rather not look at all of this stuff until I have money to spend."

"I can buy you something, silly."

"No. Please, Fanny."

"Suit yourself." Fanny let Duncan hand her down from the carriage, and Joe hopped down once again from his seat next to Duncan to follow her into the shop. He looked resigned.

"I'm staying this time," she told him when he opened her door. Wait, she could just sit in here and count the stitches in the upholstery for an hour, or she could climb up front and talk to Duncan. "If you don't mind the company, could I come up there?"

Duncan looked surprised. "Aye." He gave her his hand and helped her down from the carriage. "Just a wee minute." He pulled out his handkerchief, climbed up on the box and wiped the seat off. Then he came back down and held her hand while she climbed up onto the box.

The seat was built to hold two people, but Janie hadn't realized how close she would be sitting to him until he climbed up.

Duncan had not expected this arrangement. He noticed that his boots were still clatty with that morning's mud.

Miss Jones' eyes looked so blue today. She smelled like strawberries. She smoothed her skirts, then looked over at him."Mr. MacKinnon, I've been wondering. How did you and Elspeth end up in England?"

"'Tis a long story, Miss."

She grinned. "Did you fail to notice how long Fanny spent in that last shop?"

Duncan chuckled. "Och, I suppose we do ha' the time, then. Well, my mother and I came to be in London because the Laird we worked for married an English lady. She wanted to stay in their house in London most o' the time."

"How long did you live in Scotland?"

"Until I was thirteen. My father was carriage driver for the Laird, and my mother was a housemaid."

"What were they like, your parents?"

"My father died when I was a wee laddie; I only remember he was a great, braw man, and he was kind. 'Twas said he could do anything wi' horses. My mother was very bonnie, the bonniest lass in the district."

"Did she die too? Sorry, you just sounded so sad. I don't mean to pry."

"I dinnae mind tellin' ye." Duncan was surprised to realize it was true. He had never told anyone his story except the minister at the kirk. "Aye, she died. Much too young." He looked away, choosing his words.

"The Laird had a brother who came to visit him in

London." Duncan's right hand had fisted, and he flexed it out. "He forced himself on my mother and got her wi' child. When she couldn't hide her condition anymore, The Laird's wife dismissed her frae service without a reference or even her last month's wages."

Miss Jones gasped. "That's terrible! What did y'all do?"

"I was nae mair than a laddie then, but I wanted to kill the man. As a servant, I couldnae even ca' him oot."

"Call him out?"

"Challenge him to a duel. My mother had nae living relations back in Scotland, and she thought we had a better chance to find work in London. We rented a room, and we did whatever odd jobs we could, but we couldnae keep up wi' the rent, and then we were oot on the streets." He swallowed the lump in his throat. "Right before her time."

Duncan looked over at Miss Jones. He hadn't planned on telling her this part, but now he wanted to. He took a deep breath. "I was desperate to get my mother intae lodgings, anywhere. I took to stealing, to my shame. There was a man who would gie money for things withoot asking questions. In the end, it wasnae enough. My mother died giving birth, and the bairn wi' her." He looked down at the hands that had been powerless to save her or the baby.

"I'm so sorry, Mr. MacKinnon." There was no condemnation in her eyes, only compassion. They sat in silence for a minute. "Elspeth told me you adopted her. What did she mean?"

Duncan couldn't help but smile at that. "Aye. I suppose I did. That's a wee bit of a story, too. After my mother died, I went on stealing, and I learned to fight. All I could think aboot was taking revenge on that man, until I met a minister who was preaching on the streets. He was frae Scotland, too, and he took me in. Mr. MacDonald gave me a job at the kirk and a place to stay, and he taught me aboot God and His forgiveness through Christ. It changed me. I didnae want to steal anymair or take revenge. I decided to leave it to God."

"Your minister reminds me of my father. That's just what he would do."

Duncan smiled. "That same year, somebody left a wee bairn on the steps o' the kirk. He took her in, too."

"Elspeth."

"Aye. I asked if I could name her after my mother. We decided to give her my last name, so she could be my sister."

"So Elspeth is actually English."

"Perhaps. We raised her, though, so she's a Scot, too."

"But how is it that you're both here in Kent, instead of London?"

"Mr. MacDonald arranged for me to get this position. He knew I was pining after the country, and he had some connection wi' the Knight family. Last year, Mr. MacDonald died, and Elspeth came here, too. I ha' never seen her so happy; Susanna Sackree is like a mother to her.

Elspeth thinks the world o' ye too, Miss Jones, for letting her act as your lady's maid."

Miss Jones grinned. "I couldn't do without her."

Duncan was thoughtful. He would never in a hundred years have imagined he would share his secrets with a highborn lady, but Miss Jones was different. She wasn't like anyone he'd ever known.

David's bones! What rotten luck! Having been informed that the ladies planned on shopping, Raven had picked the poshest looking place in the village. It had looked like a sure thing, but Miss Knight came in with only a sad-looking lackey.

So Miss Jones was still outside with her blasted steel-fisted guardian angel. At least Raven now knew his disguise worked; Miss Knight clearly did not recognize him. He bought the cheapest thing he could find and slunk out of the shop.

Janie wasn't too surprised to see that Fanny had bought another stack of parcels. Duncan helped Janie down and back into the carriage, and he and Joseph arranged the packages inside. Then he handed Fanny into the carriage, which was considerably more crowded than it had been on their way into the village.

"I've got a present for you! I'll show you when we get home. I think this shop is losing its touch, though. There was quite a vulgar, common man shopping in there today. Why were you sitting up there instead of inside?"

"It was too boring to sit by myself, so I went to talk with Mr. MacKinnon."

"See, you should have come in with me. Then you wouldn't have had to talk about bridles and saddles."

"I like bridles and saddles."

CHAPTER 13

For a' that and a' that, our toils obscure and a' that,
The rank is but the guinea-stamp, the man's the gowd for a'
that.
~Robert Burns, "A Man's a Man for a' That"

Fanny's Diary- 6 Oct. 1813

Yesterday before dinner, I gave Janie the adorable bonnet I bought for her in Chilham. It has blue ribbons and the sweetest sprig of forget-me-nots on it. She looked so pretty in my blue gown that I just knew the blue bonnet would become her. The facial preparations, however, are failing us! Her freckles are as bad as ever. Cook has a recipe for lemon cream, which we will try next.

Speaking of Miss Jones, she is at this moment in the back parlor, giving Louisa and Cassandra their first violin lesson. She warned me that they would sound terrible at first, but there are no words to convey how truly horrible are the screeching noises coming from that room!!! I hope my sisters improve soon, or I shall have to alter my schedule so that I am out of doors during their lessons!

Janie now has an occasion for wearing her new bonnet. Yesterday, I asked Cook to prepare a large picnic hamper for today, in hopes that the fine weather would continue. Happily, it is a beautiful, sunny day, and the ground is no longer wet. Another happy circumstance is that Mr. Plumptre is to stop here with us for the rest of the week, then travel back to Oxford with my brothers. I didn't even have to beg them to join our picnic, since it means they may have a game of cricket, the only thing they love more than shooting. The younger children can play battledore and shuttlecock. I'm sure that Aunt Jane can be persuaded to leave her writing box at home and join in the fun.

They could simply have walked down to the river, were it not for the ginormous picnic hamper. "Where is Duncan?" Janie asked Fanny, when an open carriage, with the hamper strapped to its back, pulled up to the front door. An older man she had never seen before was driving it.

"How should I know? I suppose he has other things to do. Duncan doesn't usually drive us, anyway; he's just a stablehand. Gabriel is our coachman and head groom.

Duncan was filling in for him while he was ill, but it looks like he is better now."

How odd it was to be handed up into the carriage by this stranger. And disappointing.

Fanny had chosen a lovely spot down by the river. Besides Fanny's brothers and sisters, Janie was surprised to see that two of the footmen, with a cart full of additional supplies such as cushions for lounging, paddles and shuttlecocks for playing, and umbrellas to protect them from the sun, were already waiting for them there when they arrived. The children all wanted to have lunch before playing their game, so the hamper was unloaded forthwith, and Fanny supervised the distribution of china plates and crystal glassware to her younger siblings on some blankets under the willow trees.

A good deal of preparation had obviously gone into this outing. The picnic fare included cold roast beef and lamb, fresh bread, pickled vegetables, rout cakes, and lemonade. It was a far cry from the sandwiches and chips, eaten from paper plates, which Janie's family had on their picnics. The fanciest thing the Joneses ever did was to chill a watermelon in the creek.

Janie was struck again by the unreal quality of her own memories. It was almost as if they were a dream. Like a dream, could those memories fade away altogether? It was a terrifying thought.

After lunch, all of the boys except young John played a single wicket game of cricket. John had asked his Aunt Jane to take him to feed bread crumbs to the fish in the river.

Lizzy and Marianne watched the cricket game, while Fanny and the two youngest girls showed Janie to play battledore and shuttlecock, which resembled badminton without a net. As they batted the shuttlecock around, Janie asked Louisa and Cassandra about their lessons—which subjects they liked, and which they didn't, which seemed to be most of them. Miss Clewes had her work cut out for her, it seemed.

When Janie got tired, she and Fanny sat on some cushions to watch the rest of the cricket game. Fanny's brothers were incredibly good players, and they had a good-natured competitiveness that made them fun to watch. Mr. Plumptre didn't fare well by comparison with such natural athletes. He looked more and more wilted as the game went on, and his relief when it ended was obvious. Janie couldn't help saying, "Poor guy," under her breath.

"Excelling at sport is not everything. He is a very good scholar," Fanny said.

Edward came over and flopped down on the grass next to his sister. His tousled hair was even wilder than usual. "I almost asked you to sub in for Plumptre, Fanny," he said with a grin. "You're a far better batsman than he is. Besides, the fellow's done to a cow's thumb."

"Ned! You wouldn't!"

"Lud, I'm just teasing you, Fan. He may not be a Corinthian, but Plummy's a capital fellow, top o' the trees, and just the chap you want when you've got a big exam coming up."

William ambled over. "Come on, Ned, we're going fishing!" He held up a rod. "Begging your pardon, ladies," he said, with a roguish wink at Janie.

Edward leapt nimbly to his feet, grabbed the rod, and made a quick bow. They ran down to join the others at the river.

"That little brother of yours is dangerously charming, Fanny. He can't be any older than— what, sixteen? I think you need to have a talk with him."

"Will is fifteen, the cheeky boy. He will be sixteen on the tenth."

"And the oldest one is dangerously good looking, but there's not much you can do about that."

Fanny's eyebrows went up. "You find Ned handsome?" She smiled.

"Don't get any ideas!" Janie laughed. "Besides, I can't understand half of what he says."

"The boys do tend to show off the cant they've picked up at Oxford whenever Papa's not around."

Miss Austen and John returned from the river, and Miss Austen settled herself onto some cushions next to Janie. "I have been wanting to talk with you," she said. "I have been thinking a great deal about all that you said in the library, and how I responded. I was rather rude to you, and I am sorry."

"There is no need to apologize. I probably rocked your world."

"What an apt expression that is! Yes, in a way, I suppose you did; you opened up to me a reality I had never considered possible. You did not shake the foundations of my beliefs, however, if that is what you mean. God Himself is outside of time, is He not? He chose to step into time for our sake, in the incarnation. I have always known that there are 'more things in heaven and earth than are dreamt of in my philosophy,' Miss Jones. Now I find that I am filled with curiosity about the world you come from."

"What would you like to know? I need to be careful about what I say because of this thing called the butterfly effect, which may or may not be real, but just in case it is—"

Miss Austen looked confused, and rightly so. Janie was duffing it. She took a deep breath and tried again. "The idea is that anything I say or do now could possibly change the future in some way. It might cause someone to make different choices, for example. Especially someone important like you."

Miss Austen blushed. "I must protest that adjective, but I confess that after you told me those things in the library, I was tempted to write to my sister Cassandra and ask her to burn every single letter I ever wrote her, and those silly stories I wrote as a young girl."

"No! Please, please don't do that! She will save too little, as it is! Also, promise me you won't decide to write stories about time travel, or any of the future stuff I tell you about. Just write what you have always intended to write, as if I was never here." Shoot, this was starting to feel like a really bad idea.

Bad idea or not, Janie spent the rest of the afternoon satisfying Miss Austen's curiosity. She told her about women in universities, emancipated slaves, automobiles, movies, and a great many other things. The tree of knowledge had also borne some very bitter fruit in the last two centuries, but Janie didn't want to talk about those things. This was Jane Austen, whose pen did not dwell on guilt and misery. Had Janie been sitting under a willow tree with Fyodor Dostoyevsky instead, she probably would have had a very different conversation.

"One more thing," Miss Austen said, after they had spent nearly an hour talking about the marvels of the future. "The other day in the library, you said I would write six novels. Only one of those you mentioned I haven't started writing yet."

Janie nodded. "*Persuasion*." She didn't like where this was going.

"Does something happen that keeps me from writing anymore, or—"

"Oh, Miss Austen, I—" Janie bit her lip.

Miss Austen stood up. "I'm sorry. I know I shouldn't have asked. I am going to go look for blackberries." She turned and started walking away from the river.

"Fanny says the birds have eaten them already," Janie called after her.

Miss Austen waved her words away and continued on.

When they arrived home, Janie told Fanny she was going for a little walk. She grabbed an apple from the sideboard in the parlor, in case her walk might just happen to take her by the stables.

The carriage was parked in the stable yard, and Duncan

was unhitching the pair of bays that had brought them to the river. Janie waved when he looked up.

"Miss Jones! Is there something ye need? Did ye leave something i' the carriage?"

Dang, that would've been less obvious, wouldn't it? Too late now. "No, I just wanted to see Nan. I brought her an apple."

"Och, don't let Pretty Pie see ye gie it to her. She'll be that jealous."

"I didn't think of that. I should've brought two. Maybe we could cut it in half."

Duncan held his hand out for the apple, and Janie gave it to him. He grinned and took a bite. "Mm, that's good." He pulled a pocket knife from his waistcoat pocket and cut what was left of the apple in half before handing it back to Janie.

"I guess I should have brought three," she said, laughing.

The two mares were stalled next to one another. "I've missed our rides together," Janie said as she fed the first half to Nan, stroking her nose.

Duncan's heart did a wee flip. She missed him, too! Nae, eejit, she was obviously talking to the horse. He went back to currying the bay.

When Miss Jones had fed the two mares, she came back to the open area of the stable, where Duncan was working. "May I help?" she asked, picking up another brush from the shelf. "I actually really enjoy doing this."

"Aye, if ye like."

She brushed on the other side. "I have a horse back home in America. His name's Apple Jack, but I just call him Jack. My father gave him to me when I was a little girl. He's a dapple grey; Dad picked him because of his spots."

Her expression was dreamy, as if she saw far-off things. "My father loves to say, 'Glory be to God for dappled things.' That's a line from his favorite poem; it's about seeing beauty in things that are imperfect– things that have spots or freckles, like my mom and me, and my brother and sisters." She looked at Duncan then, and smiled. She went back to brushing.

Duncan smiled, too. He liked those freckles across her nose.

"What's his name?"

"Broon Horse."

"Brown Horse?" Miss Jones laughed. She had the kind of laugh that made one feel joyous inside. It was like hearing the church bells ringing on Christmas morning.

""'Tis not very original, I ken, but wee Miss Cassandra Knight named him."

"Ah, yes. Some of the names I gave to my grandfather's horses when I was a little girl were real doozies."

Duncan laughed. "Doozies, is it?"

"Yeah, you know, doozies. I think my best one was Mr. Sloppysocks."

"Och, that is terrible!"

"Hey, I was really proud of that one," she laughed. More bells.

They had curried Brown Horse twice over already, but Duncan didn't want Miss Jones to leave. "May I ask ye something? What is it like in America?"

"Oh, it's so different from here. I keep catching myself saying that, but it's true."

"Aye, no side-saddles." Och, he had her blushing now; he hadn't meant to. "What else?"

"I was going to say it's more of an idea that makes America so different— a different way of thinking. Of course, the most important thing is the freedom to believe what you want and say what you want, but you can also become what you want, if you're willing to work hard enough. That's the idea, anyway. There's no royalty, no aristocracy. Nobody can tell you that you are below them. You can fall in love with and marry whoever you want."

Did she glance at him when she said that? Nae, he imagined it.

"You can run for president, even if you grew up on a farm, or whatever. America's not perfect, and I'm not saying that nobody there is poor, or even homeless. Not very many people there live in a mansion like Godmersham Park; I sure don't. But you have the chance to work for your dream, whatever it is. I don't think I really appreciated that until I came here. There are a lot of differences, but I think those are the main things."

America sounded far too good to be true to Duncan. Just like the notion that maybe Miss Jones had really come by today just for the purpose of seeing him.

As she left the stables, Janie had the disconcerting feeling that she was being watched. She felt a prickling of fear, and wondered if she should turn back and ask Duncan to walk with her. She looked around her, but she could see no sign of her attacker. There were several outbuildings, though, and he could be hiding behind one of them. Should she run the rest of the way? No, the house was quite close, and she was being paranoid. Hold your head high and walk with purpose, she told herself. As she approached the house, Janie saw an upstairs curtain fall back into place.

CHAPTER 14

I spied a pretty fair maid, she appeared like a queen
In her costly fine robes and her mantle so green.
~Traditional, "Her Mantle So Green"

Janie was more than a little surprised that the scratching at her door did not preface the entrance of Elspeth. Instead, it was the pretty maid who had sat next to Duncan in church. Janie now knew her name was Susan, and that she was a parlormaid. Susan had in her arms a green silk gown that Janie hadn't seen yet.

"Elspeth is busy. I'll be attending to you this evening, Miss Jones," the maid explained, dumping the gown unceremoniously on the bed. The "Miss Jones" sounded as if she meant, "you scum."

Susan was obviously less than thrilled to have to do the job. Janie was tempted to say she didn't need any help, but she doubted she could manage to fasten the gown by herself, so she said, "Thank you." She let Susan help her out of the blue day dress and into the green silk gown.

Thank goodness Elspeth didn't dress her like this every day, yanking on the corset strings and jabbing half of the pins into her flesh before putting them through the fabric of the dress! Either Susan was having a very bad day, or she resented having to do a job that wasn't hers. Janie was curious about where Elspeth was, but she didn't ask. Better to forgo conversation, the sooner to be done.

Janie seated herself at the dressing table and allowed the maid to pull the comb rather roughly through her tangles. Susan dressed her hair and secured it with combs; Janie winced when one of them jabbed into her scalp. It was the price for beauty, right?

When Susan was finished, Janie couldn't help but admit that her hair looked even more lovely than when Elspeth did it. "Thank you, Susan. My hair looks wonderful." Janie smiled, and she saw a momentary glimmer of pleasure cross the maid's face before her expression hardened again. Susan leaned in closer and spoke to Janie's reflection in the gilded mirror.

"I've been watching Sara Sayce do hair for a long time, much longer than that chit Elspeth, and I am the one who will be moving up to lady's maid. Take my advice, Miss Jones. Stay away from where you don't belong, and who you don't belong with." Susan's eyes narrowed. "And don't go telling the Knights I said so, or you will regret it." Then she slipped out of the room as quietly as a snake.

Janie could see why Susan might feel threatened by the experience Elspeth was gaining, but why had she made such a weird threat? Janie had never even spoken to her before, other than the occasional "hello" when she saw the maid in the drawing room or the hall.

Janie decided to put it out of her mind, and she gave herself one last look in the mirror before going downstairs. The gown was lovely. It was almost the exact shade of green as Janie's formal concert dress. How appropriate, since she and the Knight children were to present their drawing room concert tonight after dinner. Wait, she should wear her necklace! Janie went over to the little corner closet, where her own green dress was folded neatly on one of the shelves. There was no way she would be wearing that dress here, since sleeves were a must in 1813. On the shelf above it was her emerald and diamond necklace. Sackree had wrapped it in tissue paper.

The necklace was a family heirloom that Janie's dad had given to her mom when they got married. He said he wanted Janie to wear it, once he saw the emerald green gown she picked out last year.

Janie did the clasp at the back of her neck. After one last look in the mirror, she left her room to go downstairs for dinner.

Janie had discovered that dinner was a comparatively simple affair when the Knights didn't have a bunch of guests. There was no row of footmen; only the butler was there to pour the wine. Fanny had put Janie between her oldest brother and Miss Austen. Fanny and Mr. Plumptre sat across the table from her. Janie turned to Miss Austen. "How is your new book coming along?" she asked quietly. She was fairly sure no one else could hear her; Fanny's brothers were too busy talking with their father about the day's fishing.

"Rather well, I think," Miss Austen answered, also in an undertone. "I am in the initial stage of outlining the characters and the plot."

"I know you think no one but you will like your Emma, but I've always loved her."

"You say something like that, and I feel compelled to cross myself in the old Romish manner! It's awfully hard to eat one's Cornish hen in complacency when sitting next to a prophet, Miss Jones."

Janie chuckled. "Sorry! I'll try not to say anything too disturbing, I promise. I just wanted to say that now that I've gotten to know your niece, I see a lot of her in Emma—the way she's so devoted to her father, for one thing. She's also 'handsome, clever, and rich.' Then there is her love for matchmaking, of which I have firsthand experience."

Jane Austen laughed, covering her mouth with her napkin. "Oh, dear. Poor you!"

"Yes. The less said about that, the better." Was she herself Harriet, then, dressed up as she was in Fanny's clothes? "Anyway, I was wondering if perhaps you based the character partly on her."

Miss Austen raised one eyebrow. "Perhaps." She smiled.

"Though you did give the name Fanny to a totally different character in *Mansfield Park*, so—"

"There you go again! It is too uncanny! That hasn't even been accepted for publication yet; I just finished it! No more, please," Miss Austen laughed. "Do try some of the raspberry fool, Miss Jones. It's quite delicious."

An hour after dinner, the gentlemen joined the ladies in the parlor. Their pianoforte duet began the program. They were followed by Fanny's four younger sisters, who each played songs they had recently learned on the pianoforte. The applause was loudest for seven year old Cassandra, who started her piece three times, but persevered to the finish. Last of all, Janie rose from her seat and picked up the precious violin and its bow carefully from the side table. She walked to the front of the room and began to play the piece she had chosen, Chopin's Nocturne in E-Flat Major. Never mind that Chopin hadn't written it yet; the Guarnerius seemed to want to play that piece. What could it hurt? A hush settled over everyone as the pure strains of the violin filled the room. Janie noticed that Mr. Knight's eyes were wide with surprise. He was probably shocked at how beautiful this violin that he'd been ready to give away actually sounded. Janie closed her eyes, letting the music wash over her as she played.

When Janie finished, she looked out at the applauding audience with a smile. Her smile was reflected in every face but one. Edward Knight was scowling.

Miss Clewes and Sackree were ushering the children out of the parlor as Mr. Knight came back in with two footmen at his heels. "Miss Jones, may I speak with you for a moment?" he asked. Fanny grinned at her.

"Sure." Janie followed him into the great hall. The footmen stood on either side of Mr. Knight. It felt weird; something was up.

"Miss Jones, explain yourself."

Oh, no. Had he heard something about her time travel? "Wha— what do you mean? What do you want me to explain?"

"Explain how you came to be wearing my late wife's necklace. The necklace I have been saving to give to Fanny on her next birthday. The necklace that was locked away in my study, and is no longer there. I just checked."

"Wait, no— this is mine! It was my great-grandmother's. My dad gave it to me."

"I cannot believe you are brazen enough to lie about it

to my face! I have extended hospitality to you. You have received nothing but kindness from me and my family. My precious daughter has been your friend. It is too monstrous!" His voice was now raised enough that Janie was sure that the rest of the family could hear everything he was saying.

"I'm sorry, sir, but you're wrong. Maybe it looks a lot like it, but it's not! Ask Sackree. She knows I was wearing it before, when I first came."

For a moment, Mr. Knight looked unsure, but then his expression hardened. "You could have stolen it earlier, before we returned home. The jeweler created this design for my wife; there is not another just like it."

Fanny and Miss Austen were now standing in the hall, too. Janie shot a look of appeal to them. Would they stand up for her?

"I don't know if you are aware, but I happen to be the magistrate. Miss Jones, I am placing you under arrest for theft." Mr. Knight nodded. Suddenly, the two footmen were gripping her arms. "Jane, will you please remove the necklace from her?"

Janie's heart sank as Jane Austen stepped behind her and undid the clasp.

Fanny started crying and ran back into the parlor.

Janie sat alone on the bench in the hall, trying to will herself not to cry. It wasn't working. A footman had tied her wrists together in front, but she managed to wipe her eyes with the back of one hand. Her nose was going to start running. She leaned her head back against the wall to enlist the help of gravity. The chandelier above her was as stunning as she had imagined it would be, but seeing it only made her feel more wretched. Sweet Fanny had asked Johncock to have its candles lit this evening in honor of their concert, even though it was just a family gathering, simply because Janie liked to see it all lit up.

Miss Austen came into the hall from upstairs. She had a long coat draped over her arm. "Miss Jones, the carriage is ready." She put a handkerchief between Janie's tied hands. "Here," she said. Then she draped the coat around Janie's shoulders. "Please borrow my pelisse. It will be cold in there, I'm sure."

"Thank you," Janie said. "I didn't do it, you know. I didn't do it."

"Try not to worry. I am certain that we will get it all sorted."

The front door opened, and there was Gabriel, ready to help her into the carriage. Not Duncan. She couldn't tell if she was disappointed or relieved.

The jailer kept a tight grip on her arm. He set his lantern down and unlocked the cell with an absurdly large key. He drew back an equally large bolt. The hinges screeched painfully as he pulled the heavy door open. He yanked Janie through the low doorway, and she nearly fell over when he suddenly let go of her arm.

The cell smelled like a mixture of moss and something else— was it urine? Ugh, probably. The jailer turned abruptly away, and the room went dark as he ducked out through the doorway. Janie had the disorienting sensation that she was standing on the ceiling instead of the floor, and she was going to fall off. "Wait! Is there a bed or something? I can't see."

The jailer stuck his arm back in and swung the lantern to the right. "O'er there."

She could barely make out a bench against one wall. Janie quickly wobbled over to it and sat down. It would be so dark in there when the jailer was gone. He couldn't leave yet! Her head was spinning with so many questions. "Wait! How long until my trial? What happens if I'm convicted? What's the penalty for stealing a necklace?"

"After Lent 'sizes." He sounded like he had a mouthful of rocks.

"After what?"

"Assizes. In th' spring."

Spring? That was in what, six more months? "Wait, wait!" Janie yelled as the door swung shut with another shriek and a clang. "What about the penalty?"

The jailer's gruff voice was muffled by the door, but his answer was clear enough. "That be a hangin' offense."

CHAPTER 15

Fareweel, ye dungeons dark and strang, the wretch's destinie!
MacPherson's time will no be lang on yonder gallows tree.
~Traditional, "MacPherson's Rant"

A hanging offense. She could be hanged. Hanged! At twenty-two! She hadn't even finished school yet. She hadn't found her one true love. She had hardly even begun to live! Janie was shaking all over, and her teeth chattered uncontrollably. "Oh, God, Oh, God, Oh, God, Oh, God" eventually became a more coherent prayer. "God, please help me. I don't know what to do. Help me get out of here and show them I didn't do it. Amen."

Peace settled over Janie's soul like a comforting blanket. Her mind stopped its out-of-control spiral, and the violent shaking subsided. She knew in the deepest part of her being that God had heard her.

The cell was damp and cold, and Janie was grateful for the coat's extra layer of warmth over her thin dress. She said another prayer of thanks for Jane Austen. There was no one more clever than she. It was a reassuring thought; if anyone could prove Janie hadn't stolen the necklace, it was Miss Austen. She knew Janie was innocent, didn't she? Even so, would she cross her own brother in defense of a virtual stranger? Miss Austen might try to explain about the time travel. If she did, wouldn't Mr. Knight just think Janie was crazy? Ending up in a place like Bedlam might be worse than being hanged.

Fear threatened to clasp Janie in its frigid arms again, and she forced her thoughts to move in another direction. She thought of her family, so far away in the future; it was strange and disturbing, but their faces had recently taken on an out-of-focus, dreamlike quality. Janie didn't want to put her family through the pain of losing her this way. Then again, they would never know she had been hanged in another century, would they? At least they would be spared that much. As far as her family would know, she had simply disappeared. But they had already lost her mom, and no one should have to go through that kind of pain twice.

Janie told people her mother was dead, but the truth was more complicated than that.

The summer Janie turned sixteen, her mom spent three weeks traveling around Ireland. She was there to do research for a book she was writing on the role of poetry in the history of rebellion in Ireland. As her mom said, it was "publish or perish," and if she wanted to preserve her tiny office in the musty halls of the history department, she must go ever further afield and ever deeper into obscurity. She seemed to be loving every moment, though, according to the ecstatic descriptions of everything she wrote on the backs of the two beautiful postcards of the Emerald Isle which she posted home. The postcards arrived, but she never did.

On the day before her mom was supposed to fly back home, a couple out for a walk with their dog found an abandoned rental car. It had apparently run off the road and into a low stone wall. The keys were still in the ignition of the car, which had suffered surprisingly little damage. In the back seat, they found a backpack and a small suitcase. Not a single thing seemed to be missing from the luggage: the driver's money, passport, clothing, and notebooks full of research notes were all there. Everything was there but the driver.

The hikers called the local garda, the Irish police, who contacted the area hospitals and the American embassy. A lengthy investigation involving local and international police turned up nothing. Nothing at all. It was as if she had simply vanished from the face of the earth.

Janie suddenly shot up straight from her huddled position on the bench. How had she not seen it until this moment?

Janie's dad had always said that he *knew* her mom was still living. As husband and wife, they were one, he said, and he believed he would know in his heart if she were dead. After all of the years without a single reported sighting, she was officially presumed dead. Janie's father presumed something different: she must have hit her head in the accident and suffered total amnesia. There was a chance that one day her memory would return, and she would come back to them.

That was the reason why they had never moved, in spite of the memories of Janie's mom haunting every room of their house like spectres. Even after her dad's father died and he inherited the farm in Kentucky, along with the beloved 100-year old house he had grown up in, they did not move into it. Instead, her dad paid a salary he couldn't afford to a caretaker who watched over everything. They would all move back there after their mom came home, he said.

Her dad's fellow pastors thought the reason he felt so strongly that his wife still lived was because she was in heaven now, more alive than she had ever been. Less generous people thought her dad was in denial to the point of delusion. Some even assumed her mom had simply abandoned the family. A small, secret part of Janie had always wondered if they were right, if her mom hadn't loved them enough to come back. An even more secret part of her wondered if maybe things would have been different if Janie were more like her mother, if she were someone her mom could be proud of.

As much as Janie adored her dad, she hadn't shared his optimism for a long time. Hope was just too painful, followed as it always was by the crushing weight of disappointment. She had gotten in the habit of tamping hope down whenever it surfaced in her heart. As months and then years went by, it was easier just to accept that her mom was dead. She would see her in heaven someday, but never again on this earth.

Now, for the first time in years, Janie did not extinguish the spark of hope she felt. She desperately needed its warmth.

At first, only the crosshatched bars on the window and the small spaces between them had been visible in the moonlight, and Janie could barely even make out the shape of her own hands, which the jailer had shackled together at the wrist in narrow iron cuffs. At least he had agreed to let Janie slip her arms through the sleeves of Miss Austen's coat and buckle its belt beforehand.

Now that her eyes had adjusted, they confirmed what she had already concluded: the cell contained nothing that could help her escape. There were iron restraints bolted firmly into the wall and a bucket underneath the bench, nothing more. At least the jailer hadn't chained her to the wall, at Mr. Knight's request. Mr. Knight was not unkind; he was only doing what he thought was right, she told herself. Janie just prayed he could be convinced that what was right was to have her released.

As the night wore on, Janie found her thoughts returning again and again to her family, and her memory of their faces, voices, and mannerisms began to come back to her. One by one they stepped out of the shadows: her father, with his tousled, salt-and-pepper hair, wire-rimmed glasses, and hazel eyes that crinkled at the corners when he smiled, always ready with a hug and an encouraging word for everybody. Then came Lottie and Charlie, so startling in their similarity, with their curling auburn hair and hazel eyes, that people who didn't know much about twins assumed they were identical rather than fraternal, especially when they were younger. Janie could almost hear them laughing at the jokes no one else got, least of all their little sister Christie, whose green eyes looked at the world so seriously. Christie looked the most like their mother, with her beautiful red hair. All of the siblings had their mother's freckles, to some degree.

It was such a relief to see them all with clarity again. They were not lost to her, after all. In spite of everything, she had the curious feeling that all would be well.

Janie was just slipping into sleep when she heard a soft but unsettling sound—a kind of scritching on the stone of the floor. Something was skittering across the cell. She sat up again and arranged her coat so that it covered even her ankles and feet. Sleep was out of the question now. She would have to think of something else to do.

If Dad were in her position, he would probably be singing hymns at the top of his lungs like Paul and Silas and waiting for the doors to swing open. The thought made her smile. There were worse ways to pass the time than singing.

So Janie sang. It was a song that she had sung many times before with her folk band, but she had never sounded so good; the cell's acoustics were amazing.

Oft in the stilly night,
Ere slumber's chain has bound me,
Fond memory brings the light
Of other days around me;
The smiles, the tears,
Of childhood's years,
The words of love then spoken;
The eyes that shone,
Now dimmed and gone,

The cheerful hearts now broken.
Thus, in the stilly night,
Ere slumber's chain has bound me,
Sad memory brings the light
Of other days around me.
When I remember all
The friends, so linked together
I've seen around me fall,
Like leaves in wintry weather;
I feel like one
Who treads alone
Some banquet-hall deserted,
Whose lights are fled,
Whose gardens dead,
And all but he departed.
Thus, in the stilly night,
Ere slumber's chain has bound me,
Sad memory brings the light
Of other days around me.

It was a sad, sentimental song, but it was perfect for her just then—a woe is me, I'm all alone in jail in the middle of the night in the wrong century, and I miss my family song, and somehow it lightened her heart. Her musician friends often said the same thing about singing the blues.

CHAPTER 16

Morning finally came. Waking with a sudden jerk, Janie was surprised to realize that she had actually slept a little bit. The arms that she had wrapped around herself in the cold were stiff and sore. She sat up and took in her surroundings. It must still be early; the light slanting in through the bars on the window above her head was soft. The cell was larger than she had thought— it had seemed more coffin-like in the dark of night. Where was the chamber pot? Oh, yuck— it had to be that wooden bucket beneath the bench! She would hold off on *that* as long as possible. She would also not be using her handkerchief anymore; it had fallen to the floor in the night. Janie shuddered.

The gray stones of the walls were visibly damp, and

patches of something green and slimy-looking were growing on them. Gross, she had been leaning against that all night, and now she was sure it was all over the back of the beautiful brown silk coat Jane Austen had loaned her.

At least whatever was running across the stones last night was gone. It was safe now to unfold her legs and lower her feet to the floor. Or was it? She pulled her feet quickly back up to the bench. Were there trap doors that were triggered by springs beneath the stones? Could the walls start to close in on her? She almost laughed aloud at herself. Too many Gothic novels, just like Catherine Morland in *Northanger Abbey*! With that thought, her mind went to Miss Austen. Did the author think, as her brother certainly did, that Janie was a criminal? Did Fanny? What about Duncan? The thought that he might believe she had stolen from the Knights was too much to bear, and her eyes filled with tears that threatened to overtake her completely.

That's quite enough of that, she scolded herself, and she wiped her snotty nose on her coat sleeve. Oh dear, Miss Austen's coat! She quickly wiped the sleeve on her dress. Oh, no, Fanny's dress! This time she did laugh out loud, rather hysterically. Yikes! Would she go mad in here? "Run mad as often as you choose, but do not faint!" she quoted aloud, and it echoed a bit in the empty room. Now she was talking to herself— possibly a sign of madness, but the Austen quotation made her laugh again, a real laugh, and she felt a little better.

Janie had walked the length of the cell fifty-eight times so far in an effort to warm herself up. She was trying very hard not to wonder if pacing was another common sign of impending insanity, and if counting one's paces was yet another, when she heard a tiny, fluttering sound behind her. She turned to see something white on the floor beneath the window.

It was a paper, elaborately folded into an airplane. With difficulty, Janie opened it up and read, "Take courage. I have a plan to get you out. Don't do anything stupid." It was signed, "A friend." There was an ink blot at the bottom of the paper. She thought it looked a little bit like a bird.

It was probably mid morning when the cell door opened with a rattling, scraping sound. The jailer stuck his head in, bringing with him a gust of warmer air from somewhere. Janie jumped up from the bench. What did this mean? Was she free?

"Visitor, Miss," the jailer said in his mumbling way. Then he shuffled out sideways as Jane Austen stepped in.

"I've brought you some breakfast, Miss Jones. Ever the

clergyman's daughter," she said with a self-deprecating grin. "I do hope you are— um, in good health."

"I'm okay, I guess."

"Oh-kay. That's good, right?"

"Yeah, it is. Thanks." Awkward because of her manacled hands, Janie took the basket that Miss Austen held out to her. She was suddenly very aware not only of the no-longer-empty bucket, but also the state of the borrowed silk coat. She was pretty sure Miss Austen could tell it was much the worse for wear, even in this poor light.

Miss Austen laid a hand on Janie's arm. "Let me assure you, Miss Jones, Fanny and I believe you. I know you're not responsible for the missing necklace. It's completely absurd to think that you would steal it and then proceed to wear it in full view of everyone! While I admit I enjoy a good laugh at the ridiculous— look for it, even, I can't see you doing such a stupid thing. You're far too rational a creature. So, I've questioned the servants in hopes of shedding some light on the matter. I find that servants don't miss very much that goes on in a house, even one as vast as Edward's. So far, no one seems to know anything helpful. All I've been able to discover is that the parlormaid, Susan, seems quite eager to have the blame put on you. That could mean something, but I'm not sure what. Oh, and the stablehand— who seems rather enamored of you, by the way, protests quite vehemently that you're innocent. He is ready to swear in court that he saw the necklace on you when he found you. I'm afraid he may try to storm the prison in your defense," she added with a grin. "At any rate, I will not give up until I have uncovered the truth and secured your release."

Duncan believed in her! Why that should mean any more to her than the faith of Fanny and Miss Austen, she did not allow herself to ponder. Weak-kneed with relief, Janie dropped to the bench.

"Oh, dear! Do have something to eat and drink, Miss Jones. You must be ravenous by now." Miss Austen sat down next to her, took a jar from the basket, and opened it. "Here." She held it up to Janie's lips. It was tea, strong and hot, but not too hot. Perfect.

Janie hadn't realized how thirsty she was. She drank all of it and felt surprisingly revived. No wonder the Brits considered a "cuppa" to be such a cure-all! Miss Austen unwrapped the parcel that was left in the basket, revealing thick slices of toasted bread with some kind of cheesy topping. She handed one to Janie, who tried not to think about having handled that disgusting bucket earlier. Dear God, don't let me die of dysentery, she prayed silently. "Thank you so much," she said, and she took a gooey bite. It was warm, and it was delicious. Melted cheese, egg, and something else— was it mustard? "Oh, my gosh, what is this? It's amazing! How can it still be hot?"

"Toasted cheese. It's one of my favorites. The jailer let me use his fire to make it."

" If I ever get out of here, you've *got* to show me how to make this. "

"I trust that will be very soon. Fanny is surely pleading your cause with my brother even as we speak." She paused, took a deep breath, and let it out again. "Don't think badly of him, Miss Jones. Last night, Edward was acting as he knew a magistrate should act, but I am hoping we can convince him to allow you to come back to Godmersham, maybe even this evening—" Her gaze faltered for a moment. "Possibly still under house arrest, though. To let you stay in this place another night would be unthinkable. It's not as if you were dangerous, and I believe we can prove your innocence before the trial. There *must* be a way to do so without betraying your time travel secret, and I am determined to find it. 'Be strong and courageous,' Miss Jones!"

"That reminds me. Thanks for the note you sent earlier."

"But I didn't send a note. Someone else must have done it." She looked thoughtful, then said brightly, "Surely that means you have other supporters."

Now that she thought about it, it *was* hard to imagine Miss Austen telling her not to "do anything stupid." Even harder to imagine her making a paper airplane. Who could it have been?

There was a rattling and sliding of the bolt on the door, and the jailer poked his head in.

"Visit's over."

Miss Austen clasped Janie's hand in both of hers. "I feel quite sure my brother will send someone for you soon."

She turned to the jailer. "Be expecting someone with orders from the magistrate to come for her. By the way, I believe she is innocent, and I will prove it."

"Oh, I knows it. Heard her singin' like an angel of heaven last night. Brought me near to tears."

Only a few hours had passed before Janie heard the bolt on the door sliding open. Thank God! Someone had come for her already!

She could hear the jailer's gravelly voice at the door. "We'll be keepin' them shackles, sir. Hope you brought yer own— mad folks can be uncommon tricky. I even thought she were an angel."

"No need," someone answered. "The wagon will be locked, it will." The voice was familiar, and it sent a shiver up her spine. It was the voice of the man who had attacked her in the stableyard.

CHAPTER 17

I've neither brocht your silken cloak, nor your golden key,
But I am come to set you free frae this green gallows-tree.
~Traditional, "The Maid Freed From the Gallows Tree"

Fanny's Diary- 7 Oct. 1813

Although it was on Papa's orders that Janie was arrested, I'm sure he is as relieved as I am that my Aunt Jane has found the proof to exonerate her at last! The instant she returned from Canterbury, Aunt Jane asked if she could take a look at the necklace itself. She examined it with the help of a quizzing glass, and lo! She discovered that there are inscriptions on the back of two of the gold collets. One reads, "Beth 1921," and the other reads, "Love, Eric."

She showed them to Papa, who confirmed that my mother's necklace bears no such inscriptions. Aunt Jane pointed out the impossibility of Janie's having taken it to a jeweler in London or even Canterbury to have the engraving done, since she has been continually in our company. She reminded Papa that Duncan had identified it as the same necklace Janie was wearing when he found her in the road, before she had any access to the house.

Papa is understandably indignant that the jeweler, who had insisted the design was one of a kind, must have either made more than one or copied our necklace from another. But of course, he realizes Janie is guiltless in this matter, and he will have her released. I am so glad!

It still doesn't solve the mystery of what happened to Mama's necklace, though. Aunt Jane said Susan might know something, since she seemed to be trying to place the blame on Janie. She said she had another idea about the matter as well, though she wasn't at liberty to share it. "Time will tell," she said. She was being very mysterious, and I asked her what she meant. All she would say was that she wouldn't be at all surprised if our own necklace reappeared in Papa's office one day, as if by magic. Whatever could she mean?

The man had shaved his whiskers and gotten a terrible haircut, but he was definitely her attacker. Janie noticed the big, purple bruise on his jaw with satisfaction.

"You'll be coming with me now, Miss Jones. Let's go," he said.

"No, I won't!" Janie appealed to the jailer. "Please don't

make me go with him. He attacked me the other day!" She turned back to her attacker. "Plus, he called me fat."

"I did not. I called her a *twmffat*. It's Welsh. It means idiot."

"Oh, and idiot is *so* much better!" She turned to the jailer again. "I don't want to go anywhere with him."

The jailer looked uncomfortable. "Sorry, Miss. He's got a magistrate's order to take you o'er to yon lunatic asylum in West Malling."

"What? No! The magistrate's order is supposed to be for me to go back to Godmersham Park! It has to be fake. Let me see it."

"Ignore anything she says, mate. She's *gwallgof*, barmy. She thinks she's from the future, she does. Could you give us a minute in private?"

The jailer nodded and stepped out of the cell. The hinges shrieked as he closed the door.

What was going on? Could Miss Austen have betrayed her? Janie didn't think so. "Wait– who told you that? What do you know about me?"

"Come with me, and I'll explain everything. I'm here to help you get home."

Could he really do that? "Hey, was it you who sent me that note? Are you a time lord? Do you have a Tardis or something?"

"Yes, sort of, and no. That's just on the blasted telly. That's not how things work."

Oh, my gosh! He knew about television. He really was

from the future! But why did he try to abduct her before, instead of explaining things? "Why should I trust you?"

"Because you have no choice. You want to get out of prison, don't you?"

"Of course, but Jane Austen is working on that for me. Someone's coming for me tonight."

"I'll use force if— What? Jane Austen, the author?"

"Yes."

"Are you *kidding* me? Now the blasted Literary Protection Division will have to get involved! David's bones!" He looked like he was trying to pull his hair out— what was left of it, anyway. "Beg pardon for my language, Miss, but my holiday! Aagh!"

What on earth was he talking about? He didn't look scary anymore. He looked harassed and tired. Janie almost felt sorry for him— almost, until she remembered how he had terrified her the other day, grabbing her arm and dragging her like that. "Who are you?" Janie asked. "Why didn't you just say you were there to help me before, instead of scaring me to death? How can I even believe you? I'm not going to end up in an asylum for real, am I?"

"*Bobol bach,* you are so difficult! That's too blasted many questions at once. You keep doing that! One: forget about who I am. My name's not important. Two: I was in a hurry; needs must. Three: I can't even remember that one. See? Too many."

This guy was way too evasive. "That's no excuse. Why won't you tell me your name? Wait, let me guess. It must be

Rumplestiltskin!" Janie didn't even try to keep the sarcasm from her voice.

He shook his head. "It's no joke! A person's name has power in it. Besides, there is more truth in those fairy tales than most people would ever believe."

That made Janie pause. Her father was fond of saying that the fairy tales were true in a way because they pointed to a bigger truth. "Maybe so, but how am I supposed to believe anything you say, if you won't even tell me your name?"

"*Duw*, the conscious ones are such a pain! Alright, alright. Some people call me Raven."

"And some people call me Lark."

He gave her a withering look, but she just glared right back. It was true, actually—her bandmates called her Lark, but she wasn't going to explain. It wasn't this guy's business, anyway. "Look, Mr. um, Raven, I can't come with you now. I have to say goodbye to my friends. I promise I'll go with you later, but I won't just leave without saying goodbye. I won't." She might be crazy not to take the chance to get out of this place, but she just couldn't.

He sighed. "Fine. I'm only agreeing because now I need time to contact the blasted— pardon, Lit Div, but you must go through by Monday night. You've got four days. The rift can't remain open after that; I'm already getting the maximum extension. Do you understand?"

Not really, but she nodded anyway. "Absolutely.

Monday night." She might still be under house arrest then, but Miss Austen would help her escape, wouldn't she?

"Good. Meet me on Monday at that bridge near the Godmersham Park gates before midnight— let's say 11:30. Make sure you have everything with you that you had on you when you arrived. That's important; something that connected you to this time and place brought you here."

"What, like a talisman?"

"No, it's not superstition; it's blasted science. The principle of cohesion. Look it up. I don't have time to explain it all right now; I have to go tell the blasted Lit Div about blasted Jane Austen, thank you very much! Beg pardon."

"Okay. It must be my necklace, then. It's really old." She would have to get it back from Mr. Knight somehow.

"Good. Another thing: Beware of wolves. There are those who want to use the Timeline for their own evil ends; watch out for them."

What was that supposed to mean? How did she know he didn't have his own "evil ends," anyway? "Exactly what am I watching out for?"

"People who seem like they don't fit in. People watching or following you."

People like him, in other words.

"An agent from the Literary Protection Division will come by before Wednesday to deal with Jane Austen. Someone wearing a red hooded cape."

"What do you mean, 'deal with' her?"

"They will make sure her future works won't be altered. Her memory will be cleared of things you may have told her."

Janie felt herself blush. Yeah, she had told Jane Austen a few things. "Are they like the Men in Black? She won't forget *everything*, will she?"

"That's Hollywood; this is reality. People sign waivers. And no, the memory wipe is selective. They are very good at what they do. She'll be fine."

The man who some people called Raven went to the door of the cell, pounded his fist on it twice, and called out to the jailer, "Looks like she's not crazy enough for the asylum. I'll be going now, I will."

Duncan was sore from mucking out the stables. He was well accustomed to shoveling, but worry had left so much tension in his muscles that he felt as if he had done three times his usual work.

Fear over what would happen to Miss Jones was eating him up inside. Canterbury Gaol, that grim, forbidding fortress that was the city's Medieval western gate, was no place for someone like her. He was helpless. He could do nothing to save her, no more than he had been able to save his mother. He hated that feeling more than anything. The minister had understood that about Duncan, as he had so many things. "Dinnae despise your helplessness," Mr. MacDonald told him. "It can show you how to rely on God. In your weakness, He is strong."

Duncan leaned his shovel against the wall. He knelt down in the straw and prayed for Miss Jones.

Duncan could hear footsteps crunching in the gravel of the stableyard. Dusk was gathering, but there was light enough to see the master's sister, Miss Austen, approaching. "I have a job for you which I think you will be happy to do," she called out. "Can you get the carriage ready? You and I are going to Canterbury. I don't think we need to bother Gabriel about driving, do you?"

"Nae indeed!" Duncan hurried to get the bays from their stalls so he could hitch them up. His hands trembled as he put on their halters. Did this mean Miss Jones was exonerated?

"You care a great deal for Miss Jones, do you not?" Miss Austen asked as she watched him.

"Aye."

"You love her." It was more of a statement than a question.

How did she know that? "Aye." God help him, but he did. He expected Miss Austen to tell him he had no right to love someone above his station, but his eyes met with no answering challenge in hers.

"Then you will be relieved to know there is no longer any charge against her. She is free, and we are going to bring her back here. You may think that this is no business of mine, and you may be right, but I hope you will let her know how you feel. Life is too short and love is too precious to allow society's expectations to get in the way. Besides, where she comes from, people think quite differently, I do believe."

Janie heard the key turning in the lock and the noisy drawing of the bolt again, and her heart leaped up. "Miss Austen here for you," the jailer announced as he opened the door. "With another order from the magistrate." At last! But was she to be under house arrest, or had her name been cleared? Janie realized she was shaking.

"My brother has dropped the charge against you, Miss Jones," Miss Austen said as she entered. Someone else stood behind her in the darkness of the hallway. Miss Austen came and took her hands. "You are free, and we are here to take you back to Godmersham." The jailer unlocked her shackles in a swift, practiced movement.

Free! Janie's knees buckled, and she grabbed Miss Austen's arm to keep from falling. Suddenly, miraculously, Duncan was there. He caught her up in his arms as easily as if she were a child, and she put her arms up around his neck.

"Ssh– wheesht, noo. I've got ye," he said in that soft, gentle way of his. He carried her out of the cell, through the darkness of the prison's winding passages, and out into the fresh, evening air.

Janie didn't know whether she wanted to cry, laugh, or shout at the top of her lungs with exhilaration. She was not going to die. She was free. She was covered with the cell's grime, and she probably stank, too, but she was being carried in the perfect arms of Duncan MacKinnon, and she wasn't unconscious this time. It was glorious.

CHAPTER 18

———

All too soon, they were at the carriage. Miss Austen opened her door, and Duncan gently set Janie down inside. "Thank you, Mr. MacKinnon," she said. Her heart was too full for her to say more. Miss Austen was standing right there, anyway.

Duncan closed Janie's door, then he helped Miss Austen in on the other side. The carriage rocked gently as he climbed up top, and then they were moving. Janie leaned back into the seat. It was a poor substitute for leaning against Duncan's solid chest. She sighed. She might as well admit it; she was in love. Duncan MacKinnon was not only gorgeous, but also kind, funny, tenderhearted, strong, gentle, and humble. Janie had found the right guy, but he lived in the wrong century. She was leaving in four days. He would never know she loved him, and she would end up alone forever because there would never be anyone else like him. She sighed again, in self-pity this time.

"I have a theory about the necklace," Miss Austen interrupted, having no idea about Janie's pity party. "What if your necklace and ours are one and the same? What if it has come down to you through the years somehow, and now that you are here, it only appears that ours is missing because only the one necklace exists?"

"That's exactly what I think," Janie said, sitting up straighter.

"Edward did not notice how worn the inscriptions on the back were, and of course, I was the only one who recognized that 1921 was actually a date. In order to keep your secret, I encouraged Edward to think his wife's necklace may have been taken by someone else– a servant, perhaps. It is a deception. I hate that." She paused. "Goodness, how self-righteous I sound! I have a great many faults, I assure you. I am much too proud of my wit, for one thing, and I have a tendency to use it like a dagger, for another. I'm far less accustomed to lying. Especially to my family."

"I'm so sorry. I know what you mean; I've never lied so much in my whole life as I have since coming here. Thank you for not saying anything, for protecting me. If we are right, the Knight family's necklace should reappear in four days, though, so everything will be okay."

"Four days! You have discovered your way home, then? While you were in prison?" It was too dark in the carriage to see Miss Austen's expression, but Janie could hear the surprise in her voice.

"Yes." She told Miss Austen about Raven, and all that he had said.

"How do we explain your departure to the rest of the household? Fanny, and not she alone, will be devastated if you leave in the middle of the night without saying anything."

"I've been thinking about that. Could you arrange for a carriage from town to come pick me up from Godmersham Monday afternoon? We could say my family sent it for me, maybe. That would seem normal, wouldn't it? It could drop me off in the woods or something until night, and then I could go to the bridge to meet Raven when it's time. I don't have a watch, but it wouldn't matter if I showed up early. I'd just go once it got good and dark, and then wait for him to show up."

"More deception, then."

"Yes, but I think it's necessary."

"I agree, since it will protect you." She was silent for a moment. "There is another thing that disturbs me even more, Miss Jones. If this Raven spoke truly that someone is coming to 'deal with' my memory, and I submit to this treatment, I won't remember any of the wondrous things you told me. Indeed, I may not even remember you at all. Will I then feel bereft, as if some undefinable thing has been taken from me? It also occurs to me that other, unrelated memories may be casualties in this process.

Some of those are more precious than gold to me! I am of a mind to refuse. What happens if I refuse?"

"I don't know. You're right, though— I don't think you should do it." Janie knew all too well how it felt to have pieces of her memory missing. "I'm sorry I got you into this mess, Miss Austen. I'm sorry about your beautiful silk coat, too. I hope it can be cleaned."

"Think nothing of it. Mrs. Kennett and her daughters, who do the washing for my brother's family, are workers of miracles."

"Are ye able to walk, Miss?" Duncan asked Miss Jones when he helped her down from the carriage. He half hoped she would say no. Holding her in his arms was— well, it was like she belonged there.

"Yeah, I think so."

"We can manage," Miss Austen said, putting an arm around Miss Jones' shoulders.

"Thank you for your help tonight."

He waited to climb back onto the box of the carriage until he was sure the two ladies had made it safely to the house. Janie turned to look back at him when they got to the door. She gave a little wave, and Duncan felt his heart rise up into the starlit sky.

Everyone was already in bed when Janie and Miss Austen climbed the stairs. Only Johncock was there to greet them at the door when they got home. It was a relief not to have to face Mr. Knight right away, though. That awkwardness would wait until tomorrow. Miss Austen retrieved a chamberstick from a demilune table in the grand entrance hall to light their way up the stairs.

There was a tub of warm water waiting for Janie when she got up to her room. God bless Elspeth! A clean nightshift lay across the bed, and a dinner tray was on the dresser.

Janie had planned to stay awake for a little while, working out the details of her plan for leaving, but she fell asleep as soon as she lay down on the lumpy, wonderful mattress.

Janie woke up before dawn and closed her eyes again, wondering if it was possible to slip back into her dream. She had been riding bareback through a field behind Duncan, on the back of the black stallion. She could almost feel him in her arms still... No, it was just a pillow. Dang it. She was alone, and she was leaving in a few days.

Recapturing the dream was impossible, but as tired as she was, she did go back to sleep.

She woke again to see Elspeth opening the curtains.

"Good morning! I am so glad you are back, Miss!"

Janie was really going to miss Elspeth, she realized. Not that she wasn't looking forward to wearing clothes that she could put on by herself. She smiled just thinking about jeans and t-shirts. "So what am I wearing today?"

Elspeth put the garments she had been holding down on the bed. "This white gown and blue spencer, Miss. It will go very well with your new bonnet, will it not?"

"Yes, it will." She would probably not be able to bring the bonnet back home with her. Too bad; it was very pretty. Oh, well. She wouldn't really have any occasion to wear it, anyway. Maybe Fanny wouldn't mind if she gave it to Elspeth before she left. No, of course Fanny's feelings would be hurt; she didn't know Janie wasn't just taking a normal trip.

"Did you know blue is my brother's favorite color, Miss?" Elspeth asked as she fastened the back of the dress.

Was it? "No, I didn't." Janie's heart beat a little faster as she put on the blue spencer jacket. In spite of herself, she wondered if Duncan might like how she looked in it. She needed to think about something else. She sat down at the dressing table so Elspeth could do her hair, and she remembered what Susan had said to her in the mirror earlier. Janie hoped she didn't run into her today; she gave her the creeps. "Elspeth, may I ask you something?"

"About my brother, Miss? Did you know he's named after two Scottish kings? His middle name is Robert."

That was random. "Oh. Um, no, I wanted to ask you about Susan. She seems to dislike me quite a lot, and I have no idea why. Do you think she minds that you've been helping me? Does she think it should be her job?"

"Och, not her, Miss! The less work she has to do, the better she likes it. And it's not just you, Miss. She gives herself airs. She's not really nice to anyone but the Knights. Oh, and Duncan. She pretends to be friendly to me sometimes because I'm his sister. Aye, she's set her cap at him, for certain."

"'Set her cap at him'?" Fanny had used that phrase about the girl who hoped to marry Mr. Knight. Janie suddenly felt a little ill. Susan was so pretty, with her blonde hair and her perfect complexion. Janie reminded herself firmly that it was none of her business, anyway. She was going home soon.

"Oh, aye. She makes sheep's eyes at him all the time. He danced with her last Christmas at the servants' ball, and ever since then, she's been flirting with him something terrible. Of course, all of the girls think he's the brawest, handsomest lad here, but they don't act the way she does. She figures out ways to get next to him in church and tries to talk to him all during the service. Och, last Sunday, I even saw her toss her psalm book on the floor by his feet so he would have to get it for her. Duncan hates it."

Janie let out the breath she didn't realize she had been holding in. "He does?"

"Aye, Miss. Mrs. Driver— she's our new housekeeper— says it's disgraceful. I heard her say so to Susan after we got home from church. She won't give her the sack for it, though."

"I'm surprised Mr. Knight hasn't reprimanded Susan himself, if she's that distracting."

"Och, he's probably never seen it, Miss, with him being up front with the people of quality, such as yourself. Servants have to sit at the back, you know."

They had to? She hadn't realized that. Did the Knights also *have* to elevate themselves above everyone else? "It isn't like that where I come from. Everyone can sit wherever they like. Of course, most people tend to have their favorite spots."

"Do people at your church not have to wait outside for the gentlemen and ladies to go in first, then?"

"No." How had she failed to notice that on Sunday? She had been too busy looking at the building.

Elspeth gave a little sigh. "That must be grand, especially when it's cold and rainy."

A new jar on the dressing table caught Janie's attention. "What's this?"

"It's from Miss Knight. For your face."

Janie unscrewed the lid and sniffed the cream inside. Ugh! It smelled fermented. "Just keep using the strawberry stuff, please."

Elspeth put in the last comb and carefully arranged the curls that framed Janie's face. "There. You look bonnie, Miss."

There would be no avoiding Edward Knight that morning; he, Fanny, her four oldest brothers, and her Aunt Jane were all sitting at the breakfast table already when Janie came in. Breakfast had not yet been brought out, but the chocolate pot and cups were on the table. Mr. Knight and his sons rose from their seats when Janie entered, and Fanny rushed over to hug her, saying, "I am so glad you're back, Janie." She whispered, "You can fill me in on the ghastly details later."

The men waited until she and Fanny sat down, then they did as well. Mr. Knight looked uncomfortable. As he should. It was less satisfying to notice that his sons also looked uncomfortable, keeping their eyes on their empty plates.

Then Mr. Knight stood up again. He twisted the signet finger on his right hand around and around. "Before Johncock brings in breakfast, I would like to say something. Miss Jones, I owe you an apology. I have no excuses to make; what I did was insupportable. I put you through an ordeal you should have never had to suffer. It was unworthy of me, and I can only beg your forgiveness."

It was a very formal apology, as befitted the owner of Godmersham Park, but Janie believed it was sincere. "I forgive you, Mr. Knight," she said.

"Thank you, Miss Jones. That means a great deal to me." She thought she saw the glint of unshed tears in his eyes.

"I'm just glad your sister is such a genius." Everyone laughed, the tension broken. Even Mr. Knight laughed as he dabbed at his eyes with his napkin.

Fanny lifted her cup of chocolate. "To my Aunt Jane!" The others joined in the toast. "To Jane!"

When everyone had finished eating, Miss Austen announced, "I have some news to share. May I tell them, Miss Jones?"

Janie nodded. What choice did she have? Anyway, she trusted in Jane Austen's cleverness, whatever she was doing.

"Saturday, I met the post and saw that a letter had come for Miss Jones, and I brought it to her yesterday. Sadly, she found out that a family situation requires her to leave us quite soon. Her father is sending a coach to collect her and bring her to Southampton on Monday, so that they may journey together to America. I propose that we have a farewell party for her tomorrow evening."

Surprise was evident around the table, but so was approval of the proposed party.

The lie was perfect, vague with just enough detail. Thankfully, they seemed to buy it. Doubtless, no one questioned what Miss Austen said because they knew how honest she was. Janie knew that it cost her something to deceive her family like this.

"Thank you so much, Miss Austen," Janie said. "You are so kind. I have a different proposal to make: instead of a party, might I please give you all a concert tomorrow night? I want to say thank you to everybody. And could all of the servants who wish to attend be allowed to come, too? So many of them have been kind and helpful to me. It would be a gift to me, too; I can't tell you how wonderful it is to be able to play your family's beautiful violin."

Once again, there were surprise and approval all around. "I think that is a capital idea, Miss Jones, and a generous one," Mr. Knight said with a smile.

Miss Austen's smile had a hint of complicity in it.

CHAPTER 19

———

Should auld acquaintance be forgot and never brought to mind?
Should auld acquaintance be forgot and auld lang syne?
~Robert Burns, "Auld Lang Syne"

After breakfast, Fanny said, "I must go make plans with Cook for the party— concert, rather. We need to have food and drinks for everyone, and I want it to be special."

Janie thought she might practice and work out which songs to play on Saturday night, but Miss Austen asked her if she would take a turn through the gardens with her, and she agreed. "Let me just run back upstairs and get my bonnet," she said. Even after Elspeth had mentioned how it matched Janie's outfit, she had managed to forget it. She didn't care about getting sun on her face, but she did care about Fanny knowing how much she appreciated the gift.

After she tied the bonnet's ribbons under her chin, Janie thought to check the closet, to see if her necklace had been returned. She gave a sigh of relief; there it was, back in its place on the upper shelf. There was something else there with the necklace, too: It was a note, folded up like a packet and sealed with wax. She opened it, and a small velvet bag fell out onto the floor. The note read, "With heartfelt apologies, E.K." She retrieved the bag and opened it. Inside was a little gold brooch in the shape of a violin.

Miss Austen was already outside, looking at the birds in their extravagant cage. "I sometimes feel sorry for them," she said when Janie arrived. "They are still in a prison, for all it resembles a palace, and for all the care and attention Fanny gives them." Her eyes suddenly widened. "Oh, Miss Jones! I'm sorry! That was thoughtless of me."

"It's okay, really. I'm alright now, and in some ways, better off, after being in there. I don't know if I can explain it, but I think maybe I didn't really appreciate my life, and what a gift it is, before. Now I don't want to waste a minute of it. I want to do exactly what I was put on earth to do, and be exactly who I was meant to be. When I got out, it was so exhilarating just to be alive." And to be held by Duncan, she had to admit. That too. "I know I'll never forget that feeling, as long as I live. For another thing, I realized how important my family really is to me. I'm not like Elizabeth Bennet—"

"Is anyone?"

Janie laughed. "What I mean is, I couldn't do what Elizabeth Bennet does. She turns down two marriage proposals, knowing she is throwing away her family's best chance at security. She chooses her own happiness over theirs. Of course, it all works out in the end, but she doesn't know that's going to happen at the time, does she? I've found myself faced with the choice of either going home and bringing happiness to my family, or staying here and pursuing my own happiness, yet hurting my family terribly. I suppose I am more like Emma, who can't leave her father, no matter how much she loves Mr. Knightley. Of course, you have the power to make things work out for Emma, too, since you're the writer. I don't have that."

"Perhaps it's a choice you don't have to make. Perhaps the one you love would also be willing to leave his home in order to be with you, Miss Jones. Give Duncan a chance."

Janie gasped. "How did you know?"

"I am a genius, by your own admission, am I not?" Miss Austen laughed, then she was serious again. "Did you know I had to make such a choice once? On second thought, don't answer that. You probably know far too much about my personal life; I shudder to think that Cass won't destroy all of my letters. Eleven years ago, my neighbor, Harris Bigg-Wither, asked me to marry him. I didn't love him, but I still said yes, thinking of my mother and my beloved sister, how it was in my power to give them a secure future and a home at Manydown House. By the next morning, I knew I had to tell him I couldn't marry him after all, poor man. I chose my own happiness, and I hurt him. In a way, I suppose Elizabeth Bennet is my justification for myself."

They turned to walk away from the house, and headed, by unspoken agreement, towards the folly on the hill. After they reached it, they sat down on the bench. Miss Austen took the blue woolen shawl from her shoulders, and held it out to Janie. "Here. I want you to have this. You will need it if you are really going to return home."

"There's no 'if.' I can't stay. And thank you, but I can't possibly take your shawl, Miss Austen."

"Of course you can. You are going to be waiting outside at night, remember? The evenings have turned quite chilly. My sister and I have several shawls between us; I truly don't need it. Besides, look at all of the places I have darned it— there," she pointed, "and there, and there's a place on the back, too. In fact, I'm quite ashamed of it," she said, laughing. She thrust the shawl into Janie's hands.

"Okay, then," Janie laughed. "Thank you." She wrapped the gift around her shoulders.

"I've been thinking about what you said a little while ago," Miss Austen said. "To know why you are here and to fulfill that purpose is everything, is it not?" Her words were a ripple on the surface of the water, but something was hidden in the depths below.

Janie waited for her to reveal just what that was.

After a moment, Miss Austen continued. "I have

decided that when the person who is to alter my memory comes, I shall allow it, as long as I have the assurance that I will lose only those specific things." She gazed out over the hillside. "I know what I was put here to do, and I want to do just that. My novels are my own dear children, and I don't want to endanger them. They are all I have to give, my bequest to the world." She turned to look at Janie. "I know we both agreed yesterday that I should refuse, but I haven't been able to stop thinking about it. I don't wish to risk the possibility of being influenced; my final works must be what they were meant to be." She looked down at her lap, where her hands were clasped together. Her voice got softer. "Of course, I would also rather not know they are to be my final works."

Miss Austen looked so vulnerable, yet so brave. Impulsively, Janie put her arm around the author's shoulders in a quick hug. "I am so proud to have been named after you."

"You were named after me?"

Janie nodded. "I'm Jane Austen Jones."

"Truly?"

"Yes. My parents both love to read, and they named all of us after novelists. My younger brother and sister are Charles Dickens and Charlotte Brontë. Those two are after your time. My youngest sister is named after Agatha Christie, who is *way* after your time. I'm the eldest, and you were their first choice. It's not as big an honor as having all of those movies made of your books and everything, but..." Janie shrugged.

"Ah, my favorite future invention! I am rather sad to lose movies."

From where they sat, they could see a coach coming up the lane to Godmersham, and they stood to go back down the hill to the house.

As if it had been conjured by their conversation, a red-cloaked figure stepped down from the coach.

By the time they reached the house, Janie was a little breathless from descending the hill so quickly. Miss Austen hadn't exactly run, but Janie could barely keep up with her; Miss Austen's legs were very long. Janie wondered if traveling back to 2025 would be as hard on her body as coming to 1813 had been; she still felt like she was recovering from some kind of long illness.

Johncock met them at the door. He handed a calling card to Miss Austen and asked her if she wished to receive the guest who was waiting in the front parlor.

"Yes," she said. "Please bring us a tea tray."

They went into the parlor, and Miss Austen welcomed her visitor, introducing both herself and Janie.

The girl looked far too young to be a government agent; she couldn't be a day over seventeen. It didn't inspire confidence. Perhaps the goal was trust, instead– she certainly looked harmless. The girl stood and curtsied. "You may call me Miss Cardinal," she said. Another alias? Janie and Miss Austen glanced at one another.

Miss Austen welcomed Miss Cardinal to sit, and they all sat. Janie couldn't help but wonder if all of the Literary Protection Division agents resembled Little Red Riding Hood, or if it was just this one. She had a lidded basket sitting on the sofa next to her.

Johncock entered with the tea tray, and Miss Austen poured tea for everyone.

"This won't take but a few minutes," Miss Cardinal said. "Do you have any questions for me first?"

"A good many, but they may all be distilled into one thing: I want your assurance that I won't be— impaired in any way by this procedure, that all of my other memories will be left intact."

"Absolutely. It will erase exclusively the memories created by your exposure to any knowledge of future events. The compounds in the serum attach themselves to anything in the neural network which is anachronistic with the past and present timeline. I can administer it right into your teacup. The main side effect is drowsiness, although some people also experience a headache. Do not try to drive or operate heavy machinery for twelve hours afterwards. I would suggest a nap."

Miss Austen nodded. "I am ready, I suppose."

Miss Cardinal turned to Janie. "And *I* suppose I need

not tell you to say nothing else of the future to her after this."

"I won't. I promise."

Miss Cardinal opened the lid of her basket and pulled out some papers. Underneath those was a set of little compartments. She set the papers on the tea table in front of Miss Austen. "Please read and sign this waiver." She pulled a vial from one of the compartments and checked its label. Then she uncorked it and poured its contents into Miss Austen's teacup. Janie saw a little swirl of black in the tea as the girl stirred it with a teaspoon. She continued stirring as Miss Austen read the papers.

When Miss Cardinal was satisfied that she had stirred enough, she pulled a quill pen and brass-lidded travel inkwell from another compartment in her basket and set them on the table.

After Miss Austen finished reading, she didn't even look up. She reached for the pen, dipped it into the ink, and signed her name at the bottom of the paper. Then she turned and handed the pen to Janie.

So many strange things had happened to her, but somehow this felt surreal in a new way. Janie felt like she was outside of time altogether. Underneath the famous signature of Jane Austen, which was nearly as familiar to Janie as her own, so many likenesses of it had she seen, Janie signed on the line labeled "witness." She watched as Jane Austen drained the contents of her teacup.

"Who was that?" Fanny asked upon entering the parlor, where Janie and Miss Austen stood at the window, watching Miss Cardinal get back into her waiting coach.

"Someone who was here to see your Aunt Jane."

"No one with whom you are acquainted, Fanny. Just someone attending to some matters of business for me."

Fanny raised her eyebrows at their evasive answers, but she didn't ask any more questions.

Miss Austen started feeling sleepy not long after the agent left, and she went upstairs to take a nap. Janie hoped she would be okay; not for the first time, she was feeling rotten about what the author was going through because of her. Fanny had been talking nonstop about her plans for the concert for the last half hour, and Janie wanted nothing more than to be alone for a little while. She needed to practice, anyway. It would feel good just to throw herself into her music.

After nodding her approval of Fanny's furniture arrangement plans, she said, "Hey, Fanny, I'm going to go find somewhere to practice outside of the house for a while, okay? Your Aunt Jane is asleep, the children are studying, and I don't want to bother anybody. Besides, I want the songs to be a surprise."

"Of course. That's a good idea."

Janie went to the back parlor to get the precious Guarnerius violin. After making sure its clasps were securely closed, she lifted the box by the handle and went out by way of the front door. She turned without thinking towards the stables. After a few yards, she stopped. What was she doing? As much as she wished she could see Duncan, she needed solitude for practice. There was the temple folly, but she didn't want go all the way up the hill. The gardens contained several benches, but she didn't want to spend the next hour sitting on cold, hard stone or iron.

Janie remembered how she had sat on the hay bale in the barn and played for Duncan, and her resolve to stay away crumbled. That would be so much more comfortable! Besides, he might not even be in there; he could just as easily be working in the carriage house, or out exercising a horse.

"Mr. MacKinnon? Are you in here?" She called out, peering into the barn. He wasn't there. Only the two mares were there, munching on their hay. The other horses were probably taking their turn to graze out in the pasture. "Do y'all mind if I play some music?" Janie asked the horses. "You seemed to like it before." They twitched their ears at the sound of her voice, and Nan looked over her shoulder at her. Janie sang a line from a song to her, "Come saddle to me my bonnie gray mare." There were gray mares in quite a few of the old ballads, now that she came to think of it.

She went and sat down on the same bale of hay as before. She tightened and rosined the bow and tuned the strings, ran through a few scales, and began to play.

She played one of her favorites after another, letting the precious violin's music wash over her. No matter what century she was in, music was where she really belonged; it brought her home.

Janie decided that tomorrow night, she would play a couple of classical pieces, but mostly the traditional tunes she loved the most, and she would also sing two or three of them. She wanted to include at least one Robert Burns song for Duncan. She had always loved Burns' songs, and apparently, that was something she and Duncan had in common. She couldn't tell him how she felt about him, but perhaps the music could speak the words she wouldn't be able to say.

One of her favorites was "A Red, Red Rose." She played and sang it through to its end:

And fare thee weel, my only love,
And fare thee weel awhile.
And I will come again, my love,
Though it were ten thousand mile.

Except Janie could not come back again, could she? No,

she would pick another song. She thought about how so many of the old songs were about two people who couldn't be together because they were separated by an ocean, or war, or death. How ironic it was that those had always been her favorite ones. If Raven spoke the truth, Monday at midnight, an ocean of time would separate her and Duncan. She started playing a different kind of song, one about joy and happy endings.

As he entered the stable yard, Duncan could hear the strains of violin music coming from the barn, and he stopped. He had heard about the concert to which the servants were invited; Miss Jones must be rehearsing for it. Should he wait to go in until she was done? That was what he probably should do, but it was the last thing he wanted to do. He wanted to drink in the sound and sight of her. Besides, the bays would not be happy if he were to turn back around when they were so close to their oats and hay. That decided it. Duncan walked them both into their stalls as quietly as he could, then he shoveled some oats into their feed bags and put them on. He needed to groom the horses too, but he could do that in a little while. He sat down on a bale where he could watch Miss Jones.

She smiled when she saw him but kept on playing. The song was one Duncan had never heard before, and the melody was so tender and beautiful that he thought it would pull the heart right out of him.

When she finished, Miss Jones rested the violin on her knee. "I hope you don't mind my coming here, Mr. MacKinnon. I couldn't think of any other place that was out of the house but comfortable enough for a long practice session."

"I dinnae mind." He felt shy, as if he had intruded into her private space, though it was closer to being the other way around. "Please dinnae stop on my account."

"No, it's been over an hour. I'm done." Miss Jones bent down and put the violin back in its case, then loosened the bow before putting it away, too.

It was probably impertinent to ask, but Duncan was going to, anyway. "Miss Jones, are ye alright, truly? After being in that awful place? I prayed for ye."

A little sob escaped her, then she smiled as if to cover it. Sudden tears in her eyes made them look bigger, bluer. "You did?"

"Aye. It must ha' been dreadful for ye." Lord, he wanted to take her in his arms and comfort her.

Miss Jones looked down at the violin case in her lap. "Yeah, it was pretty bad, but you know something?" She looked back up at him. "I prayed too, and then it was like God wrapped His arms around me, and I felt such peace. I've never had anything like that happen before. Of course, I've always believed in God; my dad is a preacher."

"Och, but ye dinnae inherit faith like ye do freckles. Ye ha' to make the faith your ain."

Miss Jones smiled shyly. "Yeah, I know. What I mean is, at that moment, I *knew* He was right there with me. The thing is, after we lost my mom, I didn't want to have much to do with God, and I thought maybe He left me. He didn't. He was there." She looked down, blushing. "Gosh, I didn't mean to unload all of that stuff on you."

"Some people never get to feel the touch o' God. I'm glad ye did."

Miss Jones stood up to go, holding the handle of the violin case with both hands. "Thanks for asking how I'm doing, Mr. MacKinnon. You're very kind."

Duncan stood, too. "Could I ask ye one more thing? What was that song ye were playing when I first came in?"

"It's an Irish tune. It's had different words through the years, but the version I know is called 'The Lark in the Clear Air.' It's always the opening song I play with my band."

"What is it aboot?"

"Um, it's about this man that is in love with a girl. The girl he loves has smiled at him, so he decides that the next day he will tell her all that's in his heart."

Duncan shouldn't have asked. His own heart was suddenly beating very fast. Lord help him, he wished he could kiss her. Instead, he asked, "What does it all ha' to do wi' a lark, then?"

Miss Jones laughed. "The guy is listening to the lark

singing, and he's full of joy like the lark because he's pretty sure that the girl loves him, too."

"Will ye sing it tomorrow, not just play it?"

"That depends. Will you be there?"

"Aye."

"I suppose I will, then."

Miss Austen woke up for dinner, but she excused herself from their card game afterwards, saying that she had no idea why she was so sleepy.

After dinner, the older boys played billiards, but the rest of the family played a game of Whist. As partners, Janie and Fanny sat across from one another at the card table. Charles took his Aunt Jane's place as his father's partner.

Janie had thought Whist looked boring at first, but she became intrigued by the challenges of strategizing and remembering which cards had already been played. She and Fanny did creditably well, but Mr. Knight and Charles still won the game.

"That was really fun! I know I was a handicap, though; you might have won, otherwise," Janie told Fanny.

"Indeed not! Perhaps I ought to have warned you that no one stands a chance when playing against Papa, save my Aunt Jane. I am accustomed to losing. It does sting to be beaten by one's little brother, however." Fanny grinned at Charles, who beamed back at her.

Janie suddenly missed her own family with an intensity that surprised her. How had she gotten so comfortable in 1813 that she had nearly forgotten them? Would she have forgotten them altogether if it hadn't been for that night in prison? She wouldn't let anything keep her from going back home now, not even the undeniable feelings she had for Duncan MacKinnon.

CHAPTER 20

————

I will tell her all my love, all my soul's pure adoration,
And I think she will hear my words and she will not say me nay.
~Samuel Ferguson, "The Lark in the Clear Air"

Before breakfast the following morning, Janie and Fanny cut dahlias in the garden to use in decorating the house for the concert. "They stay fresh much longer if they are cut early in the day, you know," Fanny said. No, Janie didn't know. She had never kept a garden; she only knew she loved being in one. It was so peaceful out here. She wished she had something like this at home. No one in her family had a green thumb except her mother, and no one particularly wanted to pull weeds, either, so they only had the small rose garden her mother had planted. Janie's father tended to it as best he could, but it looked more scraggly with every passing year. Of course, Fanny didn't have to do any work to keep this one beautiful. Thomas was already hard at work in the flowerbeds.

Janie decided she would come back out here to practice

in the garden, instead of going to the barn and risk seeing Duncan. She needed to be able to concentrate on her music. In fact, she was not going to think about Duncan MacKinnon at all today. At least, not until she got through the concert.

Fanny's Diary- 9 Oct. 1813

My brothers and Mr. Plumptre left for Michaelmas term this morning. Now I shall be counting the days until we can all be together again in December. After lunch today, I had the chance to talk with Janie about the horrors of prison. She said there were manacles and chains attached to the wall!! Papa had ordered that she be spared them, thank goodness! I was surprised to hear that she didn't see any skeletons, ghosts, or vile instruments of torture. Nor was she able to hear the groans and wails of other prisoners, but it was cold, dark, and damp, and there was at least one rat. I shudder to think of what it must have been like for her, sitting in the darkness of the dungeon and contemplating the noose!!

The seating is already arranged in the library for tonight's concert, and we have put tables around the walls of the entrance hall for food and drinks, leaving space for dancing. I am looking forward to it, but with mixed feelings. I shall miss my friend when she leaves. I think it was very kind of Janie to think of including the servants in the entertainment. Naturally, they still have to work to get all ready beforehand and clean up afterwards, but it will be nice for them to have some fun with us.

Janie has gone to her room to rest, so that she will be fresh for the concert. Small wonder that she needs some respite, after enduring the terrors of a prison cell!

I haven't decided which dress Janie should wear tonight. I think perhaps the white sprigged muslin, with white ribbons for her hair.

Duncan finished shaving, and he rinsed his face in the bowl. He had set out his Sunday clothes to wear to the concert. Why was he looking forward to tonight so much? It couldn't possibly be as perfect as it had been in the barn, where he didn't have to share Miss Jones with all of those other people, for one thing. For another, she would be leaving the day after tomorrow, returning like a magical selkie to the sea. Duncan knew his very heart would leave his chest the day after tomorrow too, and it would go with her all the way to America. How had she come to be everything to him? She was the sun that he waited for on a dreich day. All of his days would be dreich after Monday.

And yet, it seemed to Duncan that yesterday, there had

been the promise of something impossible in her words. Even if it was just for this evening.

Janie wondered if Miss Austen had also based Catherine Morland in *Northanger Abbey* partly on Fanny, too. Janie could have sworn it was Catherine asking her all of those questions about prison this afternoon. Fanny, with all of her charming contradictions, apparently contained multitudes.

While Janie was practicing the pieces for the concert, she had decided to dedicate a song not just to Elspeth, but also to each of the other people who had become special to her. It was probably not something people in 1813 even did, but that didn't really matter.

Not long after Janie returned to her room, Elspeth was there to help her get ready. She was brimming over with excitement about the concert. "You are going to look so bonnie, Miss!" she said, after helping Janie get into the gown Fanny had wanted her to wear. Being Fanny's doll had lost some of its charm, but Janie had to admit the gown was gorgeous. How many white dresses did Fanny own? This one was particularly exquisite. The material was sheer and had tiny white flowers embroidered all over it. She hadn't seen Fanny wear it, which gave Janie the impression that it might be one she reserved for special occasions.

Elspeth styled her hair in a new way, with white ribbons woven through it. Was it too much? "My goodness! I look like a bride, Elspeth."

"Not yet, Miss." Elspeth grinned at her in the mirror. Then she pinned some tiny, white silk flowers into Janie's hair, as well. "Now you look like a bride. Or an angel, which my brother says you sound like," she teased. "I can't wait to hear you sing."

"Gosh, no pressure or anything! Thank you, Elspeth. Oh! One more thing." So that Mr. Knight would know she truly accepted his apology, Janie went to the closet and got the little gold violin brooch. Elspeth helped her pin it to the bodice of her dress, making sure to put it on her right side, where it couldn't accidentally scratch the Guarnerius violin. She carefully slid the pin only through the embroidered flowers, as to leave no holes in the delicate muslin fabric. Janie decided against wearing her emerald necklace; there was no need to remind everyone of the last time.

Usually, Janie was more excited than anxious before a performance, but she felt rather nervous this time, and she knew it was more due to Duncan's presence in the front row than anything else. She had asked Fanny to tell the servants they could sit anywhere they liked for the evening, knowing that otherwise, they would probably all be expected to sit behind the family.

Edward Knight took it in good humor. "Quite right. All should be done in the true democratic spirit for our American guest of honor," he said when everything was in place, and obligingly took a seat in the back row himself. All of the servants looked to be wearing their best clothes, which was touching, somehow. They probably seldom had the opportunity to do something like this. It was so odd to see the footmen looking like individuals, without their matching outfits and powdered wigs. Janie remembered wondering earlier how many people it took to run Godmersham Park. It apparently took at least twenty-one people, if she had counted right.

Elspeth sat next to her brother, and Janie saw her squeeze his hand excitedly. He reached an arm around her shoulders and gave her a little hug. Janie's heart melted. She was glad to see that Susan had to sit somewhere else, and she wondered if Duncan had sat in the end seat on purpose. Either way, Janie was relieved not to have to watch Susan flirt with him.

"Thank you all for coming," she said when everyone had settled down. "So many of you have helped me, and I'm more grateful than I can say. I hope these songs will say it for me."

She opened with "The Lark in the Clear Air." She

played the melody through once, then alternated between singing the verses and playing. She made sure not to look at Duncan while she played, and it was a good thing, because she glanced his way when she finished, and the look in his eyes was— distracting, to say the least.

Janie had ultimately decided that most of the pieces should be traditional tunes, which might have more universal appeal, besides being her favorites. She dedicated the next one to Sackree, "who nursed me so well when I was sick," and another to "My favorite lady's maid, Elspeth, who was absolutely right about needing to put my hair up." Elspeth gave a little squeal, and Janie grinned. It didn't matter that no one else got the joke.

Then, to mix things up and to do justice to the Guarnerius, Janie played three classical pieces, which she dedicated to the Knight family—Fanny, her father, and her aunt, with thanks for their hospitality and friendship. Miss Austen smiled throughout the evening with obvious enjoyment, but Janie missed the connection of co-conspiracy that she had once shared with the author. Janie was just another houseguest to her now, a friend of her niece. But it was for the best.

To Duncan MacKinnon, "whom you all have to blame for bringing me to this house in the first place," she dedicated the Robert Burns song, "A Man's a Man for A' That."

After a brief interlude, when everyone had a chance to get food and drink, they remained in the great entrance hall with its brilliantly lit chandelier. Janie played reels and jigs so that everyone could dance. She was glad to see that the "democratic spirit," as Mr. Knight had called it, continued. Everyone, including the servants, seemed to know how to dance to the reels, which was a relief. Janie hadn't even considered until that evening that they might not.

Duncan danced every dance with his little sister, so Susan was forced to find other partners. Most people changed partners for each dance. It was nice to see Miss Clewes and Sackree have the chance to enjoy themselves in the company of other adults, while Louisa and Cassandra danced with their father and Charles. The little girls were already such graceful dancers that Janie felt more awkward than ever just watching them. After the last dance, Janie sang "Auld Lang Syne" to conclude the program, and everyone joined in.

Duncan said something to Elspeth, who smiled and went over to the punch table. Then he came over to the corner where Janie was putting the Guarnerius into its case. She ran her fingers lightly across its four strings to hear the whispered notes. "Thank you," she whispered back to it, before lowering the lid of the case and closing the clasps. "I'll never forget having the chance to play that violin," she said to Duncan, so he'd know that she wasn't in the habit of talking to inanimate objects.

"And I'll ne'er forget hearing ye play it," Duncan said.

"It made me so happy to see you with Elspeth tonight,

Mr. MacKinnon. It made me think of my own brother and sisters."

"Aye, she's a gift o' God to me."

Elspeth joined them with a glass of punch, which she handed to Janie. "This is for you, Miss. You must be thirsty. Thank you for the concert. It was a real ceilidh, wasn't it?"

"You're welcome, and thank you for this, Elspeth. It's just what I needed." She was indeed very thirsty, but she made a conscious effort not to gulp the punch down as Duncan and Elspeth watched her. She set the empty glass on a tray.

"Will ye walk out in the garden wi' me, Miss Jones? 'Tis a fine, braw night."

Elspeth grinned, then she whisked herself away to the dessert table.

"Okay." Janie picked her new shawl up from the table and draped it over her shoulders. Sure, she was torturing herself by spending more time with Duncan, but she didn't want to say no, not even a little bit. She was leaving the day after tomorrow. Wasn't that a good enough reason to spend every moment she could with him? She would have the rest of her life to mourn her broken heart.

When they got outside, Janie noticed with disappointment that they weren't the only ones who had wanted to enjoy the cool night air. There was definitely no shortage of chaperones.

Someone had hung candle-lit lanterns around the

garden, turning it into something magical. Janie sighed. She wanted with her entire being to be right there, in that place, in that moment in 1813, with Duncan MacKinnon— no matter what happened afterwards.

Duncan offered her his right arm, and Janie took it. Something like a current of electricity ran through her, and she shivered.

"Are ye too cold?

"No, I feel just fine."

Duncan felt as if he were still surrounded by the music. Certainly, the stars seemed to be dancing yet. He said, "Miss Jones, thank ye for the Robert Burns song."

"You're welcome. I thought you might like it."

Had she chosen that song for him only because she knew he liked the poet, or because she believed what it said—that rank didn't make the measure of a man? Could she possibly think that his lack of rank didn't matter? After all, she had said those things about America earlier. Och, why were there so many people out here?

Without speaking, they wandered to another area of the garden, away from everyone else, away from the glow of the lanterns. The moon was almost full, and Miss Jones' fair skin and white dress shone softly in its light.

Miss Austen's words had emboldened Duncan, but

exactly how was he to let Miss Jones know how he felt? He wanted to say, *That lad in the first song ye sang is me. I want to tell ye all my love, all my soul's adoration.* Och, maybe he should just come out and say it plainly, instead. But was that romantic enough? He wanted it to be perfect. He put his left hand gently on top of her ungloved hand where it rested in the crook of his arm.

Miss Jones moved closer, and he pulled her hand up to his lips and kissed it. She sighed, and Duncan turned to face her. His right arm pulled her close, and his lips found hers.

Then her hand was at the back of his head, her fingers in his hair, and he stopped trying to think of the perfect way to tell her.

Janie thought that nothing could be sweeter than that kiss, but then Duncan said her name. "Janie," he whispered, and it was the most intimate thing in the world. A thrill went through her body. There was a method to the last-name-only madness between men and women in 1813, apparently.

He said it again. "Janie, I love ye. I love ye wi' all my heart. I want to come to America wi' ye, if ye will ha' me. I ken I am no worthy o' ye. I am no a gentleman and ne'er will be, but—"

Janie shook her head and put a finger to his lips to stop that nonsense. "You are a gentleman, in the only sense that matters to me. I love you too, Duncan."

"Will ye marry me, Janie? I will work hard and take care o' ye, and cherish ye, and be true to ye for the rest o' my life."

"Duncan, I want to marry you more than anything, but there's something I have to tell you. Let's find a place to sit."

CHAPTER 21

Hard fate that I should banished be, gang heavily and mourn
Because I loved the kindest swain that ever yet was born.
~Traditional, "The Broom of the Cowdenknowes"

Janie's heart was pounding and the blood was thrumming in her ears as they sat down on a bench nearer to the house, in the lamplight. Duncan wanted to come with her to America! What if he really could come with her, not just to America, but to 2025? She could pull him through with her, and Elspeth too, if she wanted to come—it could work. It had to work! She couldn't stay here, and never see her family, possibly even her mother, again. No. She had been sorely tempted by the idea, but ever since that night in prison, she had known she couldn't stay in 1813. Not even for him.

"Duncan, what I need to tell you is going to be hard for you to believe, but it's the truth." She looked up at him.

His eyes were wary, but he nodded. "Gae on."

"I came here by traveling back in time. My home is in

America, but it is also more than 200 years away from now. I have to return to the year 2025 Monday at midnight." She glanced up. Now his eyes were wide with—what, disbelief? Anger? She mustn't look at him again until she finished telling her story.

She told him about waking up at Godmersham, her realization of the truth on the trip to Chilham Castle, the return of her memory when the cat ran into the barn, and Raven's visit to her in prison. Duncan was silent as Janie told him the story which had been there all along, interwoven with their story.

"Nae, 'tis all wuid, and I ken ye are no wuid." He said it so softly that she could barely hear him.

What did he mean, wood? Now she sought his gaze, but he was the one who wouldn't look up. "I know that I'm asking a hard thing, but will you come with me, Duncan? Not just to America, but to my time, to the future?"

Duncan looked up then, and his stricken face said it all: he was beyond hurt—he was crushed. Devastated.

She had ruined everything. No, there had never really been a chance, had there? She had known that all along. But love had opened the door to hope, and fool that she was, she had invited it in.

What Duncan said next, his voice choked with emotion, ripped Janie's heart from her chest. "Miss Jones, ye could ha' just said nae."

Janie finally cried herself to sleep, hours after midnight. In the morning, Elspeth came in as usual, but she didn't draw the window curtains open. She came over to the bed and laid her hand on Janie's shoulder. "Should I tell Miss Knight you are indisposed, Miss? Should I come back later?" she asked.

"Yes, Elspeth. I'm indisposed. I don't know if I'll ever be disposed again."

"Oh, Miss," Elspeth said with a sniffle. "I thought..." She gave a little sigh.

Poor Elspeth— yet another person Janie had hurt. "I thought so, too. I'm sorry."

Elspeth retrieved the chamber pot from the cabinet and went to the door.

"Just a minute. Do you know what the word 'wood' means?"

"Wuid? Aye. It means mad, Miss."

So Duncan had been saying that he knew she wasn't crazy. Obviously, he thought the only alternative was that she was lying to him. What else should she have expected, though? The self-accusation that had kept her up most of the night continued. She should have stayed away. Spending time with him, letting him see how she felt about him— all of it had just ended up hurting him. Janie had known that she was going to be hurt, but until last night, she hadn't realized that Duncan could be hurt, too— because he loved her.

Loved, past tense. There could be no doubt of that, not after he called her "Miss Jones" again. Until last night, she hadn't known a name could thrill like a caress, or burn like a hot coal. "A name has power in it," Raven had said.

Janie closed her eyes again; she did not need to look in the gilded mirror to know how red and swollen they were. She needed time to compose the face with which to face not only the people downstairs, but also the rest of her life.

Fanny's Diary- 10 Oct. 1813

Last night was Janie's farewell concert for the family. Happily, my choice of refreshments was very well received by all. We had a bowl of negus, a cold collation of chicken and ham, a molded jelly, rout cakes, fruit, and whipt syllabub. I helped Cook whip the syllabub, and I am happy to say it turned out to perfection.

In a way, it was almost like a Twelfth Night celebration with all of the staff participating, except there was no Lord of Misrule. Janie played reels during the second half, and everyone was dancing with one another, quite regardless of station. Somehow I found myself dancing with our footman, Joe. I almost didn't recognize him without his wig; he looked quite like a regular person! He is actually a surprisingly good dancer and a person of interesting conversation, too. To think that all of these years he has worked for us and I had hardly spoken to him at all, really, until last night. It truly was the most unusual evening!

A skylark flew into the church as we entered this morning. It flew to and fro, desperate to get back out again, and the sexton looked desperate too! I could tell that some of the ladies feared for their bonnets. It was all rather amusing, but it made it hard to pay attention to the service. I was sorry for Janie to miss it. She still hasn't come downstairs. I thought at first that she was feeling under the weather, but Aunt Jane says Janie is suffering from Disappointed Hopes and must be treated with tenderness today. Is she in love with Ned? Has she been devastated by his return to Oxford? She showed no sign of it yesterday morning. She must be in love with Papa, after all, though I never saw any particular symptoms of her regard for him, either. For my part, I cannot be sorry that my matchmaking attempt came to naught on his side. How could I have thought for a moment that dearest Papa could be anything other than completely devoted to my late Mama?

I suppose there is nothing to keep me from contemplating marriage. The children will always have Caky, and surely Mrs. Driver can manage the household for Papa.

I can't believe Janie is leaving us tomorrow. To think

that just over two weeks ago, I arrived from Goodnestone expecting that things would be very dull indeed here, when they have been some of the most diverting weeks I have spent in all my life! Now it will be back to the usual rounds of social calls, I suppose, with nothing at all to look forward to until the Canterbury Ball next month.

Janie still had no appetite at all, but Elspeth said Fanny had been worrying about her all day. The last thing Janie wanted was everyone fussing over her, so she went down to dinner and tried her best to look like she was feeling better. In the parlor afterwards, they did not play Whist, as they often did.

"It's Sunday, remember?" Fanny said, when Janie got the cards out of their drawer. "We can do some embroidery, instead. Here, I brought a handkerchief for you to work on."

No cards on Sundays? It was another unwritten rule she knew she wasn't going to ask about. It had been okay for her and Fanny to go riding last Sunday afternoon with Duncan, though. She couldn't think about that now. "My sister Lottie is good at embroidery, but I don't really know how," she said. She didn't feel like learning it just then, either.

In the end, Fanny and her Aunt Jane embroidered the

handkerchiefs, while Janie played some hymns on the pianoforte.

That Miss Austen still knew about Janie's broken heart, even if some of the facts had been erased from her mind, was apparent. She treated Janie with such sympathetic kindness all evening that it was almost unbearable. Janie excused herself to turn in early.

It was her last morning at Godmersham Park. Her last morning in 1813. Fanny had already told her to keep the white shoes, since they were too stretched out to fit anymore. Janie almost wished she needed Elspeth's help getting dressed, but of course, she didn't. She would be wearing her own green dress for her trip home. After she put it on, she felt stranger than ever, instead of back to normal. She clasped her emerald necklace securely around her neck with a sigh. How much it had put her through! Her shoulders felt unbearably naked until she put the blue shawl from Miss Austen over them and secured it at the neck with the brooch from Mr. Knight. She made sure the necklace was covered by the shawl as she did it. Again, no one needed reminders.

She heard Elspeth scratch at the door. "Come in."

Elspeth looked surprised to see that she was already dressed. "Oh! I guess you don't need my help today."

Janie could hear her disappointment. "Of course I do. What about my hair? I can't just shove it up into my bonnet, now, can I?" Janie sat down at the dressing table and managed a smile. Her eyes were still puffy, but at least they weren't red anymore.

Elspeth gave her a little smile in return, one with sadness in it. She combed Janie's hair gently and pulled it back into a neat bun.

"See if you can use as few pins as possible this time, and leave out the combs, okay? I don't want to take all of Miss Knight's things with me when I go."

"Aye, Miss."

When Elspeth had finished with her hair, Janie stood, turned, and enveloped her in a hug. "I will miss you so much, Elspeth. Take care of yourself and that brother of yours. Thank you for everything; I couldn't have made it here without you. In fact, I'm going to tell Mr. Knight that you deserve a raise in your pay."

That got a smile, but also a blush. "Och, Miss, don't do that. I'm paid well enough. The Knights are very good to me."

"I'm glad to hear that."

"Miss?" Elspeth paused, as if she was unsure about something. "My brother told me to tell you Godspeed. He left this morning for London."

Janie took a step back. "For London?"

"Aye. He said he needed to get away for a while."

"All the way to London, though?" She wouldn't even

get to say goodbye, much less make things right. If that were even possible.

Janie found Fanny sitting at her writing desk in the front parlor. "Oh, Janie! I'm glad you are awake. You find me finishing a letter to my cousin Mary. Of course, I will want to write to you in America, too. I've never had a friend in America before. I wonder how long it takes for a letter to cross the Atlantic? I suppose I'll find out," she said, smiling at Janie. Fanny pulled a little blue leather book from one of the pigeonholes in her desk. "What is your direction?"

Janie dictated her address, watching Fanny write it into the book with a goose feather quill dipped in ink. Janie had expected Fanny would write in a beautiful copperplate script, but her handwriting looked rather uneven and cramped, not unlike the little 800 square foot bungalow whose address she was recording.

"Your directions are so much longer than our English ones, are they not? There are a great many numbers."

Guilt settled on Janie like a heavy coat. Fanny was yet another person who would be hurt. She would wonder why Janie never wrote back; her letters to Janie would either be returned as undeliverable, or they would just be thrown out by whatever post office system Nashville had in 1813. International delivery by boat probably cost quite a bit, too.

"Is there something you wish to do on your last morning here?" Fanny asked after she had slipped the little book back into its cubby.

"I've been thinking about that. I want to stop by the stables to say goodbye to Nan, and then I would like to take a walk to the church, if that's okay."

"Of course, Janie. Whatever you'd like."

The path to the church passed under a lovely row of trees, the ones Fanny had called "limes," though they weren't fruit trees, whose leaves were beginning to turn a golden yellow. They stopped for a little while to lift some of Fanny's sisters' rabbits from their hutch and pet them. There was something very comforting about stroking their soft, thick fur, and Janie felt her heart lighten ever so slightly. Fanny didn't engage in her usual chatter, which was also a relief. They put the rabbits back and walked on in companionable silence, listening to the soft crunch of the gravel path beneath their feet and the singing of the birds. It wasn't exactly cold, but it was breezy. Clouds that looked like they had rain in them were scudding across the sky.

It had been quiet earlier in the stables, too, but it was the quiet of absence, and Janie hadn't wanted to linger once they had given the apples to Nan and Pretty Pie.

The church had yet another quietness. There was peace in the architecture of its sacred space and the accumulation of centuries of worship. The light coming in through its lancet windows was no brighter than it had been last Sunday, but it still bathed everything in a soft glow. There was no sign of the bird that Fanny had told her about last night. It must have found its way back home.

Janie sat down in the pew to their left at the very back, and Fanny sat beside her. Fanny closed her eyes, either in prayer or contemplation, leaving Janie to her own thoughts. It was impossible not to think of Duncan sitting here on Sundays, in this very spot. He must be halfway to London by now. Janie looked up at the ancient timbers of the vaulted ceiling and silently prayed that God would heal all of their hurt.

Duncan had asked Gabriel for three days' leave and the loan of Mr. Knight's best horse. What he really wished he could do was ride as fast and as hard as Bruce could go, as far as he could go. Of course, it would have been completely unfair to do that to the horse without some life or death reason, so he went at an easy pace, alternating between trotting and walking.

What would he do when he got to London? Mr. MacDonald had been dead for a year, and Duncan couldn't think of anyone else in London he had the heart to see just now. He had no plans beyond slipping into the familiar quietness of the kirk that had been a home to him. At least he could have the comfort of the place, if not the minister.

The further he got from Godmersham, the sunnier it got, but that did not suit his mood like the gray clouds he had left behind him. It was, unfortunately, turning out to be a perfectly beautiful autumn day.

He was nearing Maidstone when Bruce lost a shoe. Duncan dismounted and walked Bruce into town. He left the horse with the blacksmith while he went to get something to eat at the pub. He ordered an ale and a bowl of stew, which he ate more quickly than he normally would. There was nothing like eating alone in a strange pub, surrounded by the companionable chatter of other people, to make a person feel even lonelier.

He just wanted to collect Bruce and be on his way as soon as possible. On his way to what, he wasn't sure.

CHAPTER 22

With an aching heart I'll bid them adieu, for tomorrow I'll sail away
O'er the raging foam for to seek a home on the shores of Amerikay.
-Traditional, "The Shores of Amerikay"

Janie and Fanny got back just in time for a luncheon of salad and beef tongue with Mr. Knight and Miss Austen.

"Well, Miss Jones, this is to be our last meal together," Edward Knight said. "I suppose you are looking forward to eating your native food again. What did you call it— junk food?"

Janie grinned, in spite of her aching heart. "Yes, sir. I must confess, I am. Mostly, I just can't wait to see my family again." She hoped that Mr. Knight wouldn't ask any questions about her travel plans which she wouldn't know how to answer. Yesterday, he had almost insisted that he escort her to Southampton himself. When she assured him that everything had been arranged, he said, "Ah, your father is sending a servant with the carriage, then. Very good," and she didn't deny it. She was so tired of covering things up. "I want to thank you for the gift, Mr. Knight," she said, touching the brooch that held her shawl in place. "It's beautiful. It will always remind me of the time I've spent here with y'all. I can't believe it's been two weeks since I woke up here!"

Fanny said, "You say that as if it has been such a long time, Janie! Why, we often have house guests that stay four, five, or even six weeks."

"Or more, in my case," Miss Austen said with a grin. "I do my utmost to stay until I have emptied their larder, and they are thoroughly sick of me."

"Aunt Jane, you know we never tire of having you visit!"

"Besides, who else would read all of those expensive books I have bought for my library, if you didn't stay with us?" Her brother chimed in.

"That reminds me," Miss Austen said. "Fanny, we still haven't finished reading *The History of Modern Europe*, you know."

"I expect we shall finish it once Janie leaves. I shall be *so* bored!"

"You see how it is, Miss Jones. Her aunt is a last resort, when all other avenues for entertainment have been exhausted," Miss Austen said with a grin.

"Actually, Fanny, I would love to spend my last hour here at Godmersham Park in your library," Janie said. "You two could read your book, if you want to."

"Of course, if that's what you'd like to do. Only you needn't subject yourself to my Aunt Jane's efforts to improve my mind with the history of Europe. Read whatever you like."

It started raining almost as soon as they entered the library. It wasn't as relaxing as Janie had hoped it would be, though the same comfy sofas and cozy fireplaces were there, since she couldn't ignore the reminders of the afternoon when she had slipped up so badly and nearly given Jane Austen a stroke. She glanced at Miss Austen periodically, to see if it looked like the author was experiencing any déjà vu of last week's dramatic scene, but she only mentioned the books they had talked of, and showed Janie a poem by Cowper she thought she might like. It seemed that Miss Austen did recall everything else, yet had no memory of anything touching on the future. It was exactly the outcome for which they had both hoped.

Janie had a momentary scare at dinner the evening before, when Miss Austen said something about the inscription on the necklace: "I think the numbers are a date." Janie was relieved when she finished with, "1-9-2-1 could mean September first, 1721; you see? It was inscribed ninety-two years ago. That's why the inscription looks so worn, and why I knew it was not my sister-in-law's necklace."

It was fascinating— Miss Austen's brain must have simply filled in the gaps left by the memory serum with things that made logical sense.

After Fanny and her aunt finished another chapter of their book and Miss Austen declared her intention of going to get her writing box, Janie took the opportunity to tell her goodbye. "Miss Austen, I just want to say I'm so glad I've had the chance to get to know you. Thanks so much for all you've done for me. I'll never forget it, and I'll never forget you."

"I've enjoyed becoming acquainted with you as well, Miss Jones, and solving the puzzle presented by your necklace. I am sorry that your— matters of the heart have not worked out as we had hoped."

Janie sighed. "I wish you could write a happy ending for me, Miss Austen."

Jane Austen took hold of Janie's hands. "You shall write your own happy ending some day; I am sure of it. I wish you a safe journey home to America."

After getting Bruce from the smithy, Duncan got back on the road, but the closer he got to London, the more regret he felt. Och, what was he thinking, going to

London? It would be a thousand times worse there than in that crowded pub. He was running away like a bairn, and he was being foolish. He was so tired. He had hardly slept a wink last night and wasn't likely to get much sleep at an inn. There was plenty of peace and solitude to be found right here in one of these fields, though.

When he came to a stream running near the road, he stopped to water Bruce and then tethered him to a tree to let him graze. Duncan lay down underneath the tree for a nap.

Miss Clewes brought Louisa and Cassandra downstairs to say goodbye to their violin teacher, if a grand total of three lessons could be said to constitute that relationship. Janie and Fanny were waiting in the front parlor for the coach to arrive.

"You will be happy to hear they both want to continue their lessons, Miss Jones," the governess said with a smile. "They were quite inspired by your concert, I think."

"I'm so glad," Janie said, then she gave each of the girls a hug. "Take really good care of that violin. Promise?"

"We will," Louisa said, and Cassandra nodded.

"Their father has engaged a music master to start coming from Canterbury once a week," Miss Clewes said.

"And he teaches the harp, so I shall resume my lessons as well," Fanny interjected.

"Miss Jones, I want to thank you for the concert," Miss Clewes said. "The staff will remember that evening for a long time, I assure you."

"You're welcome. I'm so glad you had a good time." At least something good had come out of that night.

Fanny called out from where she stood at the window, "It is here!" Then she came over and hugged Janie tightly. "I shall miss you! Don't forget to write."

"I'll miss you, too," Janie said.

Fanny picked up a small, paper-wrapped parcel from the sideboard and handed it to Janie. "You'll get hungry on the way, so I had Cook pack this up for you."

"Thanks, Fanny, and you too, Johncock, " she said to the butler, who had an umbrella ready to shelter her until she got into the coach.

"Let her keep the umbrella. She hasn't got one," Fanny said.

"Oh, my goodness. Thank you!" Janie still had nine and a half hours to go before meeting Raven, and nine hours and fifteen minutes of that would be spent waiting in the rain, if the sky didn't clear.

The coach driver was jovial, despite the rain shedding

off of his greatcoat and his sodden hat. "Say no more, say no more!" he said, tapping the side of his bulbous nose with his index finger with each word in gleeful conspiracy, although Janie had said nothing but "thank you" when he helped her into the coach. "I was ordered *anonymously* to drop you off near the woods at the southern boundary of the Godmersham estate, well out of sight, and leave you there to be met by an *anonymous* someone afterwards."

"Yes. Thank you, sir." At least she wouldn't be expected to explain.

"Glad to oblige. Anything for young love, my dear!"

Young love. If only it were. She wasn't about to disabuse him of the notion that she was eloping, though; it was the perfect cover. Janie looked back to watch Godmersham Park slowly get smaller and smaller, until the trees hid it from view.

Duncan dreamed of Janie. She was standing in the field, wearing a blue dress. Her hair was unbound, as it had been when Duncan first saw her. A skylark was flying over her head, singing. Janie held out her hand, and the lark flew around her once, then landed gently in her hand. "Love believes all things," Janie said. The lark stayed in her hand, still singing its beautiful song.

When he woke up, he could hear a lark singing in the tree above him, but Janie was not there.

"I'm sure your young man won't leave you waiting long, my dear," the driver said with a wink, after he helped Janie down. "Then it's off to Gretna Green, and happily ever after, eh?"

"Thank you, sir. Goodbye." Janie opened her umbrella. That sounded a bit curt, when he was being so nice. She added a little wave.

"Quite so, quite so! *I'm* not wanted here!" He laughed as he climbed up into his seat again. He waved, and then the coach ambled on down the road.

Janie didn't want to be seen by anyone who might come down the road, so she went into the woods on the downs to wait. The skirt of her dress was getting wet, despite the umbrella. She had originally toyed with the idea of climbing the hill to the north and waiting in the shelter of the other temple folly, the one Fanny said had a "magnificent prospect" of the estate. Since it faced the house, she had decided against it, but now she regretted her choice. Would anyone really have seen her tiny figure up there through the rain? Probably not.

What she needed now was a convenient hollow tree big enough to crawl into. Those always seemed to exist in stories, didn't they? None of these trees were that big around, although most were quite tall. About a hundred yards in, she saw a cluster of three trees that seemed almost to spring from the same roots. Two of the trees grew close together and curved outward from the other. Janie leaned back against the two curved ones and put her feet up against the trunk of the third. She rested the parcel from Fanny on her stomach.

It might do. At least her feet would be up out of the puddling water. She was too tired and miserable to care about what critters might be crawling on the tree trunks. She situated the open umbrella in some branches above her head, and shut her eyes.

That Janie had fallen asleep was less surprising than the fact that she had managed to stay up there, wedged between the tree trunks. It had stopped raining. The sun was setting, so it was sometime after six o'clock. Her backside was sore, and her legs had gone completely numb. She eased herself down to the ground, but her legs weren't ready to hold her up, and she collapsed into the wet, muddy leaves on the forest floor. Yuck. Her dry-clean only dress was surely completely ruined now, so she went ahead and wiped her muddy hands down her hips. Fanny's package had fallen to the ground, but it didn't look too soggy. She picked it up and checked inside; in it were a sandwich and a wedge of cheese. Janie took a little bite of the sandwich, which was made with some of the beef tongue from lunch, dressed with pickle and mustard. It was delicious. She decided to eat the rest of the sandwich then and wrap the cheese up for later. Her rendezvous with Raven was still more than four hours away, and she might need a snack.

She was just finishing the last bite of her sandwich when she heard the wolves howl.

CHAPTER 23

*Though the nicht be dark as a dungeon, not a star to be seen
above,
I will be guided without a stumble intae the arms o' my ain true
love.
~Traditional, "I'm a Rover"*

She had been in Duncan's dreams before, but this time was different. It was as if Janie's extraordinary eyes had looked not only at him, but into him, and when she spoke, it was into his soul. "Love believes all things."

When Duncan was a lad, he had learned the thirteenth chapter of Paul's first letter to the Corinthians by heart, at the minister's suggestion. It was about *agape*, which was the Greek word for God's kind of love, Mr. MacDonald had said. The King James Bible translated it as "charity." Most of the chapter, "Love is patient and kind," and the rest, made perfect sense, but the idea that love "believes all things" had stumped him— believing *everything* was stupid. The minister had explained that loving someone meant believing the best of them. It meant taking them at their word. Believing *in* them.

The dream couldn't be clearer. Duncan had said he loved Janie, but then he hadn't believed her. What Janie had told him was wuid, certainly, but could it also be true?

He had to go back. Maybe he was the one who was crazy now, but he had to give Janie the benefit of the doubt. Janie had said she would be going back at midnight; he should just be able to make it back in time.

He took Bruce back down to the stream for a drink. Duncan refreshed himself too, drinking deeply and rinsing his face in the cold water afterwards. "I'm sorry to take ye this far again wi'out stable nor oats, Bruce," he said as he stepped into the stirrup and swung his leg over the saddle. They regained the road and turned east, towards home.

Thank God he hadn't given in to the urge to ride as hard as he possibly could for the first few miles out of Godmersham, or he would never have been able to turn back like this without the risk of an injury to Bruce. He prayed he would not be too late to catch her, nor too late to win her back.

Janie couldn't believe what she was hearing. Wolves had been extinct in England since the Middle Ages, right? At least that was what she had always heard. It had to be Castor and Pollux. Of course it was; Mr. Knight always let them out to patrol in the evenings. She had no need to be afraid of them— they knew her as Fanny's friend, right? She'd given one of them a bone. Janie had just never heard them make this sound before. It was an eerie, primal sound, and it raised the hair on her arms. They were howling together, one pitched lower than the other, in a kind of eldritch harmony. Almost without thinking, she held her closed umbrella out before her, wielding it like a weapon. It had gotten dark very quickly— instantly, it seemed, in the woods. Janie's eyes tried to pierce the gathering gloom between the trees.

There was the howling again, and it sounded a lot closer this time. The dogs hadn't sounded anything like this before, when they were chasing Raven away from the house. Could she possibly be wrong about there being no wolves?

She was most definitely wrong. Two enormous, silvery-grey shapes materialized out of the gloaming.

The wolves did not attack immediately, as Janie had imagined they would. They stood about twelve feet away, alternately sniffing the air, growling, and pacing back and forth. What if she threw the wedge of cheese? Would they be distracted enough for her to run the half mile to the church? Adrenaline was pumping blood into her newly awakened legs. Tingling before, now they were on fire. Janie was as bad at running as she was at dancing, though. Didn't running encourage their attack instinct, anyway? Or was that just bears? She had definitely heard that some animals would run away if you made a lot of racket and intimidated them by making yourself appear bigger somehow.

She shouted, "Go away!" They flinched but didn't leave. She tried shouting it over and over, while thrashing the umbrella about. They trotted a few yards further away, but they still didn't go. She pushed the umbrella open. Holding it out in front of her, she lunged in their direction, shouting, "Go on! Go! Go!" at the top of her lungs. At last, it was too much for the wolves, and they turned and ran away.

Janie ran after them, not because of some welling up of courage, but because it was the same direction the church was in. She made it to the church, slipping on a step that led down from the porch and running her shoulder into the thick, wooden door. She turned the large iron ring that served as the door handle, shoved the door open, and slammed it closed behind her, thanking God. She'd had no backup plan, had it been locked.

It was even darker inside the church, and quite cold. Janie went carefully down the six remaining stone steps into the nave, inching her way to the edge of each step. The smell of dampness seemed much stronger than it had on Sunday. It reminded her of the prison.

There had been two candlesticks on the oak altar table in the sanctuary earlier. They should still be there. She slowly made her way across the uneven flagstones to the front by feeling along the tops of the pew boxes. By the time she got to the end of the pews, her eyes had adjusted enough to make out the white cloth on the altar table, but she had forgotten the step that separated the nave from the sanctuary, and she stumbled on it, falling onto her hands and knees for the second time that night. The limestone was far less forgiving than the leaf litter in the woods, and she cried out in pain, the sound echoing in the emptiness.

It was all in vain, Janie realized when she finally stood at the altar. How was she to light the candles? She was almost certain that matches hadn't been invented yet. At Godmersham Park, the servants usually transferred fire from one place to another with candles or little twists of paper. She had only actually seen any of them start a fire a few times, and they had used a little tinderbox with flint in it. She'd never used one before, but she could give it a try if she found one.

She felt around under the table and found nothing. She felt around the vicar's pew and reading desk, then gave up. Rummaging like that in the dark was giving her the creeps. She was safe from the wolves, anyway; that was what mattered. She had finally stopped shaking, but the adrenaline was still there. At least she wasn't in any danger of falling asleep and missing her appointment.

Janie made her way to the back of the church again and slipped into the last pew, where she and Fanny had been sitting that morning. She probably should have just come in here in the first place, out of the rain, but she had been too worried about running into someone from the village. She wasn't going to beat herself up for her choice to go into the woods, though. How could she possibly have predicted wolves?

Janie's feet were freezing. She peeled off her wet shoes and criss-crossed her legs to warm her feet.

She should have asked Fanny for a watch, but she hadn't wanted to take anything that she would have no way of returning. She had been pretty confident she would be able to tell how much time was passing, but once she was in the woods, she saw how stupid that was. Even after the rain finally stopped, any stars not covered by clouds still weren't visible through the trees. She had never actually relied on the stars before, anyway, though her father had shown her how to do it once when they were camping.

It had probably been dark for an hour when she entered the church, and she had probably wasted half an hour on the whole candle thing. It was 8:20, then, at the latest. That was two "probably's" already, and she was sure to get worse at estimating as the night wore on, because she would get bored and space out. What if she missed it? Honestly, if it weren't for the wolves, she would just go hang out at the bridge right now, and risk being seen.

Janie unwrapped the cheese and ate it, thinking. Her band typically played 45 minute sets. They knew exactly how many minutes each song in their repertoire lasted, and they moved songs around based on the venue, the length of the gig, and their mood. If Janie sang four full sets, counting off the beats to the instrumental parts in her head, she could estimate three hours. Then she would leave the church and walk to the gate by 11:30. It was as good a plan as any. She started playing the intro to "The Lark in the Clear Air" in her head.

Duncan was uneasy. His original plan would have seen him safely to an inn well before nightfall, so he had not borrowed a firearm from Gabriel. This road, like many, was frequented by highwaymen in the dark of night, and riding a horse as fine as Bruce made him a target. He had to be constantly vigilant. Right now, he was far less concerned with the possibility of being robbed than with the time that being held up would cost him.

Passing the farm that he knew was only an hour away from Godmersham Park, Duncan checked his pocket watch. It was already 11:10; he had some time to make up. "Come on, Bruce," he said, signalling to the horse to go faster.

Janie finished singing "The Parting Glass." It was finally time to go to the gate and wait for Raven. She pulled her shoes back onto her feet with difficulty; they were still wet and clammy. Ew. She went to the door and pulled it slowly open. She couldn't see or hear any sign of the wolves.

She walked to the gates with her umbrella at the ready, but all was quiet. The full moon had risen, and the clouds were moving on, as if a giant were blowing them out of the way, revealing more stars than Janie had ever seen in Tennessee, maybe even more than on her grandfather's farm. She was but a tiny speck in time and space.

Someone was coming down the road from the direction of Chilham. Janie could hear him singing loudly in a gruff and tuneless voice. Was it some drunk man on his way home from the tavern, or was it Raven? Once she could make out the words, she relaxed. "If I could keep time in a bottle..." That was a 1970's song, one that her dad liked. It could only be Raven.

The moon shone on Raven's face, which seemed disembodied; his black hair and cape were nearly absorbed into the darkness. "Thank goodness it's you," Janie called out as the floating face approached. "I've already had to deal with wolves tonight."

Raven didn't seem either surprised or concerned; he simply nodded. "I warned you about those, I did."

"Yeah, well, I thought that you were speaking metaphorically."

"No, I save that for sonnets."

"I also thought that wolves were extinct in England."

"So they are, but we have to deal with them, anyway. Wolves have the ability to smell anachronicity on people, they have. They're used by various criminal elements to sniff out time travelers. Sounds like someone wanted to track and abduct or kill you."

"Oh." Janie shivered. "Well, that's just great. The wolves didn't attack me; I ran them off with my umbrella." Shoot, that totally made it sound like she wasn't scared completely out of her mind at the time, didn't it? What a joke!

"*Go iawn?*" He sounded impressed. "It was probably just the blasted— pardon, drug dealers, then."

"Drug dealers?"

"Lethe is worth a fortune on the black market. It's a component in that stuff the Little Red gave to Jane Austen. Lethe dealers have trained wolves to sniff it out, too. Time travelers are sometimes given a bottle of lethe before being returned to their native time, depending on the circumstances. My guess is they were checking you out for that." He roughed his hair up so that it stood up straight. "We may as well get on with it. This blasted— pardon, rift's not going to close itself. This way." They walked across the bridge and down the lane to the crossroad where the village was. "Here we are."

It didn't look much like the intersection where Janie had run into the signpost. Even the old-looking red brick building hadn't been built yet, apparently. "Where is it? I don't see anything."

"It's hard for the untrained eye to see, and it's impossible to see if there's no moon, it is. It also doesn't show at all in sunlight, in case you were wondering why I made you come at night." He pointed. "Do you see that place in the air that looks a little less sharp, kind of hazy-like?" He moved his finger up and down.

"Yeah, I think so." There was a very faint, rather wavy perpendicular line, like a mirage in the moonlight, ending in the mud of the road.

"This is it, then. 'Parting is such sweet sorrow,' and all that. Here is my card, twenty-first century version, in case you ever need to look me up." Raven handed her a cryptic-looking business card with nothing but a black bird and a lengthy phone number on it. "Keep that somewhere safe."

"Okay. Thanks." Janie put it in the pocket of her dress for now. "Do I need to leave the umbrella with you?"

Raven shook his head. "Nah. Are you ready, now that you've said your goodbyes and whatnot?"

No, she hadn't said goodbye to Duncan. He had told his sister to tell her Godspeed, but Janie hadn't had the chance to tell him anything. "I'm ready," she lied. "I want to go home." Then she burst into tears.

What was this? David's bones! He would never understand women! Raven had a sudden urge to go back to the pub for a drink, but instead he reached out and patted the girl awkwardly on the shoulder. She took a big shuddering breath which came back out in a wail. Raven pulled the handkerchief from his pocket. *Ych a fi*, it was very grubby, but it was too late now. He handed it to her, and she blew her nose on it.

"Sorry. I love someone, and I hurt him terribly, and now I've lost him." She blew her nose again. "I know somebody or other said it's better to have loved and lost than never to have loved at all, but it's not true, is it?"

Raven shook his head. "Nah, it's rubbish. It's that *twpsyn*, Tennyson. Fellow talks a lot of rot, he does."

Janie smiled a little bit, in spite of herself. Raven was

actually kind of sweet, in his way. She handed back the handkerchief. "Thank you." Should she give him a hug? She decided on a handshake, then she stepped up to the rift.

She looked back at Raven. At first she'd been terrified of him, and later she hadn't trusted him. A lot had changed. "Goodbye, Raven. By the way, I never told you my name. It's Jane Austen Jones."

Raven's jaw dropped. "Are you kidding me? By all that's holy, why didn't you tell me that in the first place?"

"You said never to give anyone your real name!"

"So I did. Well, it was that name of yours that pulled you into 1813, never mind any necklace! Go on with you, then, you daft girl. *Hwyl Fawr!*"

With that, Raven gave Janie a little shove, and the rift swallowed her.

CHAPTER 24

<hr>

"**I**f I could keep time in a bottle, the first thing that I'd like to do—," Raven sang, as he shoveled the precise amount of 1813 into the rift necessary to finish closing it up. " —Is to go on holiday to Ramsgate, and then—" Then he would, what? "I would sit on the beach with a beer." That wasn't half bad, though he'd butchered the metre. He chuckled and looked at his watch. 11:55. Done, with five minutes to spare!

He could feel the hoofbeats hitting the ground as well as hear them. Someone riding like a bat out of Bedlam was heading his way.

The man Janie had called Raven was standing there, but where was Janie? Nae! He couldn't be too late, not after he'd come this far! "Where is she?" Duncan cried. "What ha' ye done wi' her?" He jumped down from Bruce and ran to where the black-cloaked man stood, putting a short-handled shovel into a sack.

"Oh, it's you, Fisticuffs. You're the bloke she was crying over, I suppose. You're too late, but it's probably for the best, man." Raven slung the bag over his shoulder. "Two different worlds. Very messy." He started to walk away.

Duncan grabbed Raven's arm. "Nae! Ye cannae leave!" He gave Raven a shake. "I need ye to show me how to get there."

"Woah, there, big guy. Pax!" Raven put his palms up. "There's no call for that!"

The fellow was right; Duncan wasn't exercising much self-control. He took a deep breath. "I'm sorry. It's just that she asked me to come wi' her, and I didnae believe her at first, but I was wrong. I want to spend my life wi' her, sae I'm asking ye to please show me what to do."

"I'm sorry, too, mate. Look you, the rift is closed, and it's permanent. Government orders."

"Nae, there maun be a way!"

"Well, technically, there is, but it's a blasted pain in the bum, it is. Loads of red tape."

What did this have to do with tape? "Tell me."

"You can go to the agency's office in London and apply

for a time travel visa. Like I said, it's a pain, but that's the government for you."

"That is what I would like to do, then."

Raven shook his head. This poor dab had no idea what he was in for, did he? "Before I agree to this, you need to understand something, Fisticuffs. Traveling to the future is an entirely different cup of tea from traveling to the past. It's blasted dangerous, it is. A lot of people don't survive it, especially the brawny ones like you. Ever heard, 'The bigger they are, the harder they fall'?"

"Aye. I had a friend in London who taught me to box when I was a lad; he used to say that."

Raven rubbed his bruised chin ruefully. "Right. Well, let's just say the statistics aren't at all in your favor."

"Do ye mean it was dangerous for Miss Jones to go back? Could she be hurt?"

Bobol bach, now he'd gotten the giant riled again. "No, no. That was as easy as one plus one. She already did the hard bit, getting here. Going back to your native time is nothing." Good. He seemed to be reassured by that.

Raven had almost forgotten. "Another thing: even if your application is approved—and there's certainly no guarantee, mind you— you need to have something of hers with you to be able to make the trip. Do you have something she left behind? A love token? A lock of her hair? Her shoe?"

"Why would I ha' her shoe?"

"Come on, man, everyone's heard of Cinderella."

"I dinnae ha' anything of Janie's."

Ha! Raven suddenly realized that he had something, himself. "Well, Loverboy, you're in luck, because I just remembered I actually have something that will do the trick." He pulled his handkerchief from his pocket and handed it to Fisticuffs. "It's got some of her DNA in it."

"D and A. She talked aboot that."

Raven snorted. "*Duw*, that must have been a blasted fascinating conversation! Man, are you sure about this girl?"

"Aye, I'm sure."

"Then meet me at the White Horse in the morning, and you can travel to London with me. Not too early, mind— say, 10:00."

Duncan's heart was heavy in his chest; it was time to say goodbye to Elspeth. She was all the family he had in the world, and he might never see her again in this life. He had very nearly left without telling her goodbye. What if he had made it to Janie in time yesterday? Thank God he hadn't.

After getting home last night, he had waited for Bruce to cool down and given him his hay, but he had been too exhausted to do much else. This morning, he'd done all he could to leave the coach house, stables, and his quarters in good order.

Duncan went to the servants' door and asked for Elspeth, whose eyes were wide with surprise when she saw him. "What are you doing here? I thought you were in London!"

"I didnae make it that far. I have something to tell ye."

"Why do you have your books?"

"Because I'm giving them to ye, Elspeth. I cannae bring them wi' me. I've decided to go to America to be wi' Miss Jones— wi' Janie. Ye ken how I love her." He set the books down on a table in the hall.

Elspeth broke into a smile. "Oh, Duncan! I'm so happy for you both! She was that heartbroken about leaving you."

"And I hate to leave ye, Elspeth. Ye could come, too."

"Nae, I love it here, Duncan, you know I do. This is the place for me, not America. I want you to go, though."

She had tears in her eyes now, and it tore him apart. "Dinnae greet, Elspeth," he said, enveloping her in a hug. How wee she was! She was still so young, in spite of her grown up responsibilities and her grown up ways. Could he really do this?

Duncan was tempted to insist that Elspeth come with him. He was her guardian, after all; he could. Och, but she was so attached to this place and to Miss Sackree! This was what she had always wanted. She was happy here, and that was what mattered.

He kissed the top of her head. "If ye change your mind, I'll come for ye, no matter what. God bless ye, Elspeth. I am so proud o' ye. I'll always love ye, my wee sister; ne'er forget that."

"I'll always love you, too, big brother. I'll be praying for you. Send word to me when you get safely to America."

"I will." How, he had no idea. He would find a way.

Duncan's leavetaking of Mr. Knight was easy by comparison, although he knew he would be hard-pressed to ever find a better employer, and he felt guilty about not having a chance to give the proper notice. Mr. Knight was both surprised and disappointed, but Duncan told him that his friend Charlie, who worked at Chilham Castle, would likely jump at the chance to take his place. The fact that Charlie was also a fiddler who could play for dances made him a good catch. When Mr. Knight asked why his friend would want to leave the castle, Duncan had to admit that Charlie was courting Annie, a kitchen maid at Godmersham. Instead of being put off, Mr. Knight nodded. "I will ask after him, then."

The head groom did not share Mr. Knight's surprise at

the news. "I know well what it is like to be in love," he said, although Duncan had never said a word to him about Janie. Gabriel was cannier than he thought.

The police siren was a shock to Janie's ears. Had they always been so loud? She was wet and sore all over, but otherwise, she seemed okay. Was Grandpa Jim's fiddle still there, under the seat? She reached down, feeling the hard case there. Oh, thank God! Relief made her joints go as limp as old lettuce. She hadn't even thought to ask Raven what day it would be when she returned. It was as if no time had passed at all. She hated to think about what might have happened to her fiddle if two weeks had also gone by here in 2025.

A policeman wearing a reflective raincoat came up to her door, opened it, and ducked his head in. "Are you okay?" He put a comforting hand on her shoulder. "Everything's gonna be alright. An ambulance will be here in a few minutes to take you to the Kent and Canterbury Hospital." He noticed the windshield. "Blimey! Almost the whole thing is gone! I've never seen that happen before. Good thing you were wearing your seatbelt, innit? It kept you from flying out of the car."

Janie blushed. The seatbelt had done nothing to keep her in either the car or the year 2025, since she had failed to use it. "I'm okay. Do you need my license, insurance, and registration?"

"We can get them after the paramedics get here and check you out."

"It's fine. We can do it now." Janie reached into the back seat for her purse and gave him her license, then she got the registration certificate from the glove compartment. "My insurance is on my phone, but I'm not sure it's charged." She checked her phone. It was still half charged, after all that she had been through! Had it all really happened? She pulled the woolen shawl snugly around her shoulders— Jane Austen's shawl. Yes, it had really happened.

Janie insisted on bringing her fiddle in with her. She had her right arm around it as the ambulance paramedic put the blood pressure cuff on her left arm.

"I like your costume," the paramedic said.

"What?"

"Fancy dress party?"

He must be talking about her bonnet. "Um, not exactly. I was at a wedding."

"Yeah? That's brilliant. I went to one with a Star Wars theme once; it was really cool." He removed the cuff. "Your blood pressure is pretty high. They'll check it again at the hospital to make sure it has gone down. They'll probably x-ray you, just to make sure you haven't sustained any internal injuries. Sometimes the airbag can break ribs."

"Okay." Would they keep her at the hospital, or did she have to find a way to get back to her flat at school? If she was free to go after the examination, her flatmate could pick her up in the morning on her way home to Newcastle.

Janie only wanted to be one place right now— home. It was 6:30 A. M. in Tennessee; her dad had been up for half an hour. "May I call my father?"

"You sure can. Let me get your temperature first, then you're good to use your mobile."

"Hi, darlin'. I'm so glad you called! We miss you."

Janie started crying as soon as she heard her father's voice. Dang it, she had been so determined not to! Now he would really be worried.

She managed to tell him that she had been in a car accident, but she was okay. She was on her way to the hospital to be checked out, and she would call him back after they were done with her at the hospital. "Sorry, I didn't mean to cry," she said. "I'm totally fine. I just miss y'all so much."

"I'm on the first available flight there."

"No, Dad, I'm coming home. For good. I'll explain everything when I get there."

"Are you sure? What about school— your scholarship and everything?"

"That doesn't matter to me anymore. Please, I just want to come home."

"Of course, Janie, if that's what you want."

"It is. I love you, Dad."

"I love you too, sweetheart. I'm praying for you."

"Thanks, Dad."

CHAPTER 25

The sodger frae the war returns, the sailor frae the main,
But I ha' parted frae my love, never to meet again, my dear,
Never to meet again.
~Robert Burns, "It Was A' for Our Rightfu' King"

Duncan sat opposite Raven in the coach to London, looking out at the fields. This was going to be a very long ride if neither one of them spoke for the whole trip. He sighed. It was going to be a long ride, regardless. It wasn't nearly so bad when you were the one driving.

Raven finally spoke up. "Look you, Fisticuffs, I hope you don't expect me to be holding your hand the whole time. I'm dropping you off at the agency, I'm turning in my paperwork, and then I'm off on my blasted well-deserved holiday, I am."

"My name's MacKinnon. I'm sorry aboot punching ye."

"I guess I had it coming to me, I did. I shouldn't have grabbed your lady like that. I was just so blasted moithered that nothing was going right on this job. Sorry about that, MacKinnon."

"My lady, you said. I pray she will be." She had said she wanted to marry him more than anything. What if that was no longer true? He could be leaving Elspeth and risking his life for nothing.

"*Paid becso*— don't worry. You're fretting over nothing, man. Look, I know Disappointed in Love when I see it. That girl was crying her eyes out over you. Of course, now that I think about it, it could be it means she hates you now. Heck, I don't know."

Duncan nodded, unwilling to talk about it any more.

Raven resumed his earlier track. "They'll take care of you at the agency, though. Once your application is accepted, they'll provide lodging during the prep and conditioning and everything. There are fees, but I honestly don't know what they are. It's not my department."

"Lodging? Och, how long does this take?"

"I think it takes about six weeks, once you're approved. I hope you packed some clean shirts."

He had, and his Sunday clothes, too. But so long! Duncan's heart fell into his stomach. He had hoped he might even be able to catch the same boat to America as Janie. And there were fees; he hadn't thought about money, either, aside from the boat ticket to America. He and Elspeth had each inherited twenty-five pounds from Mr. MacDonald. He also had some money saved up towards his horse farm, but it might not be enough. There was his father's pocket watch— no, he couldn't part with that.

Raven chuckled. "I was just thinking about your Miss Jones. She's some woman, MacKinnon. She fought me like a blasted tiger when she thought I was abducting her. She pulled out a whole fistful of my hair, she did."

That made Duncan smile, in spite of himself.

"You will probably experience soreness in your muscles over the next few days, and your chest may show some bruising from the air bag, but the x-rays are clear—no broken ribs. Call me if you start to experience severe neck pain; we can do a brace. Take two Nurofen every four hours. That will help with muscle pain and any inflammation. It looks like you skinned your hands and knees pretty badly recently, too."

"Yeah. I tripped in a church, on the stones."

"What happened here?" The doctor touched her own forehead to indicate Janie's.

"I crashed into— um, glass, two weeks ago."

"It seems to be healing well enough. I noticed you also have some lesions on your head. There are at least six of them."

Oh, no. The leeches! Janie shuddered. How was she

going to explain that? Any decent doctor was sure to recognize what the little y-shaped scars were from. "Um, that was something that um, an alternative medicine guy did. He was trying to help with my headaches."

"I suspected as much. I doubt that leeches are the solution. May I recommend an excellent migraine specialist? Her name is Dr. Coles. She's right here in Canterbury."

"Thanks, but I live in America." Where she would be going as soon as she possibly could.

The coach stopped every couple of hours to change horses, but the stops were short. Duncan felt less urgency about reaching the agency quickly than he had before, now that he knew the application process took so long. There was no point in fashing himself over it.

"I don't suppose you happen to have your lady's direction there in America, do you?" Raven asked as they neared London.

"Nae, but I will find her. She lives near Nashville, in Tennessee. How many Joneses can there be in the Nashville area?"

Raven laughed. He laughed until tears came to his eyes, then he started coughing.

What was so funny? Duncan wondered.

"The cough takes me now and again, but I'm blasted lucky it's no worse," Raven said when the coughing subsided. "I worked the coal mines as a boy, I did. Here's the thing, MacKinnon: Jones is one of the most common surnames in America. For all I know, it could be at the top of the list in Tennessee."

"Then I will ask aboot until I find her. Someone will ken her."

Raven held up his hand. "Whoa, there, MacKinnon. I would guess there are around two million people in Nashville in 2025."

How was that possible? That was double the population of London! Duncan couldn't help letting out a cry of dismay.

"*Paid becso*, MacKinnon. One of the perks of working for a secret government agency is having access to a lot of information. They'll get her direction— Americans call it an address— and her telephone number for you."

"What kind of number?"

Raven scrubbed at the hair on the top of his head. "It's too complicated for me to explain. Let's just say it'll help you contact her in the future. Using the telephone is one of many, many things you'll be learning about in training, poor dab. They'll cram your head so full of stuff, it'll be coming out of your ears, it will."

Duncan must have nodded off. It was dark already. They had obviously arrived in London; he could hear the bustle of other traffic on the road, and their pace had slowed. "What time is it?" he asked. He had forgotten to wind his watch.

"It's going on eight o'clock. We'll stay the night at a decent inn I know in Westminster. It's close enough for us to walk to the agency after breakfast."

"Aye." He had figured they wouldn't be going straight to the agency.

By the time they arrived at the Blue Boar's Head Inn on King's Street, he was very hungry. The coach pulled into a stable yard at the rear of the inn. Just as it had felt odd to be a passenger inside of the coach, it felt strange not to stay outside and attend to the horses.

The dining room had a welcoming fire, and the clientele seemed to be the quiet and contented sort, Duncan noted with relief. He was hoping for a restful night in preparation for tomorrow, with all of its unknowns. After a dinner of beef pie and ale in the dining room, they turned in for the night.

The room looked plenty clean enough. Duncan was surprised to see that Raven had packed his own set of sheets for the bed, but he knew better than to tease him about it.

"What?" Raven asked, anyway. Duncan's face must have given him away. "You don't want bugs, do you?"

"Nae, o' course not."

"Hold your tongue, then, MacKinnon."

Duncan knew every stone in the Covent Garden neighborhood, but he had not spent as much time in this area of Westminster when he had lived in London. They walked down Whitehall and stopped in front of a graceful, three story mansion of brown brick. It did not look like a government building to Duncan; it looked like a private residence belonging to a wealthy gentleman.

"This is Gwydyr House. It's the private residence of Baron Gwydyr," Raven said, as if he had heard Duncan's thoughts. "It also happens to be the entrance to the offices of the Accidental Time Travel Agency."

The front entrance had stone steps leading to double doors topped by a three-light Venetian window and Ionic columns and pilasters on either side, but Duncan figured they would not be going in that way; that was the entrance for gentlefolk.

He was right. "We use the tradesmen's entrance, we do," Raven said, and he led Duncan around to a door at the rear of the building. He produced a key from his pocket and unlocked the door.

They went down a servants' hall which ended in a door. It was also locked, and Raven pulled out another key and unlocked it. It opened onto a dark stairwell leading to the cellar. There were two lanterns on hooks just inside the doorway, one on either side. Raven pulled a small tinderbox from his pocket and lit one of the lanterns, then lifted it from its hook. "Well, here goes your obligatory trip to the underworld, hero," Raven laughed as they descended the staircase into the cellar, and the sound was eerie in the subterranean darkness. Duncan had no idea what he was talking about, but Raven was so amused at himself that he kept on laughing until he had another coughing fit.

Duncan could not have retraced their route had his very life depended upon it, so many were the turns down other hallways, through other doors, and even down other stairwells; wherever they were going, it was certain they would no longer be in Gwydyr House when they got there. Raven had said that the agency was a secret, but it didn't need to be, as far as Duncan could tell. No one looking for it could have found it, anyway.

"Here we are," Raven said at last, stopping at a door at the end of one of the hallways. He pointed to the lintel of the doorway. "I've often thought we should have a sign up here that said, 'Abandon all hope, ye who enter here,' but I guess that would be a bit discouraging for you, wouldn't it?"

It would, indeed. Duncan couldn't abandon hope—it was all he had.

There was nothing to distinguish this door from any

of the others they had come through, except that when Raven opened it, they were bathed in a warm glow of light.

Raven must have noticed his surprise. "Our offices are all plumbed for gas lighting," he explained. "Good, isn't it?"

"Aye." He had seen gas lamps on one of the fancier streets in London when he was last in the city for Mr. MacDonald's funeral, but he didn't know they could be used indoors, too.

"Just wait until you see electric lights, if you think this is something! Personally, I think they are overdone in the future, but nobody asked for my opinion. We probably won't ever get them in our offices; they're that unwilling to part with a penny. We've only got a few measly electrified rooms in the whole agency. Well, MacKinnon, I have paperwork to turn in to my supervisor, so this is where we part ways. I'm leaving you in the capable hands of Mr. Davies, head of the Intentional Travel Division. Take a seat here in the waiting room, and his assistant should be with you soon. *Pob lwc*– best of luck to you, MacKinnon." Raven offered his hand, and Duncan shook it.

"Thank ye."

"Oh— one more thing, and it's really important, it is: Whatever else you do, make sure you get yourself some memory tonic, or you could forget everything about 1813. Remember Cinderella? Her *twpsyn* prince didn't take any tonic, so he couldn't even remember what she looked like.

He had to go around trying that blasted shoe on every girl he saw, he did. Memory tonic, MacKinnon."

Raven felt a stab of pity. *Bechod*, MacKinnon would need all the luck he could get, poor dab. Davies was the least sympathetic soul in the entire agency; it was probably the main reason why he'd been chosen for the post in the first place. The government was exceedingly stingy with its temporal travel visas, although with good reason. The agency's very existence was more at risk with every person who knew of it, for one thing. For another, some people sought to abuse the system for personal gain. Still others were out to destroy the Timeline altogether.

Theoretically, Davies was supposed to consider applicants with a number of reasons for requesting a visa, but in all of the years Raven had worked for the agency, he had only ever heard of Davies granting them to cases involving the utmost national security. The real reason Raven didn't know what MacKinnon's fees would be was that the government ate the costs for those national security cases. Who knew how much they would charge for anything else?

Raven felt like a heel as he walked back down the hallway to his own office. What had made him agree to bring MacKinnon all this way for nothing? He hadn't been thinking about Davies, that was for sure. It was that infuriating, beautiful girl who fought like a tiger and stood up to wolves. Her tears had done it. He was getting blasted soft, he was.

CHAPTER 26

_The water is wide, and I can't cross o'er, and neither have I
wings to fly;
Build me a boat that can carry two, and both shall row, my love
and I._
-Traditional, "The Water is Wide"

Duncan sat down on the wooden bench to wait. The room was so small he could touch the walls on either side of him. He felt like a horse in its stall. On a short table in front of the bench was a thick, red book. The cover read, "Linemen: A History." He picked it up and thumbed through it. He looked at the illustrations, which were so realistic it was uncanny. Some of the men in the pictures bore a strong resemblance to Raven. One of the chapters was titled, "During the Blitz." What did that even mean? He put the book back on the table.

A homey needlepoint picture in a long, rectangular frame hung on the opposite wall. It featured the words, "Preserve the Past From the Future" in fancy, Gothic letters worked in red thread, surrounded by roses in pink and yellow. Next to it was a wee placard that read, "The needlework mottoes on display in this department were done between 1865 and 1880 by Maisie Williams Evans, wife of the agency's first chairman."

1880. Sixty-seven years in the future. A shiver ran through him. He looked back at the needlepoint picture, which seemed strangely foreign now. Underneath it was a rack that held several different pamphlets. He chose one titled, "What is the Accidental Time Travel Agency?" Maybe this would make more sense than the book; it was a lot shorter, anyway.

The Accidental Time Travel Agency is a secret subsidiary agency within the Department for Transport. It was created by Prince Albert during the reign of Queen Victoria in the year 1849, for the purpose of monitoring and mending rifts in time. Albert, always a proponent of public works projects, was delighted to learn about the existence of time rifts. Although men had been working on rifts for centuries in Wales, with the knowledge and skills being passed down through a few families from father to son, time rifts had never before been formally regulated. The prince saw the potential for bringing the innovations of the future to his Great Exhibition. Alas for Prince Albert and his Crystal Palace, conditions for travel to the future proved to be far rarer than to the past. However, the department he created has proven to be an invaluable asset to the British government.

Linemen do the vital work of returning accidental temporal travelers to their native times and repairing time rifts. All linemen are both native Welshmen and native Victorians. However, they can work anywhere on the island of Great Britain, anywhere on the Timeline, on any given day.

Linemen of today use the same time-honored methods that were used by their ancestors, minus the mystical trappings. What was thought to be magic in the days of Myrddin the Enchanter, the Victorians understood to be science, and the old spell books have long been relegated to dusty departmental archives. The tools of their trade— the ingeniously formed picks and shovels— have remained virtually unchanged from days of yore.

Linemen still follow the tenets instilled in them by their Welsh forefathers. Visitors to the agency may see many of these inspirational maxims on display in the hallways.

Tiny print on the back of the pamphlet read, "UK Department for Transport, 2023." 2023! That was two years before the one to which he hoped to travel— Janie's year. Duncan returned the pamphlet to its place in the rack. Reading it had made him feel strangely light-headed. He leaned back against the wall and closed his eyes.

A pretty, dark-haired young lass wearing an unusual, bell-shaped yellow gown with a high neck and white lace collar entered the waiting room. She was probably several years younger than Janie. "Mr. MacKinnon?"

Duncan stood up. "Aye."

She nodded. "Follow me, please. You may experience

some slight dizziness in our hallways due to minor temporal adjustments." She spoke with a Welsh accent, like Raven. She walked with a limp, but she still moved quickly as she led the way down a long, twisting corridor with doors on either side. Each time they turned a corner, Duncan was thrown a bit off balance. They passed many more needlepoint mottoes. By the time they finally stopped, Duncan did indeed feel dizzy. He could barely read the motto, "Time is of the Essence," in front of them. To their right was a door labeled, "Temporal Visa Applications." The lass rapped on the door and opened it. "Mr. MacKinnon is here to see you," she said to the man seated there.

Mr. Davies was a stocky man wearing striped trousers and a blue frock coat. His shirt had a stiff, standing collar tied around with a red cravat in a horizontal bow. His head was entirely bald on top, but a quantity of black hair waved out on either side of it.

He stood up from his desk and held his hand out to Duncan, and Duncan shook it. Mr. Davies' manner was as starched and stiff as his collar.

"Pleased to meet you," Mr. Davies said. "Go ahead and have a seat." He had a Welsh accent, too. He gestured towards a chair facing the desk. The chair had a small writing desk attached to its right arm. Duncan was not sure he would fit in it, but then he noticed the desk portion was on a sort of hinge. He could lift it so that he could sit in the chair, then lower it into place again.

After Duncan sat down, his dizziness subsided. The sight of Mr. Davies' desk was disconcerting, though; it was completely covered in disheveled piles of paper. Och, were those the applications?

"Mr. MacKinnon, the British government recognizes only three legal reasons for intentionally traveling through time. Number one: National Security. Number two: Family Honor. Number three: True Love. Which of the three will you be claiming on your Temporal Visa Application today?"

A vision of Janie, laughing as she threw a handful of hay at him, came unbidden to Duncan's mind. "Number three."

After the doctor's examination and a chest x-ray, Janie was free to go. She slept as well as she could in the waiting room of the E.R., in between the noisy arrivals of other patients with their various injuries and illnesses. She couldn't wait to take a shower; she had to be positively crawling with germs. She waited until 7:00 in the morning to call Ann and ask her if she could pick her up.

"Oh, my gosh! Why didn't you call me right away? I would have come," Anne said when Janie told her about the accident.

"I didn't want you to miss out on your amazing room at the castle."

"Oh, my gosh! It's so brilliant! I'm sending you some pictures now."

The room looked as luxurious as Janie had imagined it would. "Wow, I'm so jealous!" The bed looked especially nice after her night spent in a straight-backed vinyl chair.

"I know, right? Anyway, I'll be there as soon as I can."

"Okay. Thanks, Anne."

"Here is the application," Mr. Davies said, handing a packet of papers to Duncan, along with a metal-nibbed pen. "Be as thorough and accurate in your answers as possible." The directive, not to mention his formal manner, seemed such a contrast to his cluttered desk.

"May I borrow an inkwell?"

"It's a fountain pen. It has the ink inside of it."

Duncan tested it on a corner of one of the papers. It worked. He began filling out the forms. He filled in his name, birthdate, and place of birth, as well as his parents'. He sighed when he came to his direction and his employment. Och, it should say "former" direction and employment; the same would be true for anyone filling this out. Unless his application was denied, that is. He shook away that gloomy thought and continued. He also had to fill in all of his former directions and places of employment, list his known living relatives, and give character references. The novelty of not having to dip his pen in ink the whole time made it more enjoyable. Thankfully, there were no questions to which he did not know the answers.

Duncan finally came to the last of the questions, and he groaned aloud: "In a 500-word essay, explain why you should be given a temporal visa."

Janie woke up as Anne's car pulled into her parking space at their flat and groaned aloud. She was tempted just to go to bed and put off all of the unpleasant things she had to do now. There was no way she was going to tell Anne everything, but she owed her some explanation for leaving her without a flatmate, and she could still tell her something true. She had some money saved, so she could help Anne with the rent through the end of the semester if she couldn't find another flatmate. She should tell Anne now and get it over with.

They went upstairs, entered the apartment, and Anne flopped down on the sofa. "It's so good to be back home! It's pretty funny, if you think about it, considering I was just at a freaking castle!"

Janie wasn't going to get a better opener than this. She

sat down on the sofa next to Anne. "That's the thing. After what happened, all I want right now is to be home, in America."

"What, for good, or just a visit?"

"For good. If you don't know somebody who can take my room, I'll still pay rent for the rest of the semester, but I need to go home."

Anne's dark eyes were wide with concern. "Why? What about school? You'll lose your scholarship and everything if you go now."

"School's not what I want anymore. I realized something about myself when I was— um, after my accident. I love fiddling, and that's all I really want to do." She wrapped both arms around the case that held Grandpa Jim's fiddle. "I don't need a graduate degree because I don't want to teach at a university anymore; it's not for me. I was trying to do something, be something that I thought my mom would have wanted me to, but I'm not an academic like her. I'm okay with that now. I still love learning about traditional music, but I've been doing that on my own for years. I don't need to go to school for that."

"Wow. That's huge. I guess it's good that you realize it now, rather than later, innit?"

Duncan was certain he had not written a total of 500 words in the whole of his life, from the time he was a wee bairn learning from his mother how to write his name, until now. Och, what should he say? How was he to convince the stiff man behind the cluttered desk?

The young lass who had ushered Duncan into the office stuck her head in. "Father, Mr. Rhys needs you in his office now. He says it's urgent, and he told me to look after the applicant."

"Very well." Mr. Davies sighed and stood up. "And Bronwen, see if you can get all of these papers back into their files today. I can't work like this. They aren't here for your reading pleasure, anyway."

His daughter came into the room, holding a book. "I will. I brought a novel today, see?" She held it up and waggled it. She sat down in her father's chair. Mr. Davies went to the door, then stopped, straightening suddenly. He turned back to the room. "Mr. MacKinnon, I am trusting in your honor, sir."

Miss Davies blushed. "Father!"

Duncan was tempted to make a joke; his whole reason for being here was to make his way to the woman he loved, after all! Seeing Mr. Davies' expression, he schooled his features into seriousness, instead. "You ha' my word I'll not move frae this seat until ye return, Mr. Davies." He might have to sit here for days, anyway, trying to write 500 words.

"Thank you." Mr. Davies pushed the door all the way

open and pushed a cast iron doorstop shaped like a basket of flowers into place to hold it open. His trust apparently only went so far.

How our story ends depends on you, Duncan wrote, and he put his pen down. He had written their story, from the first moment when he saw Janie lying in the furze on the side of the road, until today. He prayed it was good enough. He wished he could stand up and stretch. First he had ridden in a coach all day, and now he had to sit here without moving. "Do I ha' to actually count the words?" He asked Miss Davies, who was absorbed in her book.

She looked up dazedly, as if she had forgotten he was even there. "Oh! Let me see how much you have."

He held up the pages, one at a time.

"That looks like enough to me."

"Och, it feels like I wrote a whole book. I only hope it will convince your father."

"May I read it?"

"Nae, I cannae get up, remember?"

Bronwen laughed and got up from her seat, her hand out to receive the pages, and Duncan gave them to her. "Here, you can read my book while I read your book," she said, handing him the volume she had been reading.

"*Pride and Prejudice* by Jane Austen. Why, I ken this lady!

I worked for her brother. I didnae realize she wrote a book."

"Really? She wrote six of them, actually. She's my favorite author. What year did you come here from, Mr. MacKinnon?"

"1813. Am I not in 1813 now, then?"

"That's the same year this book was published! And no, not exactly. The Accidental Time Travel Agency exists in a pocket on the Timeline that was created in 1851. Didn't you feel the time shift when you came down the hallway?"

"Aye. I didnae ken what you were talking aboot when you mentioned it before."

"I want to read your essay now, so *wheesht*."

"Och, ye ha' Scots, now, is it?"

"Aye." Miss Davies grinned and started reading.

Duncan was just finishing the first chapter of Miss Austen's book when Miss Davies said, "That was the most beautiful, wonderful thing I've ever read, it was."

He looked up. Miss Davies was dabbing at her teary eyes with a lace-edged handkerchief.

Just then, Mr. Davies charged back into the room, took one look at his weeping daughter, and roared at Duncan. "What did you do?"

Miss Davies jumped up and threw her arms around her

father. "He's done nothing, Father, except to have the most perfect love story. Or he will have, after you give him his temporal visa."

"Love stories don't need visas."

Duncan's heart sank. Why had Mr. Davies even told him before that love was one of the legal reasons, then? What chance did he have now?

"This one does, Father."

Duncan realized then that young Bronwen Davies just might hold his fate in her hands.

CHAPTER 27

Oh boatman, put off your boat, put off your boat for golden money,
For I must cross the stream tonight, or nevermore I'll see my lady.
~Traditional, "Annan Water"

"**Y**ou read too many novels, Bronwen," Mr. Davies said.

"That's exactly why I can tell this is a special case, Father. This one is so wonderful because it's true. It's real."

Mr. Davies shook his head. "He could be making the whole thing up, *bach*."

"He's not. Why would Raven have brought him all the way here, then? Raven knows Janie, and he knows it's all true. Raven is about as romantic as a lump of coal, Father, and you know what a skinflint he is. He even paid for Mr. MacKinnon's coach fare and his place at an inn, didn't he, Mr. MacKinnon? She caught Duncan's eye and gave him a tiny nod, as if to say, "Go along with it."

Raven must have paid, actually. Duncan hadn't even realized that himself until just now. "Aye, he did." Och, this girl was a slyboots, wasn't she?

"Hmph. Raven'll ask the agency to reimburse him, too, he will. *Pob lwc* to him," Mr. Davies said, but Duncan could see he was wavering.

So could Miss Davies, for she pressed her advantage. "His and Janie's story reminds me so much of yours and Mama's." Objection to that was written all over her father's face, but she continued. "At first he was attracted to her for her beauty, then he fell in love with what was in her heart. Just like you always said about Mama. And Janie is a gentleman's daughter, too, just like her. Listen to what he wrote, Father: 'She made me wish I were a richer man, so I would be equal to her, but even more, she made me want to be a better man, so I would be worthy of her.'"

Mr. Davies was quiet for a moment. His chin trembled, and he nodded. He looked over at a portrait hanging on the wall. "That's how I felt about my Elin. She gave up her whole world to be with me, she did."

"That's what Mr. MacKinnon wants to do—to leave his family and his whole world, for Janie. He knows how dangerous it is, and he still wants to do it. To be with her. Please, Father."

"Very well."

Miss Davies threw her arms around her father's neck again. "You won't regret it."

"I already do," he groused, but he was smiling. "*Bach,*

you're wrong about Raven, you know. He was in love once. He wanted to marry your mother— wrote her poetry, if you can believe that— but she chose me. It broke his heart, it did. Poor dab, he could never love anyone else."

Janie did not look forward to going to her academic advisor's office and withdrawing from school. Not only would she look like the world's biggest flake, but also a total ingrate. She hoped that the university would still be able to extend the scholarship to someone else.

First, though, Janie wanted to book a seat on the next flight to Nashville. She scrolled through the different options on her phone. She was lucky that it wasn't the busy season, but it was still going to cost her a lot more than it had when she had booked her flight to England. She had done that over two months in advance and saved quite a bit. The soonest flight home at any price was over a week away, and the ones that were further out than that weren't much cheaper. She booked a seat on the earliest one and texted the flight information to her father. His return text said, "I can't wait to see you, sweetheart." Janie was grateful that he was being so understanding about school. She had called him again after her release from the hospital, and he had said he was going to handle everything with the auto insurance company for her, so she wouldn't have to worry about any of that. He really was the best dad in the world. Janie "hearted" his text.

"I'm going to walk to my advisor's office now to find out how to drop out," she called to Anne, who was in the kitchen heating something up in the microwave. It smelled like leftover curry.

"Hey, do you want me to come? You know, for support? I can eat later."

"No, that's okay. I think I'll be fine. I just want to get it over with."

"Are you sure? What if they give you a hard time about it?"

"Don't say that! You'll make me nervous."

"I think I should come. This curry's all dried out, anyway. We can go for some chips afterwards."

Mr. Davies had stamped Duncan's application with the agency's official seal of approval, and Duncan had signed his name no less than two dozen times on as many forms. By the end of the stack, he was merely skimming over the forms. Most of them were promising he would not hold the Accidental Time Travel Agency or the Crown liable for injuries, medical bills, and the like. One particularly puzzling waiver promised he would not come after them in the event of his own death.

Duncan was ready to do whatever it took. He would sign a hundred forms, if he had to. "As long as I dinnae ha' to promise ye my firstborn child," Duncan joked.

Mr. Davies' eyes widened. "Has someone approached you with an offer of that nature?"

What? "Nae, 'twas a wee joke, is all."

Mr. Davies' jaw jutted out. "Young man, this is not a laughing matter. I assure you, our agency may be secret, but it is strictly above board. We have never condoned that practice, and we are pledged to bringing the criminal element that does, to justice."

It could have been worse, but it also could have been better. Janie's advisor seemed to think it was her job to convince Janie to stay, and she was determined to do that job. Janie originally had no intention of telling Mrs. Rice anything at all personal, but she felt cornered, so she ended up telling this virtual stranger that she realized she had been trying to earn her absent mother's love and approval in pursuing a graduate degree. Janie was relieved when she and Anne were able to leave the advisor's office.

After the oversharing session, they still had to go to several other offices so that Janie could decline the scholarship and complete the withdrawal process.

"We deserve the biggest plate of chips we can get, don't we?" Anne asked, once they were finally finished.

"A big plate apiece, I think. With curry sauce."

"Brilliant!"

"Ye are a right canny lass, Miss. Thank ye for helping me oot back there," Duncan told Bronwen Davies as he followed her down the corridor to the financial office. Oddly, he did not feel all peely-wally in this hallway like he had before. They passed several stitched mottoes along the way, including "No Time Like the Present" and "Time and Tide Wait for No Man."

"Nonsense. It was all your own doing. No one could have turned down your application, Mr. MacKinnon."

Duncan was certain that Mr. Davies could have easily done so, possibly without reading it at all. "Thank ye, all the same."

"You're welcome."

They came to a door labeled, "Financial Department." The motto hanging on the wall opposite the door read, unsurprisingly, "Time is Money."

Miss Davies knocked on the door, then opened it, and she and Duncan entered another office. It resembled the other one, except that there were no piles of paper on the desk, only a large ledger book. Nor were there any portraits on the wall. In one corner of the room stood a tall clock with a large, rather mesmerizing pendulum. Its loud ticking emphasized the silence. Duncan would be completely wuid if he had to work in this office. He forced himself to focus on the man at the desk, not the clock.

"This is Mr. MacKinnon, Mr. Owen," Miss Davies said, walking to the desk and handing a paper to Mr. Owen. She gave Duncan a smile of encouragement on her way back out of the office. He was on his own this time.

Mr. Owen was a thin man with black hair, a waxed mustache, and eerily pale blue eyes. He wore a suit similar to Mr. Davies', only it was all in black. He stood and shook Duncan's hand. "Have a seat," he said, indicating a chair opposite the desk. This chair had a black horsehair cushion and curved arms. The fact that there was no little desk attached was encouraging; at least Duncan probably wouldn't have to write another essay.

"Congratulations on being granted your temporal visa. Let's get you set up for your trip, shall we? It looks like you are going to the year 2025, and your contact person is Janie Jones. Do you have her direction? Phone number?"

"Nae, except that she lives near Nashville. 'Tis in America."

"We can get that information for you, for a processing fee." He wrote something down in the ledger book. "We will take your picture and issue you a UK passport for 2025, as well. Unfortunately, the passport is quite expensive, since it can only be procured in the twenty-first century. There are other things we can do here in our offices. Then there is the transportation fee itself, of course, and some prerequisite vaccinations. Those are the essential expenses."

Just how much would all of this cost? What if he couldn't afford it? His inheritance and savings totalled seventy-five pounds. Duncan wiped his sweating palms on his breeches.

"We offer a series of classes to help you navigate the twenty-first century, as well as the six-week temporal conditioning course, which we highly recommend, if you want to ensure you survive the time travel. You will have food, lodging, and care in our infirmary during that course. I also recommend you get the memory tonic, in your case."

"Aye, I need some o' that."

Mr. Owen nodded. His finger traveled slowly down the column to the far right of the ledger page. Duncan couldn't make out any of the figures from where he sat, but he still held his breath as Mr. Owen added them up.

"Mr. MacKinnon, you can expect to pay two hundred and ninety six and a half pounds, not including tax."

Duncan gasped, but his lungs couldn't find any air to take in.

CHAPTER 28

*I would swim over the deepest ocean, the deepest ocean for my
love to find.
But the sea is wide, and I cannot cross over, and neither have I
the wings to fly.
~Traditional, "Carrickfergus"*

Och, what was that smell? Was something on fire? Duncan opened his eyes. He was slumped over into his own lap, and Miss Davies was down on her knees beside his chair, holding a vial up to his nose. Her brows were knit with concern. Duncan sat up quickly, and everything spun around him.

"Be careful, Mr. MacKinnon," Miss Davies said. "Don't try to get up too quickly."

Too late. "What happened?"

"Either the temporal shifts you've experienced this morning have had an effect on you, or Mr. Owen made you pass out."

"I beg your pardon, Miss Davies. I did no such thing," Mr. Owen said, crossing his arms.

Duncan remembered. "I've lost her." He let his head fall heavily into his hands. He just wanted to be alone, but he couldn't ask them to leave. Warm tears trailed down his fingers and into his palms.

"No, you haven't. What are you talking about? Mr. Owen, please go get a cup of tea for Mr. MacKinnon."

"I beg your pardon, Miss Davies. I think you should be the one getting the tea."

Duncan looked up long enough to growl, "I dinnae need tea!" What he needed was seven and a half more years' worth of earnings.

"Yes, you do. Please, Mr. Owen." Miss Davies gave Mr. Owen a wide-eyed, plaintive look. "Please."

"Oh, very well." Mr. Owen fairly stomped out of the office.

Miss Davies touched Duncan's shoulder and handed him her lacy handkerchief. "Here." She went over to the desk and picked up the ledger book. "*Bobol bach*! This is ridiculous! Only a very wealthy person could afford this!"

"Aye." Duncan looked at the tiny square of linen and lace she had given him, then pulled his own handkerchief from his pocket and wiped his eyes.

"How much do you have?" Miss Davies asked.

"Seventy-five poonds. And my father's watch."

"I see. Well, we will just have to make that work, then. *Paid becso.* I have some ideas."

Duncan shook his head. What could she possibly do?

Mr. Owen walked in with the cup of tea, which he handed to Duncan.

"Thank ye." Duncan took a sip. He had needed the tea, after all. It was funny how comforting tea was, although it did nothing to change one's circumstances.

Miss Davies asked, "Mr. Owen, what if he declines the classes and the training?"

"His costs go down, but so do his chances of survival. The expedited passport is the greatest expense, anyway."

"Expedited? What if he waits?"

"The least expensive one is still eighty-eight fifty."

"So he could get all of the essential things for a little over a hundred pounds, then, couldn't he?"

"Yes, if you don't consider his survival to be essential."

Miss Davies gave Mr. Owen a quelling look.

Duncan's spirits rose. He would survive; he had to. "I will ha' the money for ye this afternoon, Mr. Owen, after I sell my watch." He knew exactly where to go, once Miss Davies showed him the way to get back out onto Whitehall.

Before guiding Duncan back out, Miss Davies brought him to another door. "It's such a bother to get in and out of here that we eat down here while we're at work,"

she explained. "Here is the kitchen. I think you should eat something before you go. I'm hungry, anyway." She opened the door, and they entered a small kitchen where a woman was stirring a pot of soup over a coal-burning stove. There were two tables that seated four people, but no one else was there.

"I dinnae need anything," Duncan said.

"Yes, you do. It's my treat, it is. Besides, I don't want to eat by myself." She sat down at one of the tables, and she motioned for Duncan to sit. The cook ladled soup into two bowls and brought them to the table.

Duncan sat down, too. His stomach growled when he smelled the soup. It was not a comfortable feeling to be so dependent on a young lass, but he was ashamed of how churlish he was today. "Thank ye."

"You're welcome. I've been thinking," Miss Davies said between spoonfuls. "I actually have a bottle of memory tonic at home. You can have it. That saves you five pounds."

"Can ye really do that? Just gie it to me?"

"Sure. I don't need it, and of course, I would never sell it on the black market. It's too old for the agency to use— the flavor's gone bad. It will still work, though. I'd forgotten until now that I still had it. I used to be a Little Red." Miss Davies grinned. "That sounds funny every time I say it, it does. We call the girls who make and deliver the tonics Little Reds, because the uniform is a red cloak. I started working here four years ago, when I was fourteen.

My father wouldn't let me do it anymore after one of the wolves bit me."

"A wolf? I didnae ken we had those in England."

"We don't, generally, but they can come through the rifts. Do you want to see the bite marks?" She was already rolling her stocking down, and she stuck her leg out for him to see it. She had her dress hiked up nearly to her knee.

Duncan's embarrassment was lost in the horror of what he saw. He had once seen the scars on a man whose leg had been caught in a poacher's trap, and this looked just as bad. Some of the scars were hidden by her boot and the roll of her stocking, but enough were visible to show that the wolf's teeth had torn the flesh nearly to the bone. Lord, have mercy! It was amazing that she walked as well as she did.

"I'm sorry that happened to ye," was all Duncan could say. He was relieved when she pulled her stocking back up and put her skirt down, not only because the scars were painful to look at, but because he was imagining Mr. Davies walking in and demanding that Duncan marry his daughter for having seen her bare leg.

"Look you, if you need to use the water closet before we

go, there's one right there." Miss Davies said, gesturing to a door to their right when they left the dining room.

"The what?"

"Oh, I forgot you probably haven't seen one of these. It's a room with a sort of chamberpot that flushes everything out of a building through some pipes. Come here."

Duncan followed her over to the door.

"After you um, relieve yourself, you pull down on this chain, and it flushes." She pulled the cord, and a stream of water swished around the inside of the ceramic bowl and out through a hole in the bottom. "The ones in Janie's time have a lever or button that you push, instead of a chain. Tidy, isn't it?"

"Aye, 'tis." He could feel himself blushing, but Miss Davies didn't look embarrassed at all. She looked pleased.

"When I first started working here," Miss Davies said as they walked down the corridor, "I made up a kind of song to help me remember the path from the Gwydyr House cellar to the agency's door. If you are able to get that far, then it's fairly easy to use the mottoes on the walls as landmarks for getting from one office to another."

"If ye can see straight enough to read them. I get all dissy in here."

Miss Davies nodded. "I did the full temporal

conditioning when I started working for the agency, so I don't feel any of that anymore. Little Reds have to be able to go anywhere on the Timeline. At one time I wanted to be the first female Lineman, but now it won't happen, not with my bad leg." She sighed. "It probably wouldn't have happened anyway. It's all Victorian men around here."

"Cannae ye just go back in time to before the wolf and— shoot it or something?"

"No, it's against the rules to change the past. It's illegal, really, but since nobody outside of the agency knows the laws exist, we tend to call them rules around here. It's a bad habit, it is."

"Did ye ever go to 2025?"

"No, but I have been to that century before. Everything is very, very fast there, it is."

"How do ye mean, fast?"

"For one thing, they travel in cars— something like carriages— that can go faster than a racehorse. It's quite thrilling, actually, but I wouldn't want to do it all of the time."

"Some people ride horses there, though. Janie does."

"Even the few people that have horses don't use them very much. I expect that she drives a car most of the time, just like everyone else. Cars are positively everywhere, going very fast, except when there are so many of them on the road at the same time that they must wait in queues to get anywhere."

"Aye, sometimes the roads into London are crowded with carriages that way."

Miss Davies laughed. "It's a bit like that. Just you wait, Mr. MacKinnon. You will probably have to fly to America in an airplane, too."

"Och, that's a Banbury tale. People cannae fly. Janie didnae say anything aboot flying."

"Of course not. People would have thought she was crazy, or lying."

Duncan felt a sudden heat in his cheeks. Aye.

"She could even be flying to America in an airplane right now. It's sort of like a boat with wings that sails in the sky. I haven't been in one, but I flew in an airship once, which is almost the same. It's too bad you can't afford the classes; you would learn about all of these things. As it is, I suppose you'll just have to learn as you go, like learning to swim after being thrown into the sea."

"Aye, that I will, I reckon." Like a lot of people who lived near the water, Duncan's father had thrown him into the loch when he was a wee laddie. He had flailed and swallowed some water, but he'd figured it out. He wasn't sure if he really remembered it happening, or if his mother had told him about it years later. At any rate, he could swim now.

"Oh! We're almost to the cellar already, and I didn't even try to teach you the song for getting out. It's just as well— you probably wouldn't have remembered it all, anyway. Meet me at the back door of Gwydyr House in two hours. I'll be working on some things for you while you're gone." They walked through the cellar, and she lifted her lantern so he could see his way to the top of the stairs.

"Thank ye, Miss Davies."

She waved. "I'll see you later. *Pob lwc!* That means good luck, Mr. MacKinnon."

CHAPTER 29

Rich Owen will tell you, with eyes full of scorn,
Threadbare is my coat, and my hosen are torn.
~Traditional, "The Maid of Llanwellyn"

How strange it was to find himself back on these Covent Garden streets, as if he were a lad of fourteen again, looking for pockets to pick. Ducking into a familiar alley, Duncan wondered if his old fence was still in business. It mattered little if he was not; Duncan would find another. Such places sprang up in the city as naturally as weeds between the stones in the streets.

How strange, too, that now he was desperate to sell the one thing he had thought he could never part with. Even when he and his mother had found themselves unable to pay rent, selling his father's watch had never been an option, as far as his mother was concerned. It was all she had left of his father, she said.

"Nae, ye ha' me," Duncan told her.

"Aye, that's true, but I willnae always ha' ye wi' me," she

countered, and nothing he could say would change her mind. It had made him unbearably angry at the time, but after his mother died, he found, to his surprise, that he treasured the watch as she had.

The shop was still there, but the old man who used to fence for him was not. Duncan was relieved; if he had recognized Duncan, the old man would have assumed he was still stealing. At least now, Duncan was just another down-on-his luck customer who needed to pawn something.

The shop's new broker was a young man who wore his patched, secondhand clothes with a dandified air; his collar and cravat swallowed his neck entirely, and a brightly patterned waistcoat showed under his bottle-green coat. He pulled a quizzing glass out of his pocket with great ceremony in order to inspect Duncan's watch. He opened the watch up and looked at the works, then listened to its ticking. His eyes showed a gleam of interest, but he shook his head. "I can't give you very much for it, I'm afraid. It's nothing out of the common way."

"'Tis real silver, and it keeps good time."

"So you say. Well, I can give you two pounds."

Duncan took the watch back. "Nae, thank ye." He turned to go.

"Three pounds, then. Three pounds fifty!"

Duncan kept on walking.

After Duncan had tried the familiar pawn shops, he searched for others. The highest anyone offered was ten pounds, but the woman who made that offer had leered at him suggestively, saying they could "make an arrangement" whereby he could get even more. There was no way he would sell his father's watch to her, not for any amount.

Perhaps a shop in a different part of the city could do better, but the two hours were nearly up, and that last shop had left him feeling sick. Duncan headed back towards Gwydyr House to meet with Miss Davies. He prayed that she had come up with a solution.

Miss Davies was standing at the back door when Duncan got to Gwydyr House. She was smiling. Did she have good news? "I couldnae sell my watch," he said. "I will try another part o' town tomorrow."

"It doesn't matter! I found a loophole!" Miss Davies twirled around and clapped her hands like an excited bairn.

A "loo pole" was evidently a very good thing.

"Mr. MacKinnon, I went to 2025 for a little while to use our computer there, and I found out that UK passports are supposed to be free for anyone born on or before September 2, 1929! Father and Mr. Owen both think that it is abusing the system, and maybe it is, but I don't care. I'm sure this is the last time the government will let the agency do this, but right now, they have to let you get one for free!"

Duncan still wasn't sure what a loo pole was, but he understood enough. "Aye, I was born in 1788."

"Yes! We should go in. It's best if we don't talk about these things outside."

This time, Miss Davies sang her memory song softly as they went down into the cellar and through the tunnels. The light of her lantern bobbed gently up and down with her limping gait. The song she sang sounded like the rhymes that the children in London sang when they played their games, only longer. She was right; there was no way Duncan would've been able to remember the whole thing after hearing it only once. When they were in the agency's hallways, his dizziness seemed to be no better than before.

They stopped in front of the "Time is Money" needlepoint. "We have to go to Mr. Owen's office first, then I have a surprise I want you to see. Mr. Owen knows all about the free passport and everything. He will make up a new bill for you," Miss Davies said as she opened the door. She shook her head at Mr. Owen. "He didn't sell his watch."

Duncan sat down in the horsehair chair with a sigh. He needed to close his eyes for a wee minute. He could hear the soft scratching of Mr. Owen's fountain pen as he wrote.

"I think you will be much happier with this new figure, Mr. MacKinnon," Mr. Owen said, handing the bill to Duncan. Once the words and numbers stopped moving around, Duncan read:

```
Temporal Visa.............£ 5.
Info Processing...........£ 0.
UK Passport................£ 0.
Transport....................£ 22.50
Conditioning...............£ 33.
Vaccines.....................£ 10.
6 days Rm and Bd...... £ 4.50
Memory Tonic............£ 0.
Total..........................£ 75.
```

Miss Davies said, "I did the information processing myself, with the help of your application and essay. Here is a copy of your contact information for Janie." She handed Duncan a calling card on which she had written "Emergency Contact" and Janie's name, along with what had to be her direction— the word "Nashville" was part of it. There was also a row of numbers. "Oh, and your memory tonic." She handed him a wee glass bottle filled with a dark liquid.

He put both into his pocket. "Thank ye, Miss Davies. I'm greatly indebted to ye."

"Nonsense. You're welcome."

Mr. Owen said, "That thirty-three pounds buys you only a third of the recommended temporal conditioning time, but we believe it's enough to make sure you get there alive. If you're in agreement, you may make your payment now." Duncan nodded, and Mr. Owen signed the bottom of the bill where it said, "Received." Mr. Owen handed the receipt to Duncan, and Duncan handed him all the money he had in the world.

"I told you I had a surprise for you. It's in a room you haven't seen yet, it is." Miss Davies said as Duncan followed her down a new hallway. A motto on their left read, "No Time Like the Present." The temporal shifts she had talked about were very apparent here; Duncan felt dizzy almost immediately, and he stumbled a bit.

"Lean on me if you need to," Miss Davies said. Duncan didn't want to lean on her. He took a deep breath and steadied himself.

"It doesn't matter so much that you can't take the classes. Many of the things you need to know about you can see on the telly. That's a thing that will be invented in the 1920's. We have one in a room down this way which is wired for electricity. That's another future invention. I can't explain any of it very well; it's best for you to see it for yourself." Duncan wasn't sure how well he would be able to see any of it. "All in Good Time," the needlepoint motto they had just passed, had looked like it was moving around on the wall, his head was spinning so much.

They stopped at a door labeled, "Television Room." Miss Davies opened it and flipped a switch on the wall just inside. Bright flooded the room. "Electric light is a bit much for me," Miss Davies said. It was for Duncan, too. He also thought he might cast up his accounts then and there, as dizzy as he was. "If you lie back on this sofa, you should feel better, Mr. MacKinnon. It will take me a minute to set this up, anyway."

Duncan sat on the sofa, leaned back, and closed his eyes.

"What you are going to see will seem like magic, but it's not. People in the future will figure out a way to record images so that they can be viewed over and over. When I was investigating Janie Jones for you, I found out that the band she plays in is called Clear Aire, and then I looked that up on this thing called YouTube, and I saw her—"

"You saw Janie? Where is she?" Duncan opened his eyes and sat up. Miss Davies was putting something into a silver box with a dark mirror standing behind it.

"I didn't actually see *her*, I saw the *video* of her. I

transferred it onto a DVD for you, so you can see it on this telly. Here, watch this."

The dark mirror lit up, and there was Janie. She was playing a fiddle, and there were three young men with her, playing other instruments. He could hear the music, too. "She's not really inside the mirror, is she?" Of course she wasn't; he just wanted to make sure.

"Everyone asks that. No, the telly is just showing you something that was recorded earlier. This video is from 2024. It's about forty-five minutes long. Your Janie is beautiful, she is."

"Aye." Janie had her hair down, and it was longer than when Duncan had first seen her. She was wearing a pair of close-fitting trousers, boots, and a loose, flowing white shirt that was open at the neck. It looked almost like she was wearing some of Duncan's own clothes. They looked far better on her. Lord, have mercy.

"You can watch it as many times as you like," Miss Davies said.

"I was hoping ye would say that." *Mirror, mirror on the wall, who's the fairest of them all?* How many things in the "auld tales" were real? What was next, selkies and kelpies?

"I'm going to make you watch some other things on the telly, too. There are a lot of other things you need to know about the future besides women wearing trousers," she grinned.

Duncan blushed. Miss Davies was too canny by half.

Miss Davies went to the door. "I'll come and get you before dinner."

"Does your father ken ye are doing all o' this?"

"Of course he does— it's my job. Oh, you mean being alone in a room with you for more than ten seconds? He does. Most of us have either spent so much time in the future or watching the telly that we hardly think twice about it, but Father's different. Still, I think I've convinced him that you are devoted to Janie, and that you aren't a rake," she grinned.

Duncan had watched the video all the way through. Miss Davies had said he could watch it again, but he didn't know how to make that happen. After a few minutes, the dark mirror stopped glowing. He had just closed his eyes when the door opened, and Miss Davies came in. "It's time for dinner, then I'm going home. Dr. Williams will be here tonight, and he'll show you where you'll sleep and everything, he will. I'll be back tomorrow."

"I dinnae ken how to operate the telly."

"Oh! I'm sorry. I should have shown you before." She went through the instructions for turning it off and on, inserting the DVD, switching from DVD to the telly, and changing channels. It was complicated in the extreme. He would probably just wait until Miss Davies could do it.

"Did Janie ever say anything about Charlie, except that he plays mandolin and guitar in her band— you know, what he's like?" Miss Davies asked Duncan while they were eating roast beef and vegetables in the agency's dining room. "He's very handsome, he is."

Och, *him*. Duncan would have to be blind not to see how close that young man and Janie were, the way she smiled at him. Their voices blended so perfectly together. He didn't want to talk about it. "Nae."

Miss Davies sighed. "The YouTube notes just gave the band members' names. I would have thought that Janie would tell you something about her brother, Mr. MacKinnon. It's very vexing."

Och, o' course he was her brother! Duncan had been half in agony for the last hour for nothing. What a tumshie he was! "Only that he has a twin sister," he said, with a laugh he had no intention of explaining. "Her name is Lottie."

Dr. Williams silently showed Duncan the way to his room, which was labeled "Infirmary." The motto outside the door read, "Time Heals All Wounds." The room had a strange smell that Duncan couldn't place.

"I'm going to give you half of your vaccines now, and the other half in a few days," Dr. Williams said. "Sit down in the chair and roll up your sleeve, please." He swabbed Duncan's arm with something icy cold.

What was this? The doctor didn't explain, but Duncan did as he asked. He watched Dr. Williams put something into a vial. It had a long needle on the end of it, which he jabbed into Duncan's upper arm. Ow! What the devil? A stinging sensation traveled through his arm.

"That should keep you from getting any nasty diseases. It will hurt a bit."

"Ye could ha' said so before."

Dr. Williams said that he and another doctor, confusingly also named Williams, split shifts at the agency. He showed Duncan a red button on a little white box which he could press if he needed a doctor, then he bade him goodnight and left.

There was a telly in the room, but Duncan thought better of trying it out. He was fairly sure he would have trouble making it work, and the red button was only for calling medical help. He needed to sleep, anyway. Tomorrow the training would begin. Bronwen had told him a little bit about it, but she wasn't willing to tell him much, even when pressed. "I don't want you to worry," she said, with what she probably thought was a reassuring smile.

It must be dreadful, then. He only hoped it would all be worth it.

323

CHAPTER 30

Fair and lovely as thou art, thou hast stol'n my very heart;
I can die, but cannae part, my bonnie dearie.
~Robert Burns, "Ca' the Yowes"

In the morning, the other Dr. Williams knocked on Duncan's door. Unlike his counterpart, he explained everything first. "I'm going to run a few tests on you before your first round of temporal conditioning," he said. First, he put a little glass stick under Duncan's tongue with instructions to hold it there, but not bite it. Then he checked Duncan's pulse and listened to his heart with an apparatus that resembled a telescope.

"You won't be able to eat anything today, Mr. MacKinnon. We are going to put you in the vacuum pressure chamber. It is, quite frankly, painful, and in every way unpleasant. The pressure will increase with each session. You may choose to quit at any time, but understand that it's essential if you hope to survive temporal transportation."

"How did Miss Jones survive, then? She didnae ha' any o' this when she came to 1813."

"For one thing, she traveled to the past, which is far, far easier. For another, being a woman, she has much less muscle mass than you do. Many men don't survive even a naturally occurring rift. For another, her rift wasn't the same as our lab-created ones. Believe me, we have tried—will try, to create an intentional rift which functions exactly as an accidental one, but..." He shrugged. "And with the last name Jones, ten to one, that means she's at least part Welsh. Traveling the Timeline is in the Welsh DNA, it is."

Good thing Duncan had some of that on the handkerchief in his pocket, then.

The week took on a pattern of agony and recovery. On the days he wasn't in conditioning, he was allowed to eat and rest, and Bronwen Davies joined him in the television room to explain all of the impossible things they watched on the telly. He finally learned how to turn it on for himself and how to load the DVD player. Whenever Miss Davies had to do something else, he put in the DVD. Being able to see Janie on the off days kept him going, and thinking of her on the conditioning days kept him sane.

Sometimes he felt much too sick to watch the telly and

listen to Miss Davies' commentary. At those times, she read to him from *Pride and Prejudice* while he rested. "We willnae ha' time to finish it," Duncan remarked one afternoon. "I want to ken how it ends."

"*Paid becso*, Mr. MacKinnon. This is one book you will still be able to find in 2025."

"Your passport is ready," Miss Davies said. "Do you want to see it?"

"Aye, that I do." Yesterday, Miss Davies had taken his photograph with a camera. At first, Duncan couldn't see how holding the camera in front of her own face would work to take his likeness rather than hers, and he had asked her about it.

"Here— this is the viewer." She pointed to a wee bit of glass in the camera. "Look through that, and point the camera towards me."

He did, and there was a tiny image of Miss Davies, framed in the viewer.

"Can you see me in it?"

"Aye. Ye look very wee in there."

She laughed. "Good. Now hold it still and press that button on the top."

He did. "Is that a'?"

"No; the film has to go to the twentieth century to be developed, it does. You'll see it tomorrow."

Now here his photograph was, inside of the wee book that was his passport. It was remarkable how much it looked like him. Those pictures he had seen in that book in the agency's waiting room must have been photographs, too, although this one showed the colors, and those had not.

"Here's the one you took of me," Miss Davies said, handing it to him. "You may keep it if you like." It was larger than the one in his passport. She looked exactly as she had yesterday, when she was laughing.

"Thank ye." He put it in his pocket. He carried Janie in his heart, but he wished he had a photograph of her to put in his pocket, too.

"Do ye ha' a way to send a letter through time, Miss Davies?" Duncan asked her on the day before he was to travel. He was too tired for more television. "I promised my wee sister I'd send word to her when I got to America."

"We've never done so before; we hand deliver everything. But I could post it for you from here, if you write it now. You know, that's a great idea— I should propose a regular postal system for the agency." Her eyes were wide with excitement. "We could install a secret temporal P.O. box in all of the post offices— no, probably just three: in London, Cardiff, and Edinburgh. Secrets that are too spread out are harder to keep."

"Och, I'm no even in 2025 yet, much less America. I cannae write it yet."

"Sure, you can. Just write how you imagine it will be— no, how you *know* it will be."

Each day that went by, Bronwen Davies had become more and more like another sister to him. Young as she was, she was nonetheless his older sister, teaching him how to make his way in the bewildering world of the twenty-first century.

On the final morning, Miss Davies acted even more the older sister, if not the mother. They sat waiting on a bench in the hall outside of the rift room, under the motto "Only Time Will Tell." She kept her hand on Duncan's arm, patting it now and again, as if he was just a wee laddie in need of comfort. And fretting over.

"Do you have the DNA?"

"Aye."

"Are you sure? Check your pocket."

He did, to humor her.

"Good. What about my card, with Janie's information on it?"

"Aye." He showed her that, too. "And here's my passport." He held that up.

"How about your watch?"

"Aye." He pulled it out of his watch pocket, then slipped it back in.

"You can sell that in 2025 to help with your ticket to America. It will be worth far more then."

"Och, nae. I signed a paper that I wouldnae sell things frae the past for a profit i' the future."

"Oh, that. I'll make sure to tear that one up."

"What?"

"That's just to prevent scalping. I'm sure Father would agree that these are extenuating circumstances."

Duncan was not at all sure he would agree.

The door to the rift room opened. "It's ready, if you are," Dr. Williams said.

"Take the memory tonic first," Miss Davies said.

Duncan pulled the bottle from his pocket, uncorked it, and drank it in one swallow. "Bluh!" He stuck out his tongue. "'Tis foul!" He gave his head a shake and stood up.

Miss Davies stood up too, grinning. "I told you it would be. Alright, now give me a *cwtch*." She hugged him. "*Hwyl Fawr*, Duncan MacKinnon. You and Janie have a wonderful life."

"Thank ye. God bless ye, Miss Davies." Duncan followed Dr. Williams into the room.

Thank heaven the right Dr. Williams was the one on duty, the one who explained things ahead of time. Duncan had taken to calling him "Dr. Will" and the other one "Dr. Willnae" in his mind.

"Have a seat," the doctor said, indicating a chair next to the wall. "This rift will put you out on the lawn in front of Gwydyr House. We are assuming that someone will see you and call an ambulance— a car that transports people to a hospital, a medical facility. You may be wondering why I don't simply travel with you. That's because the medical attention you will receive in 2025 is far better than any that I can give. You'll be unconscious."

Duncan nodded. He knew that.

"Possibly even in a coma."

"In what?"

"A coma. It means a state of very deep sleep, where you can't wake up. It's a natural, last-resort defense system which keeps you from feeling pain and lets your body begin to heal. I must be honest with you: people don't always wake from comas."

Duncan nodded again. How many times would they remind him that he might die? "Where is the rift?" he asked. For some reason, it was terrifying that he couldn't see it. He felt a sudden cold sweat on his forehead and neck. God, help me, he prayed silently.

"It's right here." Dr. Williams turned off the overhead light, but he had a tubular lantern in his hand that gave off a beam of light. In its glow, Duncan could see a ripple in the air on the far side of the room, and he sighed with relief. He stood up and walked over to it.

"You're a brave young man, Mr. MacKinnon, to attempt this. *Pob lwc.*" Duncan felt a shove from behind and a painful pulling from the front. The pain in his chest intensified until he screamed. Nae, he couldn't do this! He couldn't—

CHAPTER 31

I look to the high hills and a tear dims my eye,
For the lad I love dearly lies a distance frae me.
~Traditional, "A Peer Rovin' Lassie"

Janie had done little but lay in her bed or on the sofa for two days. She tried playing her fiddle, but instead of bringing her home as it always had, it betrayed her, bringing her instead to a stable in 1813.

She had changed out all of her £10 notes after realizing that it was Godmersham Park in the background of Miss Austen's picture. The portrait hadn't looked quite right, either.

"I can tell you're going barmy with boredom already, Janie." Anne said when she got back from class to find Janie lying on the sofa, staring at the ceiling. "You should go to London early, and hang out there until it's time to go— there's so much to do there, and there are some great vintage clothing shops. That's what I would do if I were you. You could take the train. It only takes about four hours."

It wasn't a bad idea, but Janie had already spent some time in London before coming to Newcastle, and Anne was the one who loved vintage clothes so much, not her. Janie sat up. "I have actually been thinking I might travel around to all of the places where Jane Austen lived."

"That's pretty cool, too. Kind of a pilgrimage to your namesake, yeah?"

"Exactly." Janie might never have the chance to come back to England. She got a notebook and pen from her backpack, Googled "where Jane Austen lived," and started taking notes on each place. She wasn't prepared to see Godmersham Park on the list, since Miss Austen hadn't actually lived there, but there it was. A photograph accompanied the listing. The house was missing its portico now. The stables didn't show in the picture. Janie's chest tightened with longing and sadness. How long would she be like this? She went to her room and shut the door so Anne wouldn't hear her crying.

Anne had come up with the solution. "Why not do one of those group tours? That way, all of your transportation and hotels are included, and you have a guide and all that." Janie wasn't sure she wanted to be with a bunch of other people just then, but the thought of not having to plan everything herself or do the driving was appealing. She looked online for tours. There were lots of them. The year 2025 marked the 250th anniversary of Jane Austen's birth, and everyone was celebrating it.

In a matter of two days, Janie had called a company whose tour didn't include Godmersham Park, packed all of her belongings back into her suitcase, hugged Anne goodbye, got on a bus, and joined a group of tourists in Bath. She had to wear Fanny's bonnet. She'd found that she didn't want to part with it, and it would have been crushed in her suitcase. Oddly, there were two other ladies in their group wearing bonnets, and a lot of other people in Bath were wearing full Regency costumes. "You all just missed the Jane Austen Festival by a few weeks," the tour guide said. "You should have seen Bath then. You'd feel like you had time traveled!"

Janie's name gave her an instant celebrity status with her tour group that she could have done without. Some of them even called her by her full name all of the time, which was particularly weird. "Hey, Jane Austen Jones, we have room at our table— come sit with us!"

Janie's favorite place on the tour was Chawton Cottage, where Jane Austen had lived and written during the period when Janie had met her. It made her so happy to imagine Miss Austen there with her sister Cassandra, their mother, and their friend Martha Lloyd— a single sisterhood, making a home for themselves in their cozy cottage.

Some of Miss Austen's personal belongings were on display there, even the turquoise ring she had been wearing at Godmersham Park. Janie gasped when she saw the brown silk pelisse that Miss Austen had loaned to her. No, shoot— it was a replica; the original was in the care of Hampshire Cultural Trust. She would probably never know if the stains had come out. An embroidered muslin shawl of Miss Austen's was also there. Janie felt like she should donate the blue woolen shawl, too, but she had no proof of its provenance. She laughed when she imagined telling the museum that Miss Austen had given it to her so that she wouldn't be cold. No, she was glad; she could keep it and treasure it, without any guilt.

In the north nave of Winchester Cathedral, Janie's tour group laid flowers next to the tomb of Jane Austen. There were a lot of other people there, but they still had the chance to gather around to read the inscription on the memorial stone and spend a moment in contemplation.

The inscription did not say anything about Jane

Austen's novels, but it said a lot about her as a person. "The benevolence of her heart" had brought Janie comfort in the darkest moment of her life and kept her warm in the cold. "The extraordinary endowments of her mind" had saved Janie from the hangman's noose.

A few of the tourists came away misty eyed, but Janie wept openly for Miss Austen, who had been a friend to her.

Janie's family was the balm her soul needed. Strangely, she was even looking forward to sharing the small bedroom with her two sisters again. Anne had been skeptical. "Don't you feel like you're taking a step backwards? I sure wouldn't want to move back into my parents' house," she had said. Maybe it was a step backwards, but Janie didn't care. Sometimes that was the only kind of step that felt right.

She hadn't expected all of them to be waiting for her at the airport, but there they were, holding up a poster that said, "Welcome Home, Janie!" She hugged her sisters and brother until they protested that she was squeezing them to death, and then her dad enveloped her in the best of all hugs, the one that had always pictured to her the unconditional love of God. She thought surely she had gotten all of her tears out already, but still she cried all over her dad's shirt, and he held her until she was done. Then he kissed the top of her head and said, "Let's go home."

Home.

Christie made a taco salad. After dinner, they all spent a couple of hours sitting around the kitchen table while Janie told her whole story. "I need to tell y'all about what happened to me," she began. "It's going to sound nuts, but I promise it's true. Will y'all just listen, and not say anything until I am done telling all of it?" They looked around at each other, then nodded.

Her family listened, and a wondrous thing happened— they believed her, every word.

Janie stayed up late, eating popcorn while watching *The Princess Bride* with everyone, though their dad had gone to bed halfway through the movie. They had all seen it dozens of times before, but it was their comfort movie, just as taco salad was their comfort food; the two went together. She was tired, but her siblings seemed to have gotten a second wind, so they all stayed in the den, talking about their mom.

Charlie was ready to get on the next plane to Ireland, rent a car, and then crash it into something.

Lottie laughed. "You're such a goober! Be serious.

Anyway, we don't know for sure that the car crashes caused the— what are they called, Janie?"

"Rifts."

"Right. That could be coincidental."

"The two crashes weren't the same, either. Janie's windshield blew out, but as far as we know, Mom's didn't," Christie said.

Janie looked at her in surprise. She must have heard more than Janie thought she did seven years ago, but Christie had always been the observant one, hadn't she? "I didn't go to a random time, and I don't think Mom did, either. I went to 1813 because of my name, and because I happened to be in the same location as Jane Austen."

"I don't think Mom is named after anyone," Lottie said. "She was doing historical research, though. What if she found something that was connected to the past?"

"A talisman?" Charlie asked.

Janie grinned, remembering Raven's reaction to that word. "Something like that. It's certainly possible."

"I vote we tell Dad tomorrow what we're thinking about," Lottie said. "I'm sure he's thought of it too, anyway. He has all of the reports and stuff on Mom, along with her research notes. We need to study all of that. We've got a lot of work to do before we think about going anywhere."

The others nodded.

Janie thought of Raven's card, which she had locked in her jewelry box, since he had said to put it somewhere safe.

On reflection, he probably just meant she shouldn't throw it away. "So, we focus on figuring out where she is–"

"*When* she is," Charlie said.

"When she is. Once we know that, Raven should be able to tell us how to get there; I have his phone number," Janie said. "It will take time, but we'll find her. Just as long as we all understand that nobody—" She looked pointedly at Charlie— "is going to be crashing a car into anything on purpose."

CHAPTER 32

He picked her up all in his arms and gave her kisses most tenderly,
Saying, "I'm your true love and single sailor,
Who came o'er the sea for to wed with thee."
~Traditional, "The Fair Maid in Her Father's Garden"

Duncan could hear people talking. Och, why wouldn't they leave him be?

"Can you hear me? It's time to wake up now."

"Make sure to say the patient's name. A name can be a powerful thing."

"Mr. MacKinnon?"

"Try his first name."

"Duncan, it's time to wake up."

Nae, he wanted to sleep.

"Have they called his personal contact?"

"The NHS has no records of him at all. Go figure. And he doesn't have a phone or a wallet, either."

"He must have been robbed, then."

"Maybe, but he has a passport. Why would they leave that?"

"Get the bag with his stuff in it and look through the pockets again. We may have missed something."

"Looks like he was at some kind of fancy dress party, yeah?"

"Check the waistcoat. Sometimes there's a little pocket on the inside."

"Look at that– phone number and everything! Good on you."

Janie had been home for a week and a half when her phone rang with a number she didn't recognize. "Is this Janie Jones?" a woman asked.

"Yes, this is Janie."

"This is St. Thomas' Hospital in London. We are calling because we have Duncan MacKinnon here, and we have you as his personal contact. He's been in an accident."

How could joy and fear both inhabit the tiny space of a second? Duncan was in 2025! "Is he– is he okay? Can I come see him?"

"He has some swelling on the brain and some broken ribs. He's in ICU. He may have up to two visitors at a time between two and eight PM. Feel free to call us for updates."

"Thank you for calling me! I'm on the next plane there, okay? Bye." Janie's hands trembled as she looked at flights on her phone. There was an available seat on one leaving Nashville tomorrow.

"Duncan, are you ready to wake up? We called Janie for you."

Janie? He tried to open his eyes. They were so heavy.

"Did you see that? His eyelids moved."

"Duncan, Janie is coming. She's in America, but she'll be here as soon as she can, so you need to wake up."

Janie was coming.

"Duncan, Janie is coming tomorrow. Don't you want to see her?"

Aye, he wanted that more than anything.

He opened his eyes.

Janie knew she shouldn't Google the effects of swelling in the brain, but she'd done it anyway, and now she was trying to forget everything she'd read as she approached the nurses' station. Several of the nurses there looked quite young; she had read something in the hall about this hospital being a training facility. Three of them were drinking from their water bottles and gossiping quietly together as she walked up to the counter.

"Have you two seen Sleeping Beauty in room 212 since he woke up?" asked a nurse with a nose ring. The other two nodded.

The one wearing blue eyeglasses said, "Izzy's heart is broken. She wanted to be the prince that woke him with a kiss."

An older nurse looked up from her computer at Janie. "May I help you?"

"I wouldn't mind snogging him myself," Nose Ring said in an undertone. Eyeglasses laughed.

"Hi. My name is Janie Jones. I got a call that Duncan MacKinnon is here. I believe he's in room 212." She gave the three girls a look that she hoped told them in no uncertain terms that any snogging was going to be done by her, and no one else.

The young nurses' eyes widened, and they quickly busied themselves with things around the desk.

Janie could hardly believe he was actually here. Her Sleeping Beauty was still gorgeous, even as rough as he looked right now. What had Duncan put himself through to get here? He was very pale, and he had at least a week's worth of beard. It looked like he may have lost some weight, too. He had a lot of bruises, and he was hooked up to a heart monitor and an IV pump. The head of his bed was raised, so that he was halfway between lying flat and sitting.

He was wearing one of those horrid hospital gowns; no bandaged bare chest, then. But those nurses out there got to change his bandages, didn't they? Actually, now that she thought about it, broken ribs probably didn't need bandages. Good.

There wasn't a chaperone in sight. Janie sat down next to him on the narrow bed and kissed him softly on the lips. His beard was scratchy around her mouth.

Duncan woke with a gasp and sat up. The beeps from the heart monitor sped up.

"Careful, try not to move too much. You're all hooked up. Plus, a nurse might come in, and I want to have you all to myself."

Duncan relaxed back into the pillow, smiling. "Are ye real this time, lass? Not another dream? Look at your hair. Ye are sae bonnie." He reached up with his IV- free hand and stroked one of her curls with his finger, then the freckles on her cheek. "Glory be to God for dappled things." His voice sounded raspy. Did it hurt him to speak?

Janie took his hand and kissed it. "I'm real, Duncan, and I'm not going anywhere."

He sighed. His eyes shone with sudden tears. "I'm sae sorry I didnae believe ye before."

"I know; it's okay. I wouldn't have believed all those things I told you, myself. I sounded crazy. Wuid, right?"

"Aye." Duncan's half-grin was rueful.

Janie wished she hadn't used that word, as if she were still holding on to it. She didn't want him to hold on to it, either. "Can we put all of that behind us? I didn't fly across the ocean in a ship with wings to talk about the past. I'm more interested in the future." She leaned in and kissed him again.

They were going to have a proper snog now, and she just dared one of those nurses to walk in.

She was real. His dreams had never been this good. Duncan kissed her back, deepening the kiss and pulling her to his chest with his IV-free arm. Pain reminded him of his broken ribs, but he didn't care. It was more than worth it.

Janie pulled gently away, much too soon. "I would love to do that forever—"

Aye, he would, too.

"But first, can we do a reset on our engagement? She got down on one knee beside the bed. "Duncan Robert MacKinnon, will you marry me?"

"Yes. A thoosand times, yes!"

"Wait! What did you just say?"

"It's frae the movie *Pride and Prejudice*. I saw it on the telly yesterday." He nodded towards the corner of the room, where a TV screen on a swivel arm was mounted to the wall.

"I know what it's from; I just didn't expect you to say yes."

What? He hadn't come through time just to say hello!

Janie got up and sat next to him again. She was smiling, and her eyes were full of laughter.

Of course! What an eejit he was! "*Aye*, then! Aye. I will marry ye."

"*That's* the word I came four thousand miles to hear."

And the one he had come two hundred and twelve years to say.

There was one other word Janie had been dreaming of hearing, one that sent thrills through her whenever Duncan said it. She leaned in for another kiss, and at last, he whispered, "Janie." She would never be Miss Jones again. At some point, it would become commonplace to hear him say her name, but not yet.

"Say that again," she said.

CHAPTER 33

I know where I'm going, and I know who's going with me.
I know who I love, and my dear knows who I'll marry.
~Traditional, "I Know Where I'm Going"

The telly had prepared Duncan to some extent, but being out on the street in London was still a shock. The number and noise of the cars seemed much greater in person.

Janie had arranged for a car to pick them up and bring them to the airport. Like the others around them, it began moving at an incredible pace once they got out of the worst of the traffic. Where was the need for such haste? Surely, not all of these people could be in dire circumstances! Janie was unruffled by their speed, so it was apparently normal. He remembered Miss Davies saying she thought cars were exciting, and Duncan couldn't help agreeing with her. He wondered aloud how long the trip from Godmersham Park to London would take in one of these cars.

"Let's see," Janie said, and she did something on her mobile. "About an hour and a half."

Duncan laughed. "Miss Knight would want to gae shopping in London every week!"

The buildings blurred as they passed them. Some of them he recognized from the nineteenth century, only they were crowded in by newer ones. The only horses he saw belonged to the guards at the entrance to St James's and Buckingham Palace. London was the same place, yet so different. It was unsettling, almost frightening. Was this how Janie had felt that day when they were in Chilham? He reached for her hand, as if to comfort that past Janie. Or maybe himself.

She took his hand into both of hers. "Are you okay? It's kind of scary, isn't it?" she asked, echoing his thoughts.

"'Tis just sae different."

"I know."

Janie kept her arm hooked through Duncan's at the airport; she didn't want to lose him in all of the chaos. She was seeing everything as if through his eyes. It seemed like there were so many more people than there were a few days ago. Everyone was moving fast, except for the ones who were on their phones and weren't looking where they were going. Others were looking with pointed curiosity at

Duncan, who was dressed in his Sunday clothes from 1813. Why hadn't she thought of bringing something modern for him to wear?

"Hey, Mr. Darcy!" A couple of giggling girls called out.

Duncan ducked his head, blushing. Janie tightened her hold on his arm and steered him towards Security.

Duncan looked over at Janie where she slept in the seat next to him on the airplane. She had a wee bit of a smile on her lips; he hoped she was having a lovely dream. A line from her favorite song ran through his mind: "Flow gently, sweet Afton, disturb not her dream." He was the most blessed man in the world— it wouldn't be long before he would wake to see Janie beside him every morning, for the rest of his life. He sighed, resisting the urge to caress the satiny ripples of her hair. He didn't want to wake her.

Janie was probably exhausted. Two nights spent trying to sleep in the reclining armchair in his hospital room had not been easy for her. She said that the interruptions every few hours, as nurses came to check on him, made sleep even more difficult than her uncomfortable position did. She had an evident mistrust of the nurses that made no sense to Duncan; they seemed perfectly competent to him.

If he hadn't been drugged, Duncan knew he wouldn't have slept much, either, and not only because of Janie's presence in his room— which he couldn't believe was even allowed, now that he thought about it. The humming and beeping of the machinery, as well as the wee lights on everything, had been very distracting. He hoped it would be much quieter and darker in the Jones' house at night.

Janie had spent some time explaining what to expect before they got on the plane, and it was much as she had described it. He'd been prepared for the strange feeling in his stomach during the liftoff, and he knew how jarring the landing was going to feel. She had also told him about something called turbulence, which she described as "bumpiness in the air," with a wrinkle of her nose and a wee shiver that revealed her dislike of it. So far, he hadn't felt any of that. To Duncan, it was the *lack* of any bumpiness that felt strange and unnerving, so different was it from any mode of transportation he'd experienced in his century.

The best part of flying was looking out of the window as they ascended. It was thrilling to see the city of London far below him, then the ocean, then to be swallowed up by the clouds as if he were driving a carriage through a fog, and finally to be moving above the clouds. They looked like a field of pillows upon which he might stretch out and take a nap.

He looked around the plane's interior. Like Janie, some of the other passengers were sleeping. Some were watching the little telly on the back of the seat in front of them, and many of them were looking intently at their wee mobiles. Most of the people at the airport had also been looking at mobiles. Thanks to Miss Davies, he understood what they were used for, but he couldn't understand how people could stand to look at them for so long when there were so many other things at the airport to look at, or people to talk to.

He was glad that Janie wasn't like that. She had a mobile, but mostly, it stayed in her pocket. She said Americans called them phones. They had used hers to call her father from the hospital. Duncan had asked him for permission to marry his daughter, which he had given, along with his herd of Thoroughbreds, as a wedding gift to them both. Duncan still couldn't believe it; he would have the woman of his dreams and the horse farm of his dreams, too. God had been so good to him.

All of Janie's siblings had talked to Duncan on the phone too, one by one. Charlie made him laugh, which felt like being kicked in the ribs by a horse, and Janie fussed at her brother for it.

It was not only a marvel, but an immeasurably precious thing that people in this century could be so far away from their loved ones and still be able to talk with them. Duncan thought of Elspeth, and a lump formed in his throat. There was no phone in the world that could reach her. His wee sister had been dead for more than a hundred years now. When he first woke up in 2025, that realization had been even more painful than his broken ribs. At least he had written the "happily ever after" letter for Miss

Davies to send to her. He hoped it got to Elspeth safely, and that she had a long and happy life.

When Janie had arrived at the hospital, joy had driven his sorrow into the corners. He looked at Janie now, still asleep, and was consoled again. Duncan knew how grief was, that it would continue to sneak up on him sometimes, but his heart was full to bursting with love for this lady who— miracle of miracles— loved him, a stablehand.

Janie opened her eyes. Duncan was smiling at her, and she felt the responding upward tug on the corners of her own mouth. "Hi," she said, reaching over the armrest and weaving her fingers through his. "What time is it?" She arched her back away from the seat in a little stretch.

He pulled out his pocket watch. "'Tis almost four o'clock."

She nodded. "We'll be home in about half an hour, then. You'll have to reset your watch to Central Time when we land. Did you sleep?"

"Nae. How could I?"

"Oh, no! Are you in a lot of pain? You should have woken me! I have your medicine right here in my backpack." She bent over and grabbed her bag from under the seat in front of her.

"Nae, I'm no hurting that much. I meant how could I sleep, when a' I wanted to do was to look at ye?"

Janie punched him lightly in the arm. "You goober! Here I was feeling bad, thinking you were in all this pain!"

Duncan laughed. "Goober, is it? Wha' is a goober?"

"I'm not actually sure; I think maybe it's a peanut. It's just something we say in my family when we're pretending to be mad at someone, or saying they're being stupid, but in a teasing way."

"Like saying someone's a tumshie, then."

"What's a tumshie?"

"'A turnip."

She laughed. "My brother is going to love that one! He'll be calling everyone a tumshie. Not everybody here uses 'goober' that way, but it's a family thing, you know?"

"I'm a wee bit nervous aboot meeting your family."

Janie gave his hand a squeeze. "Don't be. They love you already."

There they were— Duncan recognized Charlie from the video, and the others looked just the way Janie had described them. They were all grinning from ear to ear, and one of her sisters— it had to be Lottie, since she looked so much like her brother, was fairly jumping up and down with excitement. Janie called out to them,

"Remember, his ribs are broken. No bear hugs, okay? Or back slaps, Charlie."

Everyone hugged Janie, though. Lottie and Christie kissed Duncan on the cheek, and Charlie shook his hand. "It's about time we had another guy in this family," he said with a grin.

Janie's father had the kindest eyes he'd ever seen. He shook Duncan's hand. "Hello, Duncan. I'm Richard. Welcome home, son."

Home— could this fast-paced, all-but-horseless place of electric lights and noise really be his home now?

Janie laced her fingers through his.

Aye, it could. Home was wherever Janie was.

Scots Glossary

A'- all
Aboot- about
Ain- own
Aught- anything
Auld- old
Awa'- away
Aye- yes; always
Bairn- baby; child
Bonnie- pretty; attractive
Braw- handsome; fine; really good
Brocht- brought
Cannae- can't
Canny- clever, shrewd
Ceilidh- a large social gathering, usually involving music and dancing
Clatty- dirty, muddy
Dinnae- don't
Dissy- dizzy
Doon- down
Dreich- gloomy, depressing
Drookit- soaking wet

Eejit- idiot

Fa'- fall

Fareweel- farewell

Frae- from

Gae- go

Gang- gone

Gie- give

Goon- gown

Gowd- gold

Greet- cry

Ha'- have

I'- in

Intae- into

Isnae- isn't

Kelpies- in Scottish folklore, shape-shifting water horses

Ken- know

Kirk- church

Knowes- hills

Lad- boy or young man (diminutive- laddie)

Laird- lord

Lang- long

Lass- girl or young woman (diminutive- lassie)

Loot- let

Mair- more

Maun- must

Nae- no

Nicht- night

No- not

Noo- now
O'- of
Och- interjection similar to oh
Oot- out
Peely-wally- out of sorts; pale
Sae- so
Selkies- in Scottish folklore, seals that can shift into human form
Sodger- soldier
Syne- since
Tae- to
Tak- take
'Tis- it is
Tumshie- turnip, foolish person
Wasnae- wasn't
Wee- small
Wha- what
Wheesht- ssh, hush
Willnae- won't
Wuid- crazy
Ye- you
Yon- yonder, that over there
Yowes- ewes, sheep

Welsh Glossary

Bach- dear; little
Bechod- what a shame, what a pity
Bobol bach- good grief
Cnaf- scoundrel, rascal
Cwtch- hug
Duw- God
Go iawn?- really?
Gwallgof- crazy
Hwyl Fawr- goodbye
Paid becso- don't worry
Pob lwc- good luck
Poor dab- poor thing, someone to be pitied
Twmffat- idiot
Twp- stupid; idiotic
Twpsyn- fool; dimwit
Ych a fi- how disgusting, gross

Author's Note

I borrowed some of the characters and settings in this story from the year 1813. It was an interesting undertaking to blend fact and fiction, to stay true to the essence of the historical while taking some creative liberties for the sake of storytelling.

We know that Jane Austen stayed with her brother at Godmersham Park between September and November of 1813. There is a gap in the extant letters she wrote during her stay, and I have set this story's events into this gap.

Fanny Knight really did keep diaries. Unlike my invented ones, their entries were brief and often abbreviated, as their pages were only 3″ x 4 1/2″. She was, however, wont to use exclamation points.

Susanna Sackree later became the Knights' housekeeper and stayed with the family for the rest of her life. There is a touching memorial to her at the Church of St. Lawrence the Martyr.

In the character of Miss Austen, I sought to portray the clergyman's daughter as much as the writer. My sincerest hope is that readers who look upon Jane Austen with affection will recognize her in these pages.

Acknowledgements

To Claire Farrar at the Godmersham Heritage Centre for answering my questions and showing me around the Godmersham property and church on her day off, and to Rebecca Lilley for clearing up a mystery for me. Any mistakes are entirely my own.

To Paige Hurley for her positivity and much-needed help in formatting my manuscript.

To Jo Ann Staples for sharing her expertise on Regency Era card games.

To my beta readers: Ann, Amy, Beth, Erin, and Sally, whose comments were invaluable.

To Jim Buchanan for sharing his knowledge about Guarnerius del Gesù violins, and for his wise and patient instruction of this newbie fiddler.

To all of my friends in the Jane Austen Society of North America for their support and encouragement.

To my writing buddies in Heartprint for their comments, expertise, prayers, and encouragement.

To Erin Knowles at Tern Travel for her help in planning my own Jane Austen pilgrimage; it was an amazing, unforgettable trip.

To Kate Rusby, whose songs made up most of the playlist for my writing sessions.

To Darren, my own Mr. Darcy, and the rest of my wonderful family for putting up with me so patiently.

Most of all, to God, from whom all blessings flow.

About the Author

Deborah Carroll is a Regional Coordinator for the Middle Tennessee Region of the Jane Austen Society of North America. She enjoys drawing, singing, traveling, and sewing historical clothing. This is her first novel.

Photo by Brenda Vaughan